CRITICAL ACCLAIM FOR LEIGH RUSSELL

'A million readers can't be wrong! Clear some time in your day, sit back and enjoy a bloody good read'
– **Howard Linskey**

'Taut and compelling' – **Peter James**

'Leigh Russell is one to watch' – **Lee Child**

'Leigh Russell has become one of the most impressively dependable purveyors of the English police procedural'
– *Times*

'DI Geraldine Steel is one of the most authoritative female coppers in a crowded field' – *Financial Times*

'A brilliant talent in the thriller field' – **Jeffery Deaver**

'Brilliant and chilling, Leigh Russell delivers a cracker of a read!' – **Martina Cole**

'A great plot that keeps you guessing right until the very end, some subtle subplots, brilliant characters both old and new and as ever a completely gripping read' – *Life of Crime*

'The latest police procedural from prolific novelist Leigh Russell is as good and gripping as anything she has published'
– *Times & Sunday Times Crime Club*

'A fascinating gripping read. The many twists kept me on my toes and secon~~d guessing myself~~'
– *Over The Rain~~bow~~*

'Well paced with marvellously well-rounded characters and a clever plot that make this another thriller of a read from Leigh Russell' – *Orlando Books*

'A well-written, fast-paced and very enjoyable thriller' – *The Book Lovers Boudoir*

'An edge-of-your-seat thriller that will keep you guessing' – *Honest Mam Reader*

'Well paced, has red herrings and twists galore, keeps your attention and sucks you right into its pages' – *Books by Bindu*

'5 stars!! Another super addition to one of my favourite series, which remains as engrossing and fresh as ever!' – *The Word is Out*

'A nerve-twisting tour de force that will leave readers on the edge of their seats, Leigh Russell's latest Detective Geraldine Steel thriller is a terrifying page-turner by this superb crime writer' – *Bookish Jottings*

'An absolute delight' – *The Literary Shed*

'I simply couldn't put it down' – **Shell Baker, Chelle's Book Reviews**

'If you love a good action-packed crime novel, full of complex characters and unexpected twists, this is one for you' – **Rachel Emms, *Chillers, Killers and Thrillers***

'All the things a mystery should be: intriguing, enthralling, tense and utterly absorbing' – *Best Crime Books*

ALSO BY LEIGH RUSSELL

Geraldine Steel Mysteries
Cut Short
Road Closed
Dead End
Death Bed
Stop Dead
Fatal Act
Killer Plan
Murder Ring
Deadly Alibi
Class Murder
Death Rope
Rogue Killer
Deathly Affair
Deadly Revenge
Evil Impulse
Deep Cover
Guilt Edged
Fake Alibi
Final Term

Ian Peterson Murder Investigations
Cold Sacrifice
Race to Death
Blood Axe

Poppy Mystery Tales
Barking Up the Right Tree
Barking Mad

Lucy Hall Mysteries
Journey to Death
Girl in Danger
The Wrong Suspect

The Adulterer's Wife
Suspicion

LEIGH RUSSELL

WITHOUT TRACE

A GERALDINE STEEL MYSTERY

NO EXIT PRESS

First published in 2023 by No Exit Press,
an imprint of Bedford Square Publishers Ltd,
London, UK

noexit.co.uk
@noexitpress

ISBN
978-0-85730-475-9 (Paperback)
978-0-85730-476-6 (eBook)

2 4 6 8 10 9 7 5 3 1

Typeset in 11 on 13.75pt Times New Roman
by Avocet Typeset, Bideford, Devon, EX39 2BP
Printed and bound in Great Britain by CPI Group (UK) Ltd, Croydon CR0 4YY

For more information about Crime Fiction go to crimetime.co.uk

To Michael, Jo, Phillipa, Phil, Rian, and Kezia
With my love

Without Trace *is dedicated to the man behind the*
creation of Geraldine Steel, Ion Mills

Glossary of Acronyms

DCI	–	Detective Chief Inspector (senior officer on case)
DI	–	Detective Inspector
DS	–	Detective Sergeant
SOCO	–	scene of crime officer (collects forensic evidence at scene)
PM	–	Post Mortem or Autopsy (examination of dead body to establish cause of death)
CCTV	–	Closed Circuit Television (security cameras)
VIIDO	–	Visual Images, Identification and Detections Office
MIT	–	Murder Investigation Team

1

THE GIRL LAY STILL, her fair hair fluttering in a light breeze which shook the leaves of overhanging branches. A small bird flew down, attracted by insects congregating to scavenge, and was ousted by a boisterous crow that beat its wings and shrieked in triumph. Defeated, the small bird flitted away. The black crow flapped its wings before it too flew off at the approach of a more formidable creature. The man stood for a few moments, staring thoughtfully at the corpse. His wife would be home soon, and a proper burial would have to wait until she left for work again in the evening. The fabric of his jeans stretched across his brawny thighs and knees as he squatted down and began scattering forest bark and earth over the body. Starting with the face, he let fall handfuls of leaves and soil until the eyelids were completely covered. Clumps of earth crumbled between his fingers as he sprinkled it lightly over the rest of her face. He moved on down her inert figure, until only the toes of her black shoes were clearly visible, sticking up from one end of the makeshift burial mound. It would be enough to conceal her until nightfall.

Stepping back, he rotated his stiff shoulders, and tensed and relaxed his leg muscles as he checked the site from different angles before trudging back across the lawn to disappear inside his house. At the back of the garden, the small bird returned, peering around anxiously. It hopped on the ground where leaves trembled in a gust of wind without shifting their position. A few termites struggled busily across the irregular surface of the disturbed ground. Overhead, clouds hovered and passed by without shedding their rain.

It was a wrench, leaving her like that, but she was well concealed from prying eyes looking out of neighbouring houses. On his way back to the house he had dropped a fallen rotting pear on her for good measure, then removed it for fear some scavenging creature would dig around and dislodge her covering. For now, he had to go to work and return the van where her body had been stored overnight. He had been careful to hit her on the back of her head, even though it hardly mattered if her face was damaged, where she was going. Still, her looks were what had attracted him to her, and he hadn't wanted to shatter her face. He had his standards. Whatever else happened, he couldn't afford to attract any attention by deviating from his usual routine. Everything must continue as normal, on the surface, while he hid his impatience for the day to be over so he could complete his task. All through the day, as he shifted plant pots and answered customers' queries, he was waiting to go home to her.

When it was time to return, he still had to wait. At last the sun cast a fiery glow across a bright sky before sinking below the horizon. As the daylight faded, the man emerged from his garden shed carrying a pristine shovel with a wooden shaft. The metal blade gleamed for an instant as it caught the dying rays of the sun. The man walked quickly down the long expanse of lawn to the area of trees at the back of the garden. He had to complete his task before his wife came home. She had been concerned about returning to night shifts, worried that he would object. Unknown to her, he considered it a godsend, giving him time to complete his project. But he didn't know how long he had left.

Any day now, Linda might come home and tell him that she had decided to quit working nights, and then his opportunity would slip away forever. The prospect loomed over him, making him tremble with a mixture of trepidation and longing. He had already achieved so much. He couldn't stop now, not when his efforts were beginning to show such excellent results. Everyone who came to the house commented on the beautiful garden. He was out there in all weathers, checking for signs of disease or infestation. As soon as Linda went to bed after her night shift, he would spend an hour raking and weeding before going to work at the garden centre, where he kept an eye out for ailing plants. He had rescued numerous small pot-bound plants that now thrived in the freedom of his flower beds.

A blow to the girl's head had felled her without any fuss. After removing her handcuffs and gag, he had simply pressed her face into the crumbly dry earth to make sure she was no longer breathing, and covered her over. Having hidden her from view, he had turned away. He would never have walked off had he thought for one moment that she might still be alive. He remembered exactly where he had left her under the small pear tree, but when he returned shortly after sunset, she wasn't there. There was only an indentation in the ground, beside a disturbed mound of earth and tree bark. Whether or not he had been slapdash, he hadn't finished the job; she must have regained consciousness and crawled away.

For an instant he stood transfixed, staring at the spot where he had left her concealed beneath a covering of soil and bark. Turning his head, he surveyed the area beneath the trees. The body wasn't there. Shaking himself free of his shock, he peered around. She couldn't have gone far. Reluctantly, he pulled out his torch, hoping his neighbours wouldn't notice the light and wonder what he was doing, searching in his garden after dark. The narrow shaft of light shook as he scanned the darkness for the missing girl, but there was no sign of her.

A stab of fear hit him. If she survived and remembered what had happened, everything would be over. He would never see his beloved garden again. The thought made his eyes water. On the other hand, if the girl's corpse was discovered, the consequences might be equally terrible. There was bound to be a huge fuss.

The police would investigate what had happened. With all the forensic skill at their disposal, they might track him down. There was only one possible way out of his difficulty. He had to find the girl before anyone else came across her, dead or alive. And he had to make sure she was unable to talk.

He studied the ground more closely in the light of his torch, searching for a trail, but the earth yielded nothing. Whatever trace the girl had left behind was invisible to his eyes. The police, with their equipment and bright lights, might fare better. He shuddered to think they might bring dogs to sniff and scrabble around in his garden, disturbing the plants and finding things that were best left hidden. He had read that the police had dogs trained to find corpses. If that was true, they would have a jamboree in his garden. Whatever else happened, he had to make sure no one else came into contact with his latest victim, before he found her.

Struggling to control his panic, he began a painstaking search of the garden. Systematically, he scoured every inch of the shrubbery before checking the shed, inside and out. As he hunted for clues to her whereabouts, his thoughts whirled. It was possible the girl wouldn't remember where he lived. Her recollection of the evening's events was bound to be confused. Perhaps his indignant denial would be enough to satisfy the police. But if they examined the van from the garden centre, they would almost certainly find traces of her DNA from where he had kept her for nearly twenty-four hours. He remembered with a sickening lurch that she had long hair. A few strands had almost certainly been brushed off onto the floor as he had transported her inert body. She might have scratched at the paintwork or left a drop of saliva on the floor as she lay unconscious but still, as it turned out, breathing, her heart still pumping blood through her veins. It was hard to believe she had survived his assault in the back of the van. Besides, he thought he had made sure she was dead by pushing her face into the earth. It was galling to discover she had survived all that, and infuriating that he had failed to finish the job when he had the chance. She had been right there, in his hands, unconscious, and he had let her slip out of his grasp. It seemed impossible, yet it had happened.

She had gone.

2

'OH BLOODY HELL, NOT another one,' Ian exclaimed.

'I take it you're not talking about my eggs?' Geraldine asked, as she stood up to clear the dinner plates off the table.

Although she had refrained from boasting about her success, the yolks on their eggs had neither broken nor solidified. Ian prided himself on being able to fry eggs perfectly every time, but hers generally ended up more scrambled than fried.

'What?' Ian replied, looking up from his phone. 'The eggs? They were perfect, thank you.'

She smiled, pausing in her clearing up. 'You said, "not another one". Another what?'

Ian's regular features twisted into a frown as he held up his phone. Geraldine glanced at the screen before dismissing the article as click bait.

'I'm afraid it might not be,' Ian said heavily. 'I mean, yes, of course, you're right, it's a sensational headline, worthy of the lowest form of tabloid, but there might be a germ of truth in it.'

'Wherever she's gone, surely something like that is for Missing Persons to look into. It's nothing to do with us,' Geraldine replied. 'What makes you so interested in the story? Women leave home all the time. It says she's in her twenties.'

'I'm not sure you're right about that.'

'About what?'

'About her leaving home voluntarily.'

'Why? What do you think's happening?'

14

Ian shook his head and admitted he had no idea. 'The thing is,' he went on slowly, as though unwilling to say more, 'I'm breaking a confidence to share this with you, but I'm beginning to wonder if there's something going on.'

'I've no idea what you're talking about.' Seeing the anxiety in Ian's blue eyes, Geraldine sat down. 'Go on. I'm listening. What's worrying you?'

Ian hesitated, although she knew he was comfortable confiding in her. As detective inspectors working on murder investigations, they were both accustomed to keeping quiet whenever discretion was called for. They rarely worked on the same case, and it was sometimes helpful to discuss their problems when an investigation was going badly. Still, he seemed reluctant to tell her what was on his mind.

'Something's bothering you,' she said, rising to her feet. 'You don't have to tell me if you don't want to, but you know I'm here if you decide you want to talk about it.'

'One of my football team just contacted me about this, in confidence,' Ian said, with a frown.

Geraldine sat down again and brushed one hand through her short black hair as she listened.

'He's called Jason. I may have mentioned his name before. Anyway, he's been living with his girlfriend in a turning off Heslington Lane. He thought they were getting along well, only she seems to have vanished into thin air. They'd had a row and he wanted to fix it, so he went along to the office where she worked and was told she hadn't turned up for work that day. She hadn't been in touch with any of her colleagues. One day she simply hadn't turned up and they hadn't been able to get hold of her. According to Jason, her manager was fuming. Jason had been living with her for nearly two years. Does it make sense to you that she would just disappear like that?'

Geraldine shrugged but didn't answer.

Ian resumed his account. 'He said he had no inkling she was going to leave him like that, walking out without a word. She hadn't taken anything with her, only her bag with her phone and the number was unavailable.'

'So, his girlfriend walked out on him. That's a mean thing to do, but I hardly see what it has to do with us.'

'The point is, he didn't believe she would just go off like that without telling anyone, and without taking anything with her. As far as he could tell, she hadn't taken any clothes with her – although he said he couldn't be sure on that point. You know, women and their clothes.'

Geraldine grunted.

'Anyway, he started to do a little digging. Her parents didn't know where she was. He didn't want to worry her family so he's been playing it down, but he's mystified, and alarmed. He checked the local hospital but they've got no record of her, and her GP wasn't prepared to share any information with him. That's when he asked me if there was anything I could do to help him trace her. He said he hoped my training and experience would be enough to find out where she was. He just wants to talk to her, and find out what's going on. He's afraid something's happened to her, but he doesn't want to involve the Missing Persons Unit in case she gets angry with him for making a fuss. He said he doesn't know what to do.'

Geraldine frowned. 'What did they row about?'

'He said she met her ex for a drink and someone saw them together and told him. According to her, the meeting was perfectly innocent, and she accused him of not trusting her. He just wants to find her to explain and apologise.'

'Was Jason violent?'

'No, no, nothing like that,' Ian assured her.

'So he says. Well, she might have gone to stay with her parents, and asked them not to tell him where she was.'

Geraldine said she thought Jason was right not to make a fuss, but she was troubled by what Ian had told her. He wouldn't have mentioned it to her if he wasn't concerned. They drove to the police station together the next morning. On the way, Geraldine brought up the subject Ian had raised the previous evening. As casually as she could, she asked for the name of the missing woman.

'So, you are going to follow it up?' he said. 'I thought you might.'

Geraldine smiled. 'Go on, then. I have a feeling there's more you want to tell me.'

'Well, as it happens I did take a look, just briefly, and it seems that over the past month another two girls have been reported missing, in addition to the one mentioned in the tabloid. The latest one's been missing for a month and she was living in Mitchell's Lane, which is –'

'Off Heslington Lane,' Geraldine completed his sentence.

'Those three girls all lived in the same area as my mate's girlfriend, off Heslington Lane. That makes three young women and now my mate's girl is the fourth. Is that a coincidence, do you think?'

Geraldine shrugged. 'Possibly. But okay, I'll look into it, if I have time.'

To her surprise, Ian thanked her, sounding relieved. She wondered if he had undertaken to investigate the matter to placate his friend, and had then found he didn't have time to look into it as he was involved in a complicated case.

'No promises,' she said. 'I only said I'd take a look if I have a moment.'

He nodded. 'That's really great. Her name's Lucy Henderson. Seriously, it's a weight off my mind.'

'Because you can now tell your friend you've passed it on and it's now out of your hands?' she asked with a wry smile.

'I can tell him I've passed it to the right person, yes.'

'The right person?'

'If anyone can find out what's happened to his girlfriend, it's you. I've never known you give up, even when it seems pointless to carry on.'

'I'll take that as a compliment.'

'You have to agree that four girls disappearing in a month is a cause for concern.'

'I said I'd look into it,' Geraldine said.

It crossed her mind that Ian might have told her about his friend's problem because he suspected she was bored. Although she would never admit it, she felt energised by the challenge of murder investigations, seeking justice for the victims whose lives had ended prematurely. Currently she was not working on anything at all, because she was recovering from a stomach upset. The previous week she had felt quite ill and her Detective Chief Inspector had insisted she stay at home for a few days.

'You're looking peaky,' Binita had told her.

'I'm fine,' Geraldine had lied.

'You're staying at home for a week,' Binita insisted. 'You look washed out. And when you come back, I'm putting you on desk work until you're feeling a hundred per cent again.'

At first Geraldine had been secretly relieved, but she was soon fed up. Having dedicated her working life to tracking down violent criminals, such unaccustomed enforced leisure made her feel useless. Back at her desk, she was stuck doing routine paperwork. As a rule, she would have passed an online search for a missing woman on to someone else, but the case had piqued her interest. No one had yet looked for a connection between four girls who had recently gone missing, and it was possible there might be a sinister connection between these apparently random disappearances.

3

DESPITE HIS ANXIETY HE fell asleep before going up to bed, exhausted by the stress of the night. When he was woken by the sound of the front door closing, he was surprised to find he was still downstairs. Linda was home. He stood up and rearranged the cushions on the sofa before going to greet her in the hall.

'You look tired,' Linda said when she saw him. 'Are you sure my hours aren't bothering you? I don't have to do it, you know. There are other girls who could take the night shifts, and most of them are a lot younger than me. I can tell them it's too much for me. It's quite all right –'

'Don't be daft,' he interrupted her. 'You just said they're all a lot younger than you, meaning they need your experience overnight, don't they?'

She smiled weakly at the compliment, muttering that her colleagues were all perfectly capable of doing the job and she was only a few years off retirement age anyway.

'And it's not as if it's all the time,' he went on. 'I know you love what you do. As long as you can cope with the irregular hours, it's fine with me. Seriously, it makes no difference to me,' he assured her.

That wasn't true, but she knew nothing about his real feelings. As long as she was working nights, he was free to pursue his own pastime.

'Well, if you're sure,' she replied, with a faint smile. 'But you will let me know if you change your mind? Look at me. I mean it, George. One word from you and I'll stop doing nights.'

He wanted to shout at her, 'No! No! You can't stop!' but, of course, he couldn't. It was frightening to think how close she had come to ruining his plans, but he had to remain silent. Even a sympathetic woman like his wife was likely to misconstrue his activity. It was a pity, really, because he would have liked to share the success of his project with her, but it wasn't to be. She wouldn't understand. She might even report him to the police, and he couldn't allow that to happen, not when everything was going so well.

'It's fine, really,' he replied. 'If you're looking for an excuse to resign from your job, you'll have to look elsewhere.' He smiled, knowing how much she valued her time in intensive care.

'It's serene, somehow,' she had once told him. 'I mean, it's not at all like what you might expect from the dramas you see on television. There isn't as much interaction with patients as on ordinary wards, but you feel you're right at the coal face, saving lives, and if you lose patients, you can be confident it was their time to go. I know it doesn't really make sense, but I can't explain it any better than that.'

He had assured her he understood what she meant, although, of course, he didn't. Not really. More than anything, he had been struck by the irony of their situation. Outwardly a happily married couple, one of them saved lives while the other ended them. It was a perfect example of the yin and yang she liked to talk about, the universe in harmony. It was a pity he couldn't tell her how perfectly matched they were. He had to make do with telling her he loved her, forcing himself to return the smile that lit up her homely features, reminding him of the young girl he had fallen in love with. Time had not treated her kindly. Her hair was threaded with white, her face was wrinkled, and she looked older than her years. He worried that the stress of her job was draining her energy, but she assured him she was as fit and healthy as ever. Her white hair was genetic, she explained, and inevitable.

'How was your shift?' he asked, as he always did.

It was important to behave as though nothing was wrong.

She shrugged. 'Not good,' she admitted, pulling a face.

'Oh dear. What's happened? Why don't I make us a nice cup of tea and then you can tell me all about it?'

'It was one of those terribly sad nights,' she said, when they were sitting on comfortable armchairs in the living room, with their tea. 'I mean, it's always sad to lose a patient, even when there's no hope, but this time it was a young girl who'd been found lying in the road, unconscious, not far from here. It seems she was out on her own.'

'Oh dear,' he exclaimed.

There was no need to fake his shock. He had to find out more. 'What happened?'

She shook her head. 'I'm not sure.'

'So, she just collapsed? Is that what happened? Was it alcohol or drugs?' He tried to control his panic.

'It's possible she'd been drinking, although she had a blow to the back of her head, which looked suspicious.'

'Suspicious?' A spasm of fear shot through him and he struggled to speak in an even tone. 'You mean she hit her head when she fell over?' he prompted her cautiously.

She took a sip of her tea, oblivious of his impatience. 'Maybe. Either that, or else someone hit her hard enough to crack her skull.'

He whistled but didn't trust himself to speak.

'Yes,' she went on, 'her head was bashed in.'

He was itching to know what the patient looked like so he could rule out the woman he had met earlier on, but he couldn't think how to ask. He could hardly enquire if the woman in intensive care had long fair hair and blue eyes, and was wearing a dark blue jumper with very narrow vertical white stripes. Instead, he asked whether the patient was expected to recover.

'We worked all night to save her,' Linda replied. 'We managed to stabilise her condition.'

No, no, please no, he thought, but could not utter a word. *Please don't let her wake up. Don't let her remember.* Although he didn't believe in God, he realised he was praying. Struggling to conceal his keen interest in this particular patient, he waited on tenterhooks as his wife sipped her tea.

'But in the end we weren't able to save her.'

He let out an involuntary gasp of relief.

'Oh, I'm sorry,' she said, putting down her cup. 'These things happen. I shouldn't burden you with it. There's no need to feel down. She died without recovering consciousness. She didn't suffer.'

'That's good,' he murmured, wondering what kind of evidence he had left on the girl.

If the hospital doctors suspected foul play, they would ask the police to look into the girl's death, and nothing would remain hidden from them for long. They had no record of his DNA on their database, but once they detected it on the girl, it might only be a matter of time before they traced it back to him. He had heard all kinds of stories about how much information could be gleaned from a sample of DNA. He had done his best not to come into contact with her any more than was necessary to get the job done, but he hadn't been able to avoid touching her. With hindsight, he realised how stupid he had been. But at least she was dead. He shuddered, realising he'd had a narrow escape.

It was a man working at the garden centre, he imagined her telling the police, if she had survived. *He pushed me into his van and the next thing I remember was waking up, half buried in earth. There was earth in my mouth, and up my nose, and in my ears, as though someone had tried to bury me. I don't remember who it was, but I do remember he said he worked in the garden centre. He was tall and muscly, and he had shaggy brown hair and a moustache, and he told me his name was George.*

'Are you sure you're all right?' Linda asked.

He nodded. 'Just not fully awake yet,' he replied, forcing a smile. 'Now, it's time for you to catch up on your beauty sleep.'

His comment amused her. He thought with a pang how beautiful she was when she laughed, although she never believed it when he told her. He watched her walk out of the room and a moment later he heard her padding up the stairs to bed. With a sigh, he collected their cups and took them to the kitchen. He had to make plans, and be prepared for anything. If it turned out that he had to flee the country, he was ready for that. His documents were stored at the back of a locked drawer in a rusty old filing cabinet in his garage: a fake passport, and several thousand pounds in cash which he had carefully squirrelled away over the years. Neither his wife nor his manager at work had any idea of the extent of his pilfering, but he had to have money ready in case he ever needed it. But running away would be an absolute last resort, leaving his home and his wife and, hardest of all, abandoning his beloved garden. Before long, the flower beds would be overrun with weeds, and his carefully nurtured lawn would become riddled with moss and clover. It was little consolation to know he wouldn't be there to witness its deterioration. He would know.

'Would you look after the garden if anything happened to me?' he had asked Linda once.

'What are you talking about? Nothing's going to happen to you,' she had scoffed before asking, with genuine concern, whether he was feeling ill.

'No, no, nothing like that,' he had hastened to reassure her, hating to think he had upset her. She had enough to cope with at the hospital. He was supposed to be her safe place. She had told him so often enough. 'But if it did,' he had persisted. 'You would take care of the garden, wouldn't you? For me?'

'I can't see how that would help you, if you weren't around to see it any more. But nothing's going to happen to you, not as long as I'm here to look after you.'

With care, he would evade detection and complete his project. He certainly had no intention of stopping, but he was going to have to be more circumspect than ever. He had buried three girls successfully. He only needed one more, or possibly two. Three if the opportunity arose. It was going to be a wrench when he had to stop. He would miss the thrill of spotting a young woman healthy enough to meet his requirements. But, for the rest of his life, he would be able to relive the joy that coursed through him every time he had a successful encounter.

4

GERALDINE HAD SPENT A couple of days sitting at her desk catching up on paperwork. It was keeping her busier than she had expected. She had begun researching girls who had gone missing locally, but working on her own, in stray moments, she had made little progress. By Wednesday, she was feeling physically stronger, which was just as well because midway through the morning the detective chief inspector set up a briefing. Geraldine walked down the corridor with her friend and colleague, Detective Sergeant Ariadne Moralis.

'What's this all about?' Ariadne asked, as they made their way to the incident room.

'Search me,' Geraldine muttered in response. 'No one's told me what's going on, but I'd say something must have happened.'

'No wonder they pay you to carry out detective work,' Ariadne chuckled and Geraldine smiled.

Wondering whether they were about to hear that a murder had been committed in York, Geraldine suppressed a faint tremor of anticipation. She glanced at her colleague. With a brusque movement, Ariadne swept her long loose hair back from her face into a ponytail. Admittedly, it looked more businesslike than when her shoulder-length black curls swung freely around her face, which now wore a strained expression. They entered the incident room, where several officers had already gathered and were talking in hushed tones. An air of expectation rippled around the room as their senior officer, Binita, came through the door with the brisk stride and determined air of someone

25

who had important information to share. She looked around the assembled detectives with a grave expression.

'A young woman died in the intensive care unit at York Hospital in the early hours of this morning,' she announced. 'The medical team suspect she was the victim of an assault which left her unconscious. Since they believe her death occurred as a direct result of the attack, we are opening a murder investigation. As yet we have no identity for the victim who was discovered yesterday evening by a passing couple who spotted her lying on Heslington Lane just off Fulford Road, at the junction with Grants Avenue. They summoned an ambulance and she was taken straight into intensive care. She never recovered consciousness and died several hours after being admitted.'

'Was it a hit and run?' Ariadne asked.

'The medical team thought that unlikely, given the nature of her injuries,' Binita replied. 'Her clothes and hair were full of earth, and they found more in her nose and mouth and ears. She appeared to have been covered in it.'

'Earth?' a constable echoed.

'Yes, it almost looks as though someone had tried to bury her,' Binita said quietly.

She turned to display an image of woman with long fair hair. It was difficult to tell what she had looked like while she was alive, but in death she was horribly pale. Her eyes were closed but there was nothing about her face to suggest she might be sleeping peacefully as was sometimes the case with the dead. Staring at the blank face on the screen, Geraldine recalled what Ian had told her about the disappearance of his football friend's partner.

'I may have a possible identity,' she murmured.

Instantly everyone turned to look at her, and she hesitated.

'Go on,' Binita urged her. 'Do you recognise the victim?' She paused, watching Geraldine hopefully.

'No, I'm sorry, I haven't seen her before,' Geraldine said, suddenly unsure of herself. 'It's probably just a coincidence and nothing to do with us at all. I need to make a few enquiries before I can come up with a name.'

'Very well,' Binita replied, clearly disappointed. 'In the meantime, we need to find out everything we can about this woman. Check your allocated tasks and let's get started.'

On her way to the mortuary, Geraldine called Ian who answered straightaway.

'How are you feeling?' he asked, before she had a chance to speak.

'I'm fine. I just need the name of your friend's girlfriend.'

'Who are you talking about?'

Geraldine took a breath. 'You told me one of your football mates has lost track of his girlfriend. I think you said her name was Lucy Henderson?'

'Why? Have you found her?'

'I don't know.'

Quickly, she explained about the woman who had died in hospital that morning. At the other end of the line, she could hear the concern in Ian's voice as he confirmed the name: Lucy Henderson.

'Jason sent me a photo,' he added. 'I'll ping it over to you. I take it you've seen an image of the victim?'

Geraldine confirmed that she had. Ian had been keen for her to stay on desk work until she had fully recovered from her stomach bug, so she held back from telling him she was on her way to the mortuary to see the body for herself. He would find out soon enough that she was working on a murder investigation. In the meantime, she was fine now and there was no reason for him to fuss.

'I'll let you know if I get anywhere with this.'

Ian thanked her and she rang off thoughtfully. There was no proof yet that her suspicion was right, but there was a chance she had found Jason's missing girlfriend.

'Lucy Henderson,' she repeated softly to herself.

If her hunch proved correct, not only would they have a name for the dead woman, but they would have a potentially useful lead to learn about her life, and possibly her death as well. Smiling grimly, Geraldine put her foot down, impatient to reach the mortuary. A moment later her phone buzzed; Ian had sent her a picture of Lucy. Now she just had to check the image against the dead woman's face. As soon as she reached the hospital and parked, she took a look at Ian's picture and compared it with the image of the corpse already stored on her phone. The two faces were almost certainly the same person, but Geraldine wasn't sure. The dead face was hard to match with that of a vibrant woman smiling flirtatiously at the camera, full of life and mischief.

With a sigh, she made her way to the entrance to the mortuary where the pathologist was expecting her.

5

THE ANATOMICAL PATHOLOGY ASSISTANT, Avril, was a friendly young woman who seemed far more interested in her own forthcoming wedding than the dead woman recently brought in for a post mortem. Geraldine didn't comment that she was hardly an appropriate person to offer advice on wedding arrangements. Instead, she listened politely as Avril related her latest series of problems, most of which seemed to relate to a cousin who had fallen out with Avril's sister after the invitations had been sent out.

'What does she expect me to do about it?' Avril moaned, running her manicured fingers through her blonde hair. 'I can hardly tell her she's no longer welcome, can I? I mean, the invitations have gone out. I didn't even want to invite her in the first place. Everyone warned me it's a nightmare organising a wedding but, really, this takes the biscuit. You'll never guess what happened.'

Geraldine did her best to sound sympathetic but she was beginning to lose patience when Avril stopped herself in mid-sentence. 'Sorry, sorry,' she muttered, looking shamefaced. 'I shouldn't keep going on about it like this. You have to get back to work, and so do I. It's just that this is driving me nuts and it's difficult to focus on anything else.'

Geraldine was pleased to see the familiar face of Jonah Hetherington, a pathologist she had worked with several times since her transfer to York. Although they had never met outside the mortuary, they had become firm friends. He was excellent at his job, but what Geraldine appreciated almost as much as his expertise was the strong bond of trust that had grown up between them. Knowing she could rely on Jonah's discretion, she felt able to speak without constraint in front of him. Other than the pathologist, only a cadaver was present to witness her words. Aware of the need to restrict herself to the evidence, nevertheless Geraldine found it helpful to speculate about how victims might have met their deaths. With Jonah she could discuss various possibilities without fear of her theories being shared with anyone else, a freedom she found invaluable.

'You have no idea how useful this is,' she had told Jonah once. 'I mean, being able to air ideas with you like this.'

'You flatter me,' he replied, his pug-like face beaming. 'We both know I'm just the butcher here. You're the one doing all the brain work.'

She hadn't pursued the matter, but she hoped he realised how sincerely she appreciated his help, not only for the physical evidence he was able to share from his examinations of the victims.

Entering the room, she stared at the dead woman before holding up her phone to show Jonah an image of Lucy Henderson.

'Is this her?' she asked. 'It's difficult to tell. I mean, it could be the same woman, but she looks so different.'

Jonah inclined his head. 'Death changes people's physical appearance, some more than others,' he said softly as he leaned forward to scrutinise the picture on Geraldine's phone. 'I'd say it almost certainly is the same woman, but I could be mistaken.'

Geraldine nodded. It would be easy enough to acquire a sample of the missing woman's DNA, and check for a match.

'So, you think it's worth looking into?' she asked.

'I'd say so, definitely. Who is the woman on your phone? Presumably someone who's gone missing?'

'Exactly. I'll get that checked out. So, what can you tell me about this body?'

They both stared at the dead woman in silence for a few

seconds. She appeared even paler than she did in the images Geraldine had seen.

'She looks like a ghost,' she said.

Jonah grunted. 'You're looking a little under the weather yourself,' he murmured, raising one eyebrow quizzically. 'Are you well?'

Geraldine shook her head impatiently. 'It's just a bug I'm throwing off,' she replied.

Jonah took a step back in mock horror and mimed feeling faint. 'I'm not used to dealing with the problems of living bodies.'

Geraldine laughed at his antics before enquiring how the woman had died.

Jonah frowned. 'This is a tricky one to call. The cause of death is cerebral haemorrhage. It looks very much as if someone hit her on the head with an implement which could have been metal and was probably flat, looking at the shape of the contusion. Whatever the object used, the blow was violent enough to crack her skull, so the attacker was strong. Probably a man.' He pointed to a bald patch where he had shaved the dead woman's hair to expose a blackened area of skin, which had been very neatly sliced open. 'But the curious thing is, we found a significant amount of dirt on her: earth and leaf mould and fragments of twigs and such like, common detritus picked up from the ground. Forest bark. There were fragments in her hair, her nose, her mouth, her ears, under her fingernails and clinging to her clothes everywhere, not just on one side. It's almost as though she'd been completely encased in earth.' He frowned.

'Buried, you mean?'

Jonah nodded uncertainly. 'The odd thing is she was found on the pavement at the side of the road, where she wasn't in contact with any earth or mud.'

'Is it possible she was buried alive and then recovered consciousness and somehow dragged herself out of her grave?' Geraldine failed to suppress a shudder at her macabre theory.

'It sounds highly unlikely,' Jonah replied, 'but it is the most obvious explanation for the state she was in when she was found. Perhaps the only explanation. If that *was* the case, then she wasn't buried very well, and she must have still been breathing, but unconscious. It's altogether an odd one.' He shook his head. 'It doesn't really make sense, but then murder very rarely does. Why would anyone do that? Hit her on the head and then attempt to bury her? If that was the intention, all I can say is the killer wasn't very adept at what he was doing, because he didn't kill her, at least not straightaway, and his attempt to bury the evidence was botched.'

Geraldine stared at the dead woman's face, wondering what it must have been like to recover consciousness in a shallow grave.

'And why would the killer leave her like that without making sure she was dead?' Jonah added, almost under his breath.

'He might have been disturbed,' Geraldine suggested, 'or too frightened to stay any longer for fear of discovery. Or maybe he was convinced she was dead. But I agree, it seems odd. Apart from anything else, how could she have survived that?'

Jonah nodded. 'Either bury the body properly, too deep to be found, or don't bury it at all. He seems to have been in a temper.' He indicated a bruise on the dead woman's cheek. 'He gave her a violent slap on the face here. I'm afraid this is – well, I don't really know what to say, except that I'm glad it doesn't fall to me to try and make sense of it all.'

Geraldine sighed. 'We'll get to the bottom of it,' she promised him.

But she wasn't convinced that would be possible. All the murders she investigated were strange in different ways, but this one seemed utterly bizarre.

She turned back to the body. 'We'll find whoever did this to you,' she murmured. 'We'll find them, no matter how long it takes.'

But she had a sinking sensation this killer might prove impossible to track down.

6

IAN GAVE GERALDINE THE address she needed. She didn't invite him to accompany her to his friend's house. Apart from the fact that Ian wasn't involved in the investigation into the unidentified body, meeting his friend under such circumstances might be awkward for both of them. Although Geraldine was only going to gather a sample of his missing girlfriend's DNA, it was possible that Jason might become a suspect in a murder enquiry, should DNA establish the dead woman was his missing girlfriend. If only for Ian's sake, Geraldine hoped the body would not turn out to be Lucy.

Geraldine went to see Jason with her colleague, Naomi Arnold, who had recently been promoted to detective sergeant. Naomi drove them to Heath Moor Drive, which ran parallel to Heslington Lane, not far from the police station. The houses were detached, with sizeable front gardens whose well-tended lawns were bordered by a variety of hedges and shrubs, giving the street a pleasant green aspect. They pulled up a few doors along from their destination, a house which was smaller than some of the others. It was early evening, and the heat of the day had given over. A light breeze ruffled the leaves in the gardens. Under other circumstances Geraldine would have enjoyed the short walk, but the thought that she might have to tell Jason that his girlfriend had been killed cast a shadow over the gathering dusk.

Ian had told them he thought Jason was likely to be at home at that time, and he was right. The door was flung open almost as soon as they knocked by a young man who gazed out hopefully. On seeing them, his face fell.

'I thought – I thought – you were – someone else,' he stammered, staring at them in dismay. 'I'm sorry, I don't want to buy anything and I'm afraid I'm not looking for God. I can't help you.'

Before he could close the door, Geraldine stepped forward.

'Are you Jason Anderson?' she asked.

As she introduced herself, holding up her identity card, Jason's disconsolate expression changed to one of alarm. Geraldine studied him covertly. He was sturdily built, with light ginger hair that was almost blond, and rugged good looks. Probably older than he appeared, his boyish features made him look younger than Ian, who was almost forty. Meeting Jason, Geraldine understood why Ian sometimes complained that he struggled to keep up with the other players on his football team.

'Is it about Lucy? Have you found her?' Jason asked.

His voice expressed barely suppressed panic and his green eyes were almost closed, as though he couldn't bear to look at Geraldine. Carefully, she explained that they were pursuing a possible lead, and had come to ask for a hairbrush or a toothbrush belonging to his girlfriend. There was no need to tell him they were examining a body.

'You want a sample of Lucy's DNA because you've found her,' Jason whispered, his voice sounding choked. 'You've found her body, haven't you? She's dead, isn't she? What happened? Tell me what happened. Where – where is she?' His voice rose and he visibly struggled to control his distress.

As gently as she could, Geraldine confirmed that a body had been discovered and the police were exploring the possibility that it could be Lucy.

'We don't yet know the identity of the dead woman,' she reiterated. 'Lucy is just one of several possibilities,' she added untruthfully. 'So, if you could let us have a toothbrush, or a hairbrush, we can find out, and, of course, we'll let you know as soon as we can. I appreciate how difficult this must be for you, but please be patient while we look into this. The woman we've found may not be Lucy. There's no reason why it should be her rather than someone else. It's only that you reported Lucy missing, so we need to confirm, one way or the other, whether we've found her. Whoever she is, we need to identify this woman as soon as possible so we can notify the family.'

'Where did – where was she found?' he asked.

'I'm afraid we can't discuss anything further with you at present.'

She nearly added that an identity for the woman would help the investigation into her murder, but she stopped herself. Assuming the dead woman actually was Lucy, and Jason was innocent, he didn't need to be tormented by learning the circumstances of her death yet. And if he had murdered Lucy, the less he knew of the police suspicions the better, until he was arrested and locked up. And there was still a chance that the body wasn't that of his girlfriend at all. Whatever the truth, it wasn't looking positive for Jason and Lucy's relationship. If she wasn't dead, she might conceivably have met with an accident. The best he could hope for seemed to be that his girlfriend had deserted him.

Jason nodded and disappeared into the house. A few seconds later they heard him pounding up the stairs. When he returned clutching a pink electric toothbrush, he seemed perfectly composed.

'Here you are,' he said, almost cheerfully. 'Take it and do whatever you need to do. I don't suppose she'll want it back after you've mucked about with it. You realise I'm going to have to buy her a new one when she gets back. A bloody electric toothbrush!' His voice was calm, but there was a slightly manic gleam in his eyes as he spoke.

'We'll let you know the outcome of the test as soon as we can,' Geraldine assured him.

'Oh, don't worry. It's not her. It can't be. She's just gone away for a few days. She'll be back.'

With Jason's hollow assurances ringing in her ears, Geraldine walked back to the car. In a way, she hoped he was right, although that wouldn't help move the investigation forward. And if the dead woman wasn't Lucy Henderson, it wouldn't alter the fact that a woman was dead. If Jason hadn't lost his partner, someone else had lost a person they loved.

As it turned out it didn't take the forensic team long to analyse DNA on the pink toothbrush and confirm the dead woman's identity. Jason would have to be told that his optimism was misplaced. His girlfriend had been murdered.

7

'HE'S IN THE WAITING area with one of your colleagues,' Avril told Geraldine. 'He's been protesting too much.'

Geraldine nodded. She had encountered that reaction before, where next of kin refused to acknowledge the identity of a corpse, even when the evidence was irrefutable. The occasions where a body was impossible to recognise were relatively rare, and heartbreaking, but DNA evidence was conclusive. All the same, Lucy's father had insisted on viewing the body so he could confirm the identification for himself. Geraldine didn't blame him for that. She would probably have done the same.

'You people make mistakes all the time,' Mr Henderson told her, with an authoritative air, as though dealing with murder investigations was an everyday occurrence for him.

He was a tall, gaunt figure with a strained expression which was perhaps habitual, or could have been due to the situation. His wife was not with him. According to her husband she was busy, but Geraldine understood Lucy's mother was afraid to risk seeing the dead body in case it was her daughter. It was difficult to believe that Mr Henderson could really be convinced his daughter wasn't lying in the mortuary, in spite of his confident assertion to the contrary. After greeting him solemnly, Geraldine did her best to prepare him before leading the way to the viewing room where Lucy lay, her eyes closed, her expression peaceful. Her father gave a small start on seeing her. Recovering himself quickly, he nodded.

'That's her,' he said shortly. 'That's Lucy.'

Leaving the shocked father with a family liaison officer trained to deal with bereavement, Geraldine reported the identification and went back to the police station to begin investigating Lucy's life in earnest. By the time she arrived at her desk, everyone at the police station knew about the identification. Binita summoned the team to a short briefing where the duty sergeant allocated their tasks. Before speaking to Jason, Geraldine went to find Ian and explain what was happening.

'I know what's going on,' he replied bleakly.

There was nothing more to say, so Geraldine left on her sombre mission. A uniformed constable drove her to the premises where Jason worked, a building company with a head office in a block of serviced offices in York, just off the A19. It was only a couple of miles from the police station, not far from his home near Heslington Lane. They found a parking space easily, and she went into the building to ask for him. Holding up her identity card, Geraldine hoped she could rely on the receptionist's discretion. Assuring the girl she was there on a routine enquiry, she explained that she needed to see Jason straightaway. The receptionist nodded and checked her screen before issuing directions. Geraldine hesitated before saying it would be better if Jason came to the foyer to see her. She didn't add that she had some news that he might not want to hear in full view of his colleagues. With a fleeting scowl, the receptionist nodded and Geraldine went to sit on a bench that stood against the wall opposite the reception desk.

Although she had been in this position before, many times, Geraldine was still undecided how she was going to share the news when Jason came into view hurrying along a corridor leading off the entry hall. Geraldine recognised him at once. His face fell as he approached her.

'I was afraid it was you,' he muttered.

'Can we have a quiet word, please? Somewhere private?'

'What is it?' he asked, shaking his head with a fierce urgency. 'What's happened?'

Geraldine spoke softly. 'I'm afraid I have some bad news,' she said, glancing around. 'Would you like to sit down?'

The receptionist lowered her gaze as soon as she saw Geraldine looking in her direction, but she would have needed exceptional hearing to understand what was being said on the other side of the hall.

Jason shook his head and remained standing. 'What is it you've come here to say?'

'I'm really sorry to tell you that Lucy's father has identified her body,' she said softly. 'It was all over very quickly. She wouldn't have known what was happening,' she added. That wasn't necessarily true, but Jason looked so stricken she wanted to do what she could to soften the terrible news.

'No!' Jason looked down, realising he had raised his voice. 'It can't be her,' he added under his breath. 'I know it's not her.'

Geraldine invited him to sit down. He shook his head, but she insisted he take a seat before she continued. With a sigh, he slumped down beside her, and stared at the floor.

'I'm afraid the DNA evidence allows no room for doubt, and Lucy's father has identified the body of his daughter.'

'What – what happened?' Jason stammered, refusing to meet Geraldine's eye. 'How could this have happened to Lucy, of all people?'

'Of all people?' Geraldine queried.

'She was so – so full of life –' He broke off, as though he had only just realised who had brought him the terrible news. 'You – you're a detective, aren't you? An inspector? Why are you here? What's this got to do with detectives? What happened to her? Tell me, please. I need to know.'

He hadn't shifted from his position, head lowered, hands hanging between his thighs, but now he looked up and Geraldine saw tears in his eyes. There was no way of knowing whether they were a sign of grief, or guilt. Perhaps both.

'I'm going to have to ask you to accompany me to the police station,' she said gently. 'There are a few questions we need to ask you.'

'Can't you ask me here?'

'I'm afraid not. We need to question you at the police station.'

Jason sighed. 'Oh, very well. I know where it is. I'll come along later. I want to go home now.'

He rose to his feet, but Geraldine stopped him. 'I'm going to have to ask you to accompany me now,' she said. 'I'm afraid this can't wait.'

'Now?' he repeated.

'Right now.'

'Look,' he began and his voice cracked. 'Look,' he resumed, 'you've just told me my girlfriend's dead. You refuse to tell me how she died, and now you're saying I can't go home. I don't understand what's happening.'

'Jason, you need to come with me now. I don't want to have to summon my constable and make a spectacle of detaining you in front of your colleague over there, the one who's been watching us.'

'Can I at least tell my manager what's happened?'

'One of my colleagues will speak to him and explain. Now come on, please.'

With a bewildered sigh, Jason followed Geraldine out of the building.

8

LUCY HAD BEEN DISCOVERED, unconscious, on Tuesday evening and had stopped breathing during the night without coming round. By Thursday, her body had been identified and her boyfriend was at the police station, waiting in an interview room. Once the duty brief arrived, Geraldine was ready to begin questioning Jason about his relationship with the dead girl and his whereabouts at the time of her death. All in all, the investigation was proceeding at a cracking pace, and it looked set to conclude very soon. A neighbour had reported hearing Lucy and Jason arguing on the Sunday before she was killed. His friends had been questioned and several of them had admitted that Jason had been angry with Lucy for going out for a drink with her ex-boyfriend. It seemed they had found a motive for a jealous boyfriend to have hit his girlfriend, and this murder was probably unrelated to the other three girls who had gone missing.

Only Ian was not pleased. 'I don't want to rain on your parade,' he said to Geraldine, 'but I can't believe Jason would do such a thing. For a start, he adored Lucy. I know what you're going to say – that's got no bearing on whether or not he might have killed her – but he's not the sort of guy to lose his temper. He's laidback about everything. And from what he said she was a gentle girl, and not the kind to go provoking an argument.' He shook his head. 'It just doesn't add up. And yes, I know you think I'm being subjective, he's my friend, I get that. But I don't believe for one moment that he killed her. He simply hasn't got it in him. And he certainly wouldn't try to bury her to conceal what had happened.'

41

Geraldine sighed. 'What do you want me to say, Ian? I'll take your views into account, of course, I will, but I can only go through the process and see what an interview throws up. I'll keep you posted, of course,' she added quietly.

Ariadne's attitude was very different. 'This is going well,' she beamed. 'We've got our suspect behind bars, and we know he had motive and opportunity. Even Eileen would be impressed at how well the case is going, and that's saying something.'

Geraldine wasn't convinced their previous detective chief inspector would have been completely satisfied with their progress. Eileen had been notoriously impatient, and by now would doubtless have been agitating for a formal arrest and a full confession. But Geraldine agreed with her friend that things were progressing well, and she was glad Binita seemed pleased. Where her colleagues had sometimes felt undermined by Eileen's constant chivying, Binita's positivity was having an energising effect on the team. At the same time, there was no denying that, under Eileen's leadership, the investigative teams had invariably achieved good results in record time. Perhaps an impatient senior investigating officer was a necessary constituent of a successful team. Not for the first time, Geraldine wondered how well she herself would have fared in a position of such responsibility.

At one time, Geraldine had been heading for promotion, and expecting to lead a team of her own one day. But demotion had put paid to that prospect several years ago, and she was lucky to have kept her job. Now she had to be content with watching other people succeed where she had failed so spectacularly. It had taken her a while to come to terms with her own professional failure. She had been demoted after saving her twin sister from trouble. She remained convinced that she had done what was right, harsh though the outcome had proved for her personally. In time she had regained her rank as a detective inspector, but she would never now rise any higher. She wasn't unhappy with her situation, and thanks to her intervention her sister was safe.

One consequence of the success of the current investigation was that it was more difficult to conceal the murder from the public. They all knew they couldn't remain silent for long, but to have a suspect so soon after the discovery of the body made it virtually impossible to keep the case out of the media. Word soon spread among people who knew Jason that the police had been to his house. His friends knew that his girlfriend had gone missing, and rumours inevitably spread. By Thursday afternoon, the story was being broadcast on the local news, and reports had begun appearing in the press.

'The killer's probably reading this and laughing at us,' Geraldine said.

'Assuming the boyfriend didn't kill her,' someone else pointed out.

'If Jason is guilty, I don't imagine he'd be very amused at seeing his arrest all over the local news,' Naomi added.

'He's not been arrested yet,' Geraldine pointed out, a little vexed by her colleagues' slapdash comments.

'Do you think it will make him come forward and confess? I mean, if Jason is innocent, the pressure on the real killer must be hard to bear,' Naomi said.

Ariadne admonished her for being naive. 'You're talking about someone who goes around killing people,' she said. 'Why would he care if the wrong person is arrested? Seriously? Do you think this killer, who buries people alive, would feel that kind of moral scruple about anything? If he reads the local paper, my guess is that he's feeling triumphant because he thinks he's got away with it.'

'It might make him feel guilty, if he thinks someone else is taking the rap for him,' Naomi insisted.

Geraldine shook her head. 'You're imagining this killer is someone who might have a conscience like any normal, sane person. If you ask me, I'd say we're looking for a vicious maniac. Here's hoping Jason turns out to be the man we're after but, if it turns out he's not, I don't think a person like this killer is likely to crack under pressure. Ariadne's right, for all we know, he's enjoying himself reading about the investigation.'

No one wanted details of the investigation appearing in the media, but somehow information held by the police seemed to be leaking out into the public domain. Binita was resigned to it.

'There's bound to be all sorts of wild speculation flying about,' she said. 'Our job is to focus on our investigation and not allow ourselves to be distracted by anything, not even by journalists indulging their irresponsible urge to sensationalise the truth.'

Early that evening, Jason faced Geraldine and Ariadne across an interview table. A dishevelled duty brief was seated beside him, looking completely uninterested in the proceedings. His shock of grey hair shook every time he glanced down at his watch which he did frequently. With a crumpled jacket and an untidily trimmed beard, he looked barely respectable, an impression compounded by flakes of dandruff that powdered his shoulders every time he moved. Jason sat quietly, seemingly overwhelmed by the situation. Stifling a sigh, Geraldine tried to dismiss the thought that Jason was Ian's friend as she cleared her throat and began.

9

UNSETTLED BY WHAT IAN had told her, Geraldine rattled uncomfortably through the preliminaries. Even so, it seemed to take a long time before she was finally able to start questioning Jason. He stared straight ahead throughout, looking dazed, while his solicitor sat stony-faced, glancing surreptitiously at his watch from time to time. Having completed the obligatory preamble, Geraldine began with a few gentle questions about how long Lucy and Jason had been living together.

'So, that's nearly two years,' she repeated. 'But you had no plans to get married?'

Jason stared at her and narrowed his eyes. She wondered if he was thinking that she and Ian were in a similar position, and had to force herself to focus on the interview. She repeated her question and waited.

'We had no plans to get married,' he echoed woodenly.

'Really,' the solicitor interrupted irritably. 'I fail to see any justification for your intrusive questioning. If that is all you have to say, then I suggest you call it a day and stop wasting everyone's time. It's not a crime to live with someone.'

'I'm just trying to establish the nature of the relationship between Jason and Lucy,' Geraldine replied quietly.

'And how is their marital status relevant?'

Geraldine shrugged. 'Jason,' she said, turning back to the suspect. 'You're not in court here. I'm just trying to understand what happened to Lucy.'

'She's dead, isn't she,' he replied without looking up. He phrased the words as a question, but his voice was flat.

Carefully, Geraldine revealed that Lucy had been assaulted before she died. She didn't mention the exact circumstances of the attack, only referring to a head injury the victim had sustained, without giving any details.

'She was discovered lying at the side of the road in Heslington Lane, at the junction with Grants Avenue. That's very close to your house in Heath Moor Drive, isn't it?'

Jason nodded.

'She was discovered lying in the street,' the solicitor said pointedly.

'We are investigating the exact location of the attack,' Geraldine said, dismissing the implication of his words: if Lucy had been attacked on a public highway, anyone passing could have been responsible for her injuries. She leaned forward and studied Jason as she put her next question. 'Lucy was found very close to where she was living with you. When did you last speak to her?'

Jason heaved a sigh that seemed to shake his whole frame. 'We were together all day on Sunday,' he said. 'She wanted to go shopping for our trip, so we drove out to Monks Cross.' He fell silent, staring down at his feet.

'You went shopping for a trip?' Geraldine prompted him.

Jason nodded. 'Yes. We'd booked a holiday. We were going to Amsterdam in August. We'd booked – we were going away. She wanted to get some sandals.' His voice tailed off as the memory overwhelmed him and he sat, blinking furiously.

'And then?' Geraldine asked.

'She found the ones she wanted. She was so happy –' He faltered and dropped his head in his hands, unable to continue.

Gradually, Geraldine heard how Jason and Lucy had gone out for lunch before returning home laden with new clothes for their holiday.

'She liked to go shopping for clothes,' he said. 'She spent a small fortune on things for the holiday.'

'Did that make you angry?' Geraldine asked.

Jason shook his head with a faintly puzzled frown. 'What?' He turned and glanced at the lawyer who was drumming the stubby fingers of one hand on the table.

'Were you annoyed with Lucy for spending so much on holiday clothes?'

'Annoyed? No. Why would I be annoyed with her? It was her money.'

After their shopping spree, Jason had suggested they drive somewhere out of town and go for a walk, but Lucy had wanted to go straight home to try on all her new clothes. He hadn't spoken to her since Sunday. She had still been asleep when he left for work on Monday morning, so although he had seen her early on Monday morning, Sunday was the last time they had actually spoken together.

'And how did she seem on Sunday?'

Jason shrugged. 'Normal. She was excited about the holiday.'

'Did she say anything else?'

'We were talking about the garden.'

'What about it?'

He sighed. 'She wanted to brighten it up. That's what she said.'

'When did you first notice she was missing?'

'When she didn't come home on Monday evening. It was unusual. I mean, sometimes she went out after work, but she always told me when she was going to be home late. I tried calling her but she didn't answer her phone.'

Lucy had not gone home on Monday night. Jason had tried in vain to call her at intervals throughout the following day, but she hadn't answered her mobile phone.

'You must have been worried?' Geraldine asked.

'She'd been missing for at least a day,' he snapped, suddenly irate. 'I hadn't seen or heard from her for over twenty-four hours. What do you think? Of course, I was worried.' He drew in a shuddering breath. 'I'm sorry. It's just –'

By midday on Tuesday, he said he had been convinced something terrible must have happened to her. That was when he had first voiced his concern to Ian.

'I reported her missing. The police registered her details and advised me that most missing people turn up after a few days. If something had been done then, when she first disappeared, if I'd insisted, she might have been –' He broke off helplessly. 'I should have done more. I should have done more.'

'Can you think of anyone who might have held a grudge against Lucy?' Ariadne asked. 'Anyone at all? A colleague at work? Or an aggrieved ex-boyfriend?'

Jason frowned. 'Her ex contacted her recently, but I can't believe anyone who knew her would have attacked her like that. She was – she was a good person. She would never deliberately hurt anyone. She was gentle and – and kind.'

'Tell me about her ex,' Geraldine said, with a sudden flicker of hope that perhaps Ian's friend was not guilty after all.

Jason shrugged and glared miserably at Geraldine. 'Her ex called her because he was emigrating and wanted to see her before he left. She told me there was nothing between them any more, he was saying goodbye to all his friends. She said he told her he was leaving his former life behind and wanted to leave on good terms with everyone, something soft like that. I got the impression he was a nice enough guy.'

'When did she meet up with her ex-boyfriend?' Geraldine asked.

Jason claimed he couldn't remember exactly when the meeting had taken place, but it had been about a fortnight before her death.

'You can't have been happy about her seeing him.'

'No, not especially. She told me he was going to Australia

for a year, and her name was on his list of people to see.' He gave a sour smile. 'He wanted to say goodbye to her before he left.'

'It must have made you angry that she wanted to see him?'

The solicitor broke in. 'My client has already answered that question. He said he wasn't especially happy about it.'

'One of your neighbours told us they heard you arguing with her about her seeing him,' Geraldine pressed on. 'According to your neighbour, you were very angry with her.' Jason was silent but he looked pained.

Geraldine referred to the statement that a neighbour had given. 'According to your neighbour, you shouted that she wasn't to see someone called Gary. Was that her ex?'

Jason nodded.

'You wanted to stop her seeing him but she went anyway. Is that what happened?'

Jason sighed. 'I didn't like her staying out late. You know, when you love someone, you can't help feeling protective, and Lucy was so – so innocent and naive.'

'So, she refused to listen to you and went out with her ex anyway, against your wishes, and you flew into a jealous rage,' Geraldine said. 'It's understandable.'

'No, it wasn't like that,' Jason mumbled. 'You're making this sound like something it wasn't.'

'What was it like, then?'

'We never argued about her ex. I didn't mind her seeing him. That is, I wasn't happy about it. Who would be? But the guy was leaving the country. Why would I be jealous of him? We argued because I didn't like her being out late. She wouldn't tell me where she was going, she said they were meeting at the station and she didn't know where they would go. She was the one who was angry, not me.'

'Why was she angry?'

'She thought I didn't trust her, but I was just worried about her coming home late on her own. I told her I'd meet her, or she could get a cab, but she insisted she would walk home.'

'How did you know she was going to stay out late?'

'I didn't. I was just concerned in case she did.'

'What's Gary's other name?'

'I don't know.'

When Geraldine told Jason he could go home but asked him not to leave York, his solicitor spoke.

'My client is not under suspicion here,' he said, his shaggy eyebrows lowered in a scowl.

'We may need to speak to you again,' Geraldine said, addressing Jason. 'You can go home, for now, but stay in York.'

10

ANDREW SHOOK HIS HEAD. 'I don't understand it. I mean, that's to say it's not something anyone could understand. There's nothing about it that anyone sane could possibly understand. It must have been a random attack by some maniac. There's no other way to explain it. Lucy was such an inoffensive girl.'

He pulled what he hoped was an appropriately sad face. Beth had no idea he was using her as his audience while he rehearsed what he was going to say to the police when it was his turn to answer their questions. It was irritating, having to stop work for this, but he appreciated they were only doing their job. They certainly weren't going to learn anything useful from him, but they had to go through the motions.

'So, you're saying you think there's a psychopath on the loose in York?' Beth asked, her blue eyes wide with alarm.

Andrew grunted. 'Probably on drugs,' he said.

'Shouldn't we be scared? I mean, not you, but don't you think he could be a risk to people like me? Other women, I mean.'

Andrew gazed at Beth. Almost young enough to be his daughter, she was irritatingly timid, the kind of girl who would freeze when stressed instead of thinking clearly. What she was doing working as a solicitor was a mystery to him. The work wasn't dangerous, but there were times when the staff were under pressure to produce results. Beth hadn't been there very long. She had only just qualified, and it amazed him that she had managed to complete her training. She seemed to be permanently anxious.

'Yes, definitely dangerous, probably on drugs,' he repeated with relish, watching Beth crumble.

A solicitor had no business showing weakness. If Beth wasn't up to the job, it was better the senior partners discovered her flaws as quickly as possible. Andrew certainly didn't want to be saddled with an additional workload if she went off sick with stress. He had seen it happen, and found it intensely frustrating. Once he became a partner, he would set about getting rid of anyone who failed to pull their weight, whether through incompetence or idleness.

'The streets aren't safe,' Beth murmured. 'I keep a rape alarm in my bag when I go out,' she added, with a slight wobble in her voice. 'Do you think that's a good idea?'

Lost in thought, he didn't answer. *If Lucy had carried a rape alarm, things might have turned out differently. Beth wasn't alone in needing to be careful.*

'Good luck,' Beth whispered, when Andrew was summoned.

He shrugged. As if he needed luck. He had prepared himself thoroughly for this moment. Treating the interview as if it was a job, he had done his research, viewing images of the dead girl, and practising a sorrowful expression. He had schooled himself very carefully in his alibi to avoid any possibility of giving himself away. There was no reason why the police should suspect him, but he refused to be complacent. It would be easy to slip up if he wasn't alert. It had been pure chance that the girl he had seen staggering along the street had been one of the legal secretaries working at his firm. Straightening his tie, he stepped into the office where the police were questioning all of his colleagues. Reminding himself that he was a respectable solicitor, and a married man, he smiled solemnly at the police officer seated at one of the senior partners' desks. It was somehow offensive seeing her in that chair, and almost sacrilegious.

'Good morning, Mr Whittington.'

The police officer had a firm air of authority about her that suggested she was older than she looked. Her cropped black hair and penetrating dark eyes added to the impression of someone who was efficient in her work. Under any other circumstances he would have admired her air of determination. As it was, he was wary – but not afraid. Fear muddied the process of clear thinking.

'Good morning,' she repeated her greeting. 'Please, take a seat. I won't keep you long.'

He nodded his appreciation of her civility. Curiously, his confidence deserted him and he felt uncomfortably vulnerable as he studied his interlocutor. It was important that he kept his wits about him. Above all, he mustn't betray his guilt.

'How well did you know Lucy Henderson?' the detective asked.

He nodded. 'I knew her to say good morning to,' he replied. 'We never met outside work.' He stopped abruptly, conscious that the less he said the better.

He had only met Lucy outside the office once. On that occasion, her face had been so filthy he hadn't recognised her, and there had been remnants of twigs in her hair and caught in the crinkled fabric of her T-shirt. The way she had been staggering, it was hardly surprising that he had assumed she was drunk when he stopped the car. It had been a wild impulse to invite her to get in beside him. When she had backed away, he should have driven off but some warped instinct had driven him to leap out of the car and approach her for a quick shag in the back of his car. He had even offered to pay her. Only when she had stuttered his name had he realised she knew him. He wasn't prone to panic, but he realised at once that she could identify him and accuse him of propositioning her. Even though no crime had been committed, he was only too well aware of the damage she could cause to his reputation, not to mention his marriage. Before he could back away, prepared to deny any accusation as the ravings of a drunken slag, she began to scream, a horrible thin sound that seemed to slice through the air between them as she shrieked at him to get away from her. He had only intended to shock her into silence before she could attract attention, but he hadn't appreciated her frailty. One slap had been enough to fell her.

The detective's voice cut through his reverie. 'Were you aware of any tension in the office?'

Her calm tone was reassuring. She sounded almost blasé and was scarcely looking at him as she asked the question. He reminded himself that he wasn't a suspect.

As long as he didn't give himself away, he was in the clear. No one had seen him talking to Lucy. As soon as she collapsed on the pavement, he fled back to his car and drove off. No one could possibly have spotted him. Speeding away from the injured girl, he told himself he was in the clear. Not until he drew up outside his own house had it occurred to him that her DNA would be all over the hand that had struck her. With an effort, he had regained control of his thoughts. He couldn't go home like that. Her DNA must be on the steering wheel, and the door handle, as well as on his car keys. Cursing the bitch who had caused him so much trouble – for no reward – he drove off, thinking. He hardly needed to worry about using bleach. No one was going to carry out a forensic examination of his car, because no one could possibly suspect he was responsible for an act so terrifying he couldn't even name it to himself. All the same, he was keen to wash away all trace of her. He kept his right hand in his pocket as he bought a large bottle of water and some screenwash in a garage. He scrubbed his hands, and wiped the steering wheel and the door handle as thoroughly as he could, before going home and cleaning his fingernails in the shower. The next morning he took the car for a complete valet service. If the girl survived, he had only to deny all knowledge of meeting her in the street, and no one would be able to prove a thing.

With an effort, he brought his thoughts back to the present, and licked his lips nervously.

'Tension?' he repeated, raising his eyebrows to indicate his perplexity.

'Did she fall out with anyone at work, as far as you were aware?'

'As far as I was aware, no,' he replied.

As he spoke, he wondered whether he ought to attempt to point the finger at someone else. He had a score to settle with a colleague, and it would have been amusing to cast doubt on him. On balance, he decided it was safer to say nothing, do nothing that might draw any attention to himself.

'I wasn't aware of anything like that,' he said, in a tone calculated to sound firm yet nonchalant.

The detective had to believe he had no stake in this game. And really, Lucy had meant nothing to him. She had seemed like a nice enough girl but they had had no close contact until he had mistaken her for a vulnerable tart, too pissed to resist being dragged into the back of the car for a quick shag. He had never meant to harm her. He wasn't a brute. But he had been stupid. Cursing his own carelessness, he smiled sadly at the detective.

'It's a terrible tragedy,' he said. 'She was very young.'

The detective nodded.

'The consensus in the office seems to be that she was attacked by a random stranger,' he ventured, and immediately regretted his rash statement. If no one else in the office confirmed his assertion, the police might become suspicious.

'Whoever it was, you can rest assured we'll find him,' the detective replied.

It sounded like a threat. Telling himself there was no way she could possibly suspect him, he tried to smile, but his facial muscles seemed to have frozen.

'A tragedy,' he repeated fatuously.

11

GERALDINE HAD A FEELING there was something else she ought to ask Andrew. Having gone through all her planned questions, she had no obvious reason to detain him further, but somehow the encounter felt unfinished. Keeping her reservations to herself, she watched him closely as she thanked him for his cooperation. When he was leaving the room, there was a lightness in his step that she hadn't noticed when he arrived, and he carried himself with a more upright bearing. His evident relief was predictable enough, but she realised with some surprise that his expression didn't alter when she announced he could go. She wondered why he had been at pains to hide his relief from her. Possibly he was too proud to admit that he had been scared.

The next person on Geraldine's list was a recently qualified solicitor called Beth. According to some of the staff, she had been friendly with Lucy. Beth looked terrified when she entered the office. Geraldine spent a few moments trying to put the girl at her ease, assuring her that she had only a few questions for her, and the same questions were being put to everyone. She took care to explain the reason for speaking to all of Lucy's colleagues, and pointed out that Beth was under no obligation to respond.

'No, no, no,' Beth shook her head vigorously, making her straw-coloured hair flap around her narrow cheeks. 'Of course, I'll answer any questions I can. I want to help. Lucy was – she was – she was kind, and fun to be around.' Her voice faltered and she cleared her throat. 'I just can't believe it. What happened?'

'I'm afraid we can't discuss details.'

'Everyone here's saying she was murdered. Why else would you be here, questioning everyone who knew her?'

Geraldine inclined her head, unable to refute what Beth was saying. Yet, for all her eagerness to help, Beth had nothing useful to tell the police. She insisted that Lucy had been happy with Jason, whom she herself had only met once, and described Lucy in such glowing terms that Geraldine wondered whether she had been slightly infatuated with her.

'Did you and Lucy meet outside work?'

Beth shook her head. 'We hadn't known each other very long. I did think – that is, I hoped – I thought we'd become good friends, in time. And we would have been. I know we would. With some people you just click, don't you? It doesn't happen often, not to me anyhow. I never thought – I never expected anything like this to happen. I can't believe it.'

Beth was clearly desperate to help, but she was unable to add anything to what the police already knew.

After speaking to Beth, Geraldine was due to meet with one of the senior partners in the firm. Mr Holmes was bald, with a large square head and round shoulders. He wore a slightly peevish expression that probably made him look older than he actually was. The initial impression he gave was one of unrelieved severity, but this was quickly dispelled by the warmth of his smile as he grasped Geraldine's hand and shook it vigorously before sitting down. He described Lucy as a punctual and competent secretary, while Jason had struck him as 'solid'. As far as the senior partner had been aware, Lucy and Jason had been happy in their relationship, although he had only seen them together at the office Christmas dinner, at which everyone had been convivial and probably tipsy.

'Of course, you can never tell, but he seemed very fond of Lucy. My recollection is that he was attentive to her, and well mannered. He certainly didn't strike me as volatile, but naturally you don't see a clear picture of someone's character at an office

Christmas party.' He shrugged and grinned, and Geraldine had the impression he was nervous.

Geraldine and Ariadne spent several hours questioning Lucy's colleagues, who all came up with the same response. Everyone they questioned qualified their remarks by adding that they didn't really know Lucy very well, and had only a hazy recollection of her boyfriend after meeting him at their office Christmas party. Most of them had scarcely spoken to him. But they were unanimous in voicing the opinion that he and Lucy had seemed happy together, and they all expressed sympathy for him in his loss. No one seemed to think he could be a suspect. The general reaction of the staff was one of disbelief at the idea that Lucy had been murdered.

'How could such a thing have happened?'

'Who could have done something like this?'

'It's such a pity.'

'What a tragic waste.'

'She had all her life in front of her.'

But for all their expressions of grief and shock, none of Lucy's former colleagues was able to offer the police any leads to her killer. While they all seemed eager to share everything they knew about Lucy, it actually amounted to very little. By comparison, Geraldine and her team were careful to reveal as little as possible of what they knew about the circumstances of Lucy's death. They were especially keen to conceal the fact that she appeared to have been buried alive. Binita had hardly needed to emphasise the importance of withholding that information from the media. Geraldine shuddered to imagine the headlines such a revelation might generate. LOCAL GIRL BURIED ALIVE was exactly the kind of sensational story likely to catch the public's imagination.

'You look tired,' Ariadne commented to Geraldine as they drove away.

Geraldine shrugged. 'It's been a long day,' she replied.

'And it turned out to be a complete waste of time. No one there knows anything. Most of them don't seem to know the first thing about her, not really,' Ariadne grimaced. 'There are times when I really hate this job.'

Geraldine reassured her sergeant that nothing they did in the course of a murder investigation was ever truly wasted. Ariadne was still dispirited, and she drove back to the police station in gloomy silence.

12

It DIDN'T TAKE GERALDINE long to track down Lucy's ex. A search of her social media accounts came up with the name Gary Johnson. He had been Lucy's boyfriend before she met Jason, although it wasn't clear exactly when they had split up. Lucy had posted pictures of them going out together, and holidaying abroad as a couple. He was dark-haired and slightly swarthy, in contrast to Lucy's pale face and fair hair. They had appeared blissfully happy together, but an image created on social media was not necessarily an accurate reflection of reality, and Geraldine's research revealed that this seemingly perfect relationship had lasted less than a year. She wondered whether Jason had been the cause of the split, and how the break-up might have affected Gary. Two years seemed a long time to wait before venting his rage against Lucy, but if it was true that Gary was about to move overseas, it was possible he had seen this as a last chance to punish her for leaving him.

'It could be true,' Ariadne agreed, when Geraldine suggested Gary might be a plausible suspect in the murder enquiry. 'A jealous ex-boyfriend decides to kill her before he leaves the country. If he really is going to Australia, he might have thought he'd be safe from our justice system and it was worth attacking her before he quit the UK.'

'He might not have intended to kill her,' Geraldine replied. 'If this was a "crime of passion", and he just lost his temper, it could have got out of hand. But I agree, knowing he was planning to leave the country might have made him less cautious about losing control.'

'We could apply to have him extradited if we find evidence,' Ariadne suggested.

'It would make it more difficult to arrest him and it would take time, if we could even find him. But I'll follow it up. The last thing we want to do is lock up the wrong man.'

Lucy's parents lived in a smart-looking bungalow in a pleasant tree-lined street in Heslington. Geraldine called on them, hoping to find out more about Lucy's ex. The door was opened by a delicate-looking woman, whose similarity to the dead girl suggested they were related.

'Are you Mrs Henderson?' Geraldine enquired gently.

The woman nodded with a nervous jerk of her head. 'What do you want? Who are you?'

Geraldine explained that she was hoping to have a word with Mr Henderson, before introducing herself. The woman audibly drew in a sharp breath.

'It's about Lucy, isn't it?'

'Yes. I'm sorry we don't have any new information for you yet, but we are doing our best to find out what happened to your daughter and bring her killer to justice.'

'Justice?' the woman muttered bitterly. 'What kind of justice can there be in this world?'

'There is one line of enquiry we're hoping you might be able to help us with,' Geraldine ploughed on, afraid the bereaved mother would slam the door before she had a chance to put her question.

Mrs Henderson sighed. 'I'm sorry. It's not your fault what happened. I know you're only doing your job. But Lucy was –' Her voice cracked and she slapped one hand over her mouth.

Just then, Mr Henderson appeared in the hall behind his wife.

'What is it?' he called out urgently, as he saw Geraldine on the doorstep. 'What have you found out?'

Geraldine repeated what she had just told his wife and he grunted.

'Very well,' he said. 'You'd better come in. It's all right, Ellie. I'll handle this. Why don't you go upstairs and lie down?'

Mrs Henderson threw her husband a grateful glance before she withdrew, leaving him to take Geraldine into a kitchen with a large window looking out on a garden at the back of the house. The floor was wood block and there was a small wooden table and two chairs at one end of the room, with kitchen appliances and a sink under the window at the other end. He invited Geraldine to take a seat. Refusing the offer of tea, she asked him directly about Lucy's ex-boyfriend, and he confirmed that his daughter had been in a relationship with Gary for about a year.

'What was he like?' Geraldine asked.

Mr Henderson grunted. 'I know it's a cliché for a father to say this, but he wasn't good enough for Lucy. He was good-looking and seemed personable – glib, really – but he was basically a self-centred bore.'

'So, you weren't sorry when they broke up?'

Mr Henderson appeared to think about this before he answered. 'I was neither sorry nor not sorry. We only met him a few times so I can't tell you much about him, only my impression, but Lucy was certainly smitten with him.' He leaned forward eagerly. 'Do you think he did it?'

Geraldine admitted that they were still gathering information, and had reached no conclusions as yet about who had killed Lucy. Her father would be contacted as soon as the police had anything definite to tell him. In the meantime, she assured him they were being as thorough as possible in their investigation into his daughter's death.

'Do you know anything about the circumstances of their break-up?' she asked.

'Not really. You'd need to ask Ellie, my wife, about that. Lucy confided more in her than me. But I can tell you Lucy was devastated when Gary left her for her friend.'

Geraldine felt a faint frisson of dismay. 'So, it was Gary who ended the relationship?' He nodded. 'I can't give you any more details than that, but yes, he dumped her for a friend of hers. He was shallow and superficial and she was better off without him –' He broke off and sighed, perhaps thinking that she was hardly better off now.

'And you're absolutely certain Gary left her?'

He nodded. 'She came home and was inconsolable for weeks. We were very pleased when she met Jason, although I was worried in case the same thing happened again, and he let her down too.'

'Did he give you that impression?'

'No, to be fair, he seemed to adore her, and no one could blame him for that. She was – I know I'm her father and biased, but she really was a beautiful girl, inside and out. Ask anyone who knew her.'

13

GERALDINE DECIDED TO SUMMON Jason to the police station again.

'The fact that my client was in a relationship with the victim doesn't make him guilty,' his lawyer exclaimed as the interview commenced. 'He deserves compassion and condolences for his loss, not pointless bullying. This is harassment of a very serious nature. If my client suffers permanent damage to his mental health as a result of your actions, you can be sure he'll be taking steps to gain redress.'

They both knew the lawyer was only doing his job, but he sounded genuinely angry. Geraldine sighed. 'We're doing what we can,' she assured him.

The lawyer scowled and Geraldine looked away. The dishevelled lawyer hardly inspired confidence. Nevertheless, she had learned never to judge anyone by their appearance, and she took his complaint seriously.

She went on heavily, 'You must understand that your client's girlfriend was found dying only a few minutes' walk from where they were living together. And you must also appreciate that we have to look into the murder thoroughly, and investigate every possible angle. We wouldn't be doing our job if we didn't, just as you wouldn't be doing yours if you didn't object to our questioning your client.'

'Are you going to charge him?' the lawyer demanded impatiently. 'If not, you have no reason to hound him like this. He's already told you everything he knows.'

Geraldine suddenly lost patience.

'We'll let you know,' she replied curtly and terminated the interview, leaving the lawyer muttering crossly to Jason.

'Éla, what's up with you?' Ariadne asked, catching sight of Geraldine glowering at her screen. 'You look like you've been caught in a storm without a raincoat.'

Geraldine gave a reluctant smile. 'I need to go and speak to Binita about Jason,' she replied. 'I'm not sure whether we have enough to charge him.'

On balance, the detective chief inspector was inclined to suspect that Jason deserved to be arrested. When Geraldine remonstrated at the lack of evidence, Binita dismissed her reservations with a wave of her hand.

'Naturally, he's the obvious suspect,' she said. 'They were living together. And we know he was angry with Lucy for seeing Gary. That gives him a motive.'

'He denies that he was angry with her,' Geraldine pointed out.

'Why would his neighbour lie about it?' Binita countered.

'Just because they had a row doesn't mean he's guilty,' Geraldine replied, echoing the solicitor's words. 'We've got no evidence that places him at the scene –'

'What scene are you talking about, exactly?' Binita sounded exasperated. 'As far as I'm aware, we don't even know for certain where the girl was attacked, only where she was discovered, lying at the side of the road. She could have staggered there after being assaulted, or she might have been deposited there by her attacker. We know next to nothing about the circumstances of the attack. We know she was hit on the head and buried alive, but we don't know where the assault took place, or the site of the attempted burial.'

Geraldine looked down. Binita's outburst sounded like a criticism of the investigating team.

'How are we coming along with searching Jason's property?' Binita asked.

Geraldine shrugged. 'We haven't found a shallow grave that was recently vacated,' she replied with a scowl. 'SOCOs are there now, but so far they haven't come up with anything suspicious. Lucy's DNA is everywhere, of course.'

Binita sighed. 'Tell them to work faster. We'll have to find something soon. And in the meantime, go over his alibi with him again. If we find out he's lying...'

Accompanied by her young colleague, Naomi, Geraldine went to Heath Moor Drive to see what had been discovered there. Jason lived in a pleasant semi-detached house with a small front garden that had been neatly tended.

'Have you come across anything suspicious?' she asked the SOCO leading the search team.

He shook his head. 'No murder weapons and no signs of any disturbance,' he replied.

Geraldine had not yet seen the witness who had reported hearing an argument, so she and Naomi went to speak to her. It was still fairly early on Saturday morning and, as Geraldine had hoped, they found the neighbour at home. A small grey-haired woman answered the door to the property attached to Jason's house. She peered anxiously at Geraldine's identity card.

'Oh, the police,' the woman said. 'I suppose it's about the people next door? We heard what had happened, didn't we, Andy?'

She appeared to be talking to herself. As she reached down, Geraldine saw that a small dog had stationed itself at her feet and was watching the caller warily.

'Don't worry,' the neighbour said. 'He's very friendly.'

The little dog growled.

'He won't bite,' the owner said. 'What a terrible thing to happen. I can't believe it. They seemed like such a nice young couple.'

When Geraldine enquired about the argument the woman had overheard, the woman quivered with excitement.

'Do come in,' she urged them. 'I'll put the kettle on and then we can sit down and have a nice chat and I'll tell you all about it. No, no, it's no trouble,' she assured Geraldine who had begun to remonstrate. 'We don't get many visitors, do we, Andy? You come on in and make yourselves at home. You can stay as long as you like.'

'I'm afraid we don't have time to come in,' Geraldine replied firmly. 'We just want to ask you what you overheard.'

'He was shouting at her, poor little thing, shouting that he was going to kill her.'

'Are you sure that's what you heard?' Geraldine asked.

'Oh yes, I heard him with my own ears, and what's more, I'll swear to it in any court of law. I suppose they'll send a car for me? My legs aren't what they used to be. And I'm happy for them to quote me in the papers, if it helps you.' She gazed hopefully at Geraldine. 'I've got a nice photo of me and Andy they can use. I'll go and fetch it, shall I?'

'That won't be necessary, thank you.' With a sigh, Geraldine turned to leave.

'You don't need to rush off,' the neighbour said. 'There's a lot more I can tell you.'

'Were you surprised to hear what happened to Lucy?' Geraldine asked.

'Oh no,' the woman replied. 'I knew he was up to no good. I can always tell, you know. The police could use me, because I've got the knack. I can always tell when someone's lying. If you want, I can sit in on your interviews as a kind of human lie detector for you.'

Geraldine politely declined and withdrew.

'Waste of time,' Naomi murmured when they were out of earshot.

Geraldine nodded. The neighbour was a crank. It didn't necessarily mean that she had lied about overhearing a row between Lucy and her boyfriend, but it did make it almost impossible for her to be used as a witness, if the police felt they had a case against Jason.

They approached the neighbours on the other side of Jason's house, and in the properties across the road. Everyone else Geraldine spoke to doubted that Jason would have killed Lucy, but the fact remained that she had been fatally assaulted. None of the other neighbours she and Naomi spoke to was able to add to what the police already knew. No one else had heard Lucy and Jason arguing, there had been no raised voices at their home, as far as any of their other neighbours was aware, and nothing to suggest Jason might have had violent tendencies.

Having learned nothing new, Geraldine returned to the police station to question Jason again. Not knowing the time when the assault on Lucy had taken place made it difficult to pin anything down. She had died in hospital in the early hours of Wednesday morning, but the attack had taken place at an undetermined time the previous day, or possibly even earlier than that. Not knowing when she had been assaulted made it difficult to accuse Jason of injuring her.

'Tell me again what you did from Monday morning, when you claim you last saw Lucy alive, to Wednesday morning when she died.'

Jason winced, while his lawyer cleared his throat and spoke angrily.

'My client has already told you what he was doing.'

'I'd like to hear it again,' Geraldine said mildly.

'Like I said, I went to work on Monday morning. Lucy was asleep and I didn't want to disturb her, so I left. I was at work all day on Monday and in the evening I played football.' He glanced at Geraldine and she guessed he knew she was living with a member of his football team. 'When I got home, Lucy wasn't there,' he continued, in a flat tone, repeating what he had already told the police more than once. 'I didn't do this to her. I would never have hurt her,' he cried out with a sudden burst of emotion.

Lucy had been missing from Monday morning to Tuesday evening. There was as yet no proof that Jason had been keeping her imprisoned at home, but his reporting her missing might have been an attempt to conceal his activities. It was even possible he had tried to bury her somewhere nearby. There was no sign of disturbance to the soil in his garden, but there was open ground not far away. If he had attempted to conceal her body in that ghoulish way, the site of the attempted burial couldn't be far from where she had been found. A team was sent out with sniffer dogs to try and trace her movements but she seemed to have materialised in the street from nowhere, so it looked as though she might have been brought there in a vehicle. Jason's car was full of her DNA, but it seemed unlikely he would have deposited her so near his home.

Reviewing everything they had gathered about the case, Binita agreed they couldn't charge Jason on the strength of his neighbour indicating he was implicated in Lucy's death. The other query over whether Jason had been involved in his girlfriend's murder was that two unidentified samples of DNA had been found on Lucy's face and body, suggesting that at least one other male could have been present when she was attacked. Geraldine hoped that Binita was proof against succumbing to pressure from the media, who were baying for an arrest. Ian had been convinced of Jason's innocence. Admittedly, Ian was probably biased, but Geraldine trusted his opinion and couldn't help feeling uneasy that Jason remained their main suspect.

14

LINDA STARED ANXIOUSLY AT George across the table. They were having eggs on toast for lunch. Neither of them was working that Saturday, and they were spending the rest of the day together.

'Come on, eat up,' she urged him. 'Robert will be here soon. We can sit outside. It's a beautiful day.'

George grunted.

'Are you sure you're all right?' she prompted him, when she had finished eating.

George had hardly touched his food. Ever since that stupid girl had stumbled out of the garden and been found in the street, he had lost his appetite and his sleep had been disturbed. Even when he knew she was dead and could no longer pose a threat to his safety, he continued to feel on edge, fearful of discovery. It had so nearly gone horribly wrong.

'You're not sickening for something are you?' Linda went on, frowning at his virtually untouched plate.

He shook his head. 'I'm all right. There's no need to fuss. I'm just not hungry, that's all. What makes you think anything's wrong?' He was afraid he sounded brash in his endeavour to sound confident. Linda was no fool, and she knew him so well it was difficult to conceal anything from her.

To his relief, she believed him. 'It's just that you seem tired.'

'That's because I didn't sleep very well last night,' he replied, reassured by her smile. 'You're a fine one to talk. I should be asking you if you're all right.' He began to relax.

'If you're sure there's nothing wrong,' she persisted gently. 'I mean, if there's anything you'd like to talk about, you know I'm here. You can tell me anything. You know that. Anything at all.'

George hesitated. Just as he was wondering whether he dared share his secret with her, the doorbell rang and he started.

Linda stared at him. 'Good lord, you're jumpy today.'

'Who is it?' he asked, trying to hide his alarm.

'It must be Robert. He's early. I told you, he said he'd come over for the afternoon.' She glanced at her watch. 'It's only one o'clock.'

She clambered to her feet and scurried to admit Robert and his one-year-old son, Noah. George watched mother and son through the open kitchen door.

'Sorry to be so early,' Robert said, as Linda held out her arms for the baby with a welcoming beam. 'Sharon wanted a lift to the shops so I thought, as we were out in the car anyway, I might as well come straight over. I hope that's okay. I don't want to inconvenience you, but it's such a palaver getting Noah in the car, I couldn't be bothered to take him home again. He'd only have fallen asleep and been grizzly when I woke him up to come here. We can go for a drive and come back later, if you like.'

'Don't be silly. I wouldn't hear of it,' Linda replied, hastening to reassure him that he was welcome to visit them at any time. After greeting his father, Robert followed his parents into the garden where Linda spread out a blanket on the grass for Noah to lie on. They all watched admiringly as the chubby baby rolled over and over, until he had travelled right across the blanket.

'He'll go far, that one,' Linda said, smiling fondly.

'Based on his ability to roll all the way across a little blanket?' Robert laughed and she smiled complacently at the son who had brought such joy into her life. Robert looked around appreciatively. 'The garden's looking beautiful, Dad. I honestly don't know how you do it. I watered that cutting you gave me from your peonies, like you told me, but I think it's dead.'

George gazed at the red and white rose bushes blooming along the back of his garden, their vivid colours easily visible from the house. The red flowers seemed to glisten like splashes of blood and he shivered. He wondered how Linda would react if the blood of a corpse were sucked up through the roots of the bush and began dripping from the scarlet flowers. With an effort, he shrugged off such morbid imaginings and tore his eyes away from the distant bushes. He had taken care to plant bushes with delicately coloured flowers in beds closer to the house, to ensure the soft pinks and yellows could be seen from indoors. Every single plant in the garden had been deliberately positioned for maximum effect, and his care and expertise showed. His son, by contrast, had no idea how to arrange a garden.

To be fair, most people were like Robert. George was an exception. Only professional landscape gardeners could hope to match his skill. What Robert failed to recognise was that his father's talent wasn't innate, but the product of years of study and thought. Robert had been given the opportunity to benefit from his father's dedication. He could have created an attractive garden almost the equal of George's, without having to conduct any research of his own. But he had chosen to follow his own design, which basically meant leaving everything to grow unsupervised and barely cultivated. All Robert seemed to do was mow the lawn sporadically. The rest of the garden wasn't quite a wilderness, but it was certainly horribly overgrown. George had given up arguing with his son about it, and he no longer offered to tend Robert's garden for him. He wasn't altogether sorry. Apart from the mortification of his son's rebuff, George hardly had enough time to look after his own garden.

'So, how's everything?' Robert asked cheerily.

'Your father's been feeling a bit tired lately,' Linda replied.

George scowled at her. 'That's not true,' he snapped. 'I'm fine. It's just your mother fussing and seeing problems where there aren't any.'

'Perhaps you should get yourself checked out,' Robert suggested. 'It could be a symptom of some underlying problem.'

'Like growing older?' George said, with a wry grin. 'I'm not sure they've got a cure for that. Not yet, anyway. By the time junior is my age, they'll probably have people living forever.'

He smiled fondly down at Noah, who still seemed intent on rolling his way onto the grass. Every time he reached the edge of the blanket, Linda leapt forward and placed him firmly back in the middle where he lay, gurgling and kicking his fat little legs, until he set out once more on his journey.

They passed a lovely afternoon, marred only by Linda's evident concern. Several times, George caught her looking at him with a quizzical expression. Not wishing to encourage her, he studiously ignored her attention. He had told her he was fine and she had nothing to worry about. She had no business doubting him.

15

'So, Jason is still a suspect?' Ian asked Geraldine on Saturday as they sat over supper.

Geraldine gazed out over the river, sparkling in the summer sunshine. There were no boats out on the water at that time of day, although earlier slow-moving tour boats had been chugging past at a leisurely pace, packed with visitors to the city. A small pleasure craft sped past, fleetingly interrupting the peace, and then the waterway was quiet again. She sighed, enjoying the tranquillity.

'Shame it can't always be like this,' she said.

Ian frowned. 'What? You're enjoying knowing that a friend of mine is suspected of murdering his girlfriend?'

Geraldine's attention was immediately drawn, more by the angry tone of his voice than the words he uttered.

'The girl is dead,' she replied, aware that she was sounding defensive.

'So, you had to point the finger at someone and the boyfriend is the obvious suspect?'

'Well, yes, actually. Of course, he's the most likely suspect. That's always the case, as you know perfectly well. If he didn't happen to be a friend of yours, you wouldn't have thought twice about his being questioned. Binita's hoping he'll confess, so he can be formally arrested.'

'For a crime I for one don't believe he committed,' Ian snapped.

'Well, I'm very sorry,' Geraldine answered, with exaggerated and clearly fake sympathy. 'But a girl's been murdered and we're looking into the circumstances of her death and right now your friend Jason is our main suspect. I don't suppose you'd want to talk to him? See if you can get him to crack and confess all?'

For answer, Ian merely frowned and stood up.

'Ian, I'm sorry,' Geraldine said gently, recovering from her burst of annoyance. 'I know he's your friend, but we have a job to do and we can't allow anything to stand in the way of the investigation. You know that.'

'Of course, I know you're right,' he replied sullenly. 'That doesn't mean I have to like what you're doing.'

'Well, I don't like the fact that someone's been murdered.'

'No other possible suspects then?'

Geraldine hesitated, reluctant to offer false hope.

'Well?' Ian prompted her, sensing her uncertainty.

'We're investigating her ex-boyfriend,' she replied slowly.

'Who has to be an obvious suspect, surely?'

'The trouble is, her father told us he dumped her for one of her friends, and that checks out. Naomi spoke to this disloyal former friend, who confirmed that Gary was the one who ended the relationship.'

'He could still have had feelings for her. He might have wanted her back? Or she might have pursued him and made a nuisance of herself?'

'Like I said, we're looking into him. And there was a colleague of hers who struck me as a bit shifty.'

'Go on.'

'Oh, I don't know. There's nothing I can put my finger on, but I just had a feeling he was hiding something. I don't know why. Like I said, it was just a feeling I had.'

Ian made no attempt to temper his enthusiasm. 'Well, aren't you going to question him again? I have absolute faith in your instincts, Geraldine, you know that.'

'Especially when they seem to confirm what you're desperate to hear,' she said, laughing at him.

'It's not a laughing matter,' he chided her. 'A man's liberty is at stake here, a man who may well be innocent. I'm telling you, Geraldine, Jason's one of the good guys. He's not got a dark side. And he was devoted to Lucy.' He shook his head. 'If you knew him, you'd know it's inconceivable that he could have killed her.'

'And if you weren't so blinded by loyalty to your football buddy, you'd remember that, when it comes to murder, no one is above suspicion. Just because you don't believe Jason capable of murder, doesn't mean he isn't guilty. You know as well as I do that anyone is capable of killing someone they love, given the right provocation.'

Ian stared at her solemnly. 'No. That's just not true. If I believed that, I'd never dare sleep in the same bed as you.'

He chuckled, and Geraldine smiled, relieved that he was no longer furious with her for investigating his friend. They had three possible suspects, but unless there were further developments in the investigation, it was looking likely that Jason would be charged. If that happened, she hoped the arrest of Ian's friend wouldn't drive a wedge between them. Their love for one another seemed robust, developed through years of friendship with one act of consideration after another, one kind word at a time yet, like all relationships, theirs was built on shifting sands. Geraldine wondered whether she was imagining her unease over one of Lucy's colleagues, in an unconscious desire to find a culprit other than Ian's friend.

Aware that it was important to put all thoughts of Ian's friendship with Jason out of her mind, she tried to proceed as though this was any other murder investigation. She wondered whether she would have followed up her suspicion of Andrew under other circumstances. Her conclusion was obvious. At this early stage in the investigation, she would normally have focused her attention on the actual suspect, Jason. So, that was what she decided to do.

'I'm going to look into Jason,' she told Ian. 'See if there's any way we can rule him out.'

Ian gave her a sceptical glance. 'Do whatever you have to do,' he replied. 'Don't take any notice of me. You can't let my feelings distract you from your work.'

'Have you ever known me to act unprofessionally?' she demanded, stung by his implied criticism.

It hurt all the more because she knew she was allowing Ian's friendship with the suspect to distract her from what she had to do.

16

ON SUNDAY, GERALDINE HAD arranged to visit her twin sister in London. Geraldine had barely met her biological mother, who had given her up for adoption as soon as she was born. Not until she was an adult had Geraldine discovered that she had been adopted. Her birth mother's dying wish had come as a further shock, revealing to Geraldine that she had an identical twin. Their mother had kept Helena, whom no one had anticipated would live for long. But contrary to expectations, the baby had survived to be brought up by her alcoholic mother. It was perhaps not surprising that Helena had fallen prey to drug dealers. With Geraldine's help, she had gone into rehab and had succeeded in overcoming her addiction. Helena appeared to be coping with her new life, but Geraldine lived in fear of her sister returning to her former habit.

They met in a café in Cricklewood. After their initial greetings, Geraldine asked why Helena had wanted to meet so far from the flat she was renting in North London. Helena looked solemn as she explained that she had moved from the lovely apartment where Geraldine had last seen her living.

'Thing is,' Helena said, 'things is different now to what they was.'

Geraldine sighed. 'I noticed you're not wearing your engagement ring,' she said gently.

Helena snorted. 'Yeah, well, it don't take a shit-hot detective to work out what that means.'

'You're not with him any more?'

The last time Geraldine had seen her twin, Helena had been preparing for a low-key summer wedding. She had been apologetic about not inviting Geraldine, afraid that her fiancé might realise she had led an unhealthy lifestyle if he saw her beside her identical twin.

'What happened?' Geraldine asked. 'Don't talk about it if you don't want to.'

Helena shrugged, seeming not to care that her engagement had been broken off.

'It was them kids of his, innit,' she admitted, with an impatient sigh. 'They was dead set on ruining it for us. It was all about money for them, selfish arseholes. They couldn't bear to see someone else getting a cut of the dosh.' She snorted. 'Like their father was too old to deserve a good time. Poor sod. You know he was older than what he told me?' She cackled suddenly. 'Yeah, he had his secrets too. Not that I gave a shit that he was seventy-five, he was a good bloke, innit. But those snakes got hold of my history. They hired a private investigator and spilled the dirt on me. It should be illegal to go poking around in someone else's business. Anyway, they went to Glen and told him everything, more than what even you know, and I dare say a lot more that never even happened, and he dumped me. I could see he was cut up about it, but he said his kids had given him no choice. It was me or them. I tried telling him that was a nasty kind of love he was getting off them, blackmail more like, but he said he couldn't walk away from his kids. They was his kids. Bloody hell, Geraldine, what was I supposed to do with that?'

'I'm sorry,' Geraldine said.

'What you got to be sorry about? It ain't your doing.'

'I'm sorry it didn't work out for you. It sounded like you were happy together.'

Helena nodded. 'He was a generous old git, that's for sure. So, now I'm on me own again, rent to pay and all that. The bills in that place was huge, innit, so I had to shift. I still got me job, but that don't stretch far. I know it's a cheek to ask when you already done so much for me –'

'You don't need to ask,' Geraldine hastened to reassure her.

She suspected Helena was clever enough to understand the reason for her generosity, and hoped her sister wasn't upset by this lack of trust. But she was afraid Helena might relapse if she were ever reduced to desperate straits. It was an expensive way for Geraldine to expunge her feelings of guilt, even though she was not responsible for their different upbringings. She had done nothing to harm Helena. On the contrary, she had saved her. But Geraldine had promised their mother she would take care of Helena, and she did not intend to renege on that commitment. So, she did her best to hide her disappointment at learning that Helena was once again financially dependent on her, and smiled as cheerfully as she could.

'So, what's going on with you?' Helena asked. 'You all right? You look tired.'

Geraldine almost broke down and confessed that she was feeling exhausted, but instead she smiled. 'I'm fine.'

Helena grunted sceptically. 'Don't look that way to me. Still with your fella?'

There was a time when Helena had been too messed up to think beyond her own issues, and too resentful to want to hear about her twin sister's life.

'Yes,' Geraldine replied, smiling more brightly, 'we're still together. I think – that is, I hope – we're going to stay together. We were friends for a long time before we finally started living together.'

'What were you waiting for?' Helena asked, her eyes narrowing in suspicion. 'You're not with him because you've given up hoping something better will come along?' She reached out and put her hand on Geraldine's arm. 'Don't you go settling for second best. You're worth more than that, Sis.'

Geraldine shook her head. 'It wasn't that. He was married and they split up. They never got on. She went off with someone else but then she decided she wanted Ian back. It was all pretty horrible at the time, because she was pregnant.'

'Shit. And the baby was his?'

'No, as it turned out. But she told him it was his baby and he insisted on a paternity test. He told me he wouldn't have taken her back whatever the outcome, but you never really know, do you? How a man might react in that situation? I think he was a bit excited at the thought of being a father, despite everything he said about not wanting children.'

Helena sighed. 'I sometimes think I would've liked a kid. But it's better I never did. I would've made their life hell.' She laughed. 'And as for you, it's all about work for you, innit? No time for kids messing up your life. You and me, we're the same, innit?'

Geraldine wasn't quite sure what Helena meant by that, but just then the waiter brought over their food and the conversation drifted on to other matters.

'Investigating any interesting stiffs?' Helena asked, and grinned at Geraldine's disapproving expression.

Geraldine said that she was looking into the murder of a young woman.

Helena nodded thoughtfully. 'I think I read about that one,' she said. 'Is it the one where the papers think it was the boyfriend? Blonde victim?'

'How on earth do you know that?' Geraldine asked, and Helena admitted that she subscribed to an online news site about York.

'I like to keep up with what's going on in your world, Sis,' she said, a little wistfully. 'Silly, I know, but it makes you seem less far away.'

Geraldine was touched, but didn't answer. She didn't know what to say.

17

WHEN QUESTIONED MORE CLOSELY, Jason admitted that he couldn't state with certainty that Lucy had been at home on Sunday night.

'What do you mean, you're not sure?' Geraldine demanded, too surprised to conceal her irritation.

Jason explained that he had gone to bed early with a headache on Sunday, while Lucy was out with some girlfriends. They had been celebrating something, he wasn't sure what. Lucy had warned him to expect her home late, so he hadn't waited up for her.

'But she was in bed when you got up on Monday morning?'

Jason hesitated. 'The thing is,' he muttered, 'I think she was. That is, I'm pretty sure she was there but I can't be certain.'

'How can you not notice if your girlfriend is in bed beside you?' Ariadne asked.

Jason shrugged. 'I just thought she was there. But I didn't actually pull back the covers to see. Lucy likes to sleep with the duvet pulled right up over her ears. I got up very quickly, without really looking at her, grabbed my things and got dressed in the bathroom.'

'Why did you do that?' Ariadne asked.

'Because I didn't want to disturb her. I knew she'd had a late night, and she'd been drinking. And I didn't go back into the bedroom. I just went downstairs as quietly as I could.'

Geraldine frowned as she took over, concerned that Ariadne was losing patience with Jason's befuddled statements.

'So it's possible Lucy never came home at all on Sunday night?'

Jason shrugged again and looked at her helplessly. 'I think I would have noticed if she wasn't there when I woke up. But I didn't look and I can't be sure.'

'You assumed she was there?' Geraldine repeated dispassionately.

'Yes, exactly. I assumed she was there because, well, why wouldn't she be? She hadn't called me to pick her up on Sunday night, or to tell me she was staying out all night. It never occurred to me that she might never have come home.'

'You told us earlier that you were concerned whenever she stayed out late,' Geraldine murmured. 'How come you went to sleep before she came home?'

'I knew she was with a group of girlfriends,' Jason replied. 'And I was tired.'

He repeated that he had driven straight to his football practice after work on Monday. The first time he was aware that Lucy might be missing was when he returned home on Monday evening to find the house empty. He had no idea where she was, and she didn't answer her phone when he tried to contact her. Thinking her phone battery must have run out, he was more irritated than uneasy. He guessed that, either she had forgotten to tell him she was going out, or she had told him and he had forgotten. But by Tuesday morning, when she still hadn't contacted him, he became uneasy. He called in at her place of work only to be told that no one had seen her since before the weekend. He phoned Ian to tell him what had happened, and he reported her missing, but there wasn't much more he could do. When she didn't come home again on Tuesday evening, he became seriously worried. He rang round all the local hospitals, and phoned the police again, demanding action.

'So, she could have been missing since Sunday, when you last saw her?' Geraldine asked.

Jason nodded miserably. 'I thought she'd come back. I kept waiting for her to come back. I couldn't believe anything bad could have happened to her. Not Lucy. I thought maybe she'd told me she was going to stay with a friend and I'd forgotten about it.'

'Did she often do that?'

He shook his head.

Having asked him to write down the names of Lucy's friends, Geraldine went to compare Jason's list with Lucy's contacts on social media. By the end of the morning, she had drawn up what she hoped was a comprehensive list of Lucy's associates. It didn't take a constable long to establish that Lucy had been due to go out with a group of girls on Sunday evening. Geraldine sent a small team of constables to question them all.

'They were celebrating Lydia's engagement,' one of the constables reported, adding, 'Give it a few years and I dare say the same bunch will be out drinking to her divorce.'

'You said Lucy went out with them?' Geraldine asked sternly. She wasn't interested in irrelevant speculation.

The constable frowned. 'They were expecting her, but she never turned up. They all met at six in a pub in Micklegate and went on from there. They left several messages on her phone, telling her where they were, but she never responded.'

'Did any of them try to find out where she was?'

'No, they were out on the town, having a good time, and basically forgot about her,' another member of the team said.

'Not that there was anything they could have done, not knowing where she was,' the constable pointed out.

The new information wasn't helping the investigation. It now seemed that Lucy had been missing at any time from Sunday afternoon, when she had left home to meet her friends, until Tuesday evening, when she had been found dying in the street. Binita wasn't pleased with the development.

'Why has this only just come to light?' she wanted to know.

But there was no answer to that. In the meantime, Ariadne had confirmed the date when Gary had left the UK for his posting overseas. She reported her findings which established that Gary had left the country ten days before Lucy disappeared. By the time Lucy was killed, he was already in Australia, embarking on his new life. While Ariadne had been investigating Gary's movements, Naomi had been looking into Jason's past and had learned that he had been arrested for physically assaulting a previous girlfriend. He had been eighteen at the time of the alleged incident. The case against Jason was growing stronger. Armed with the new information, Geraldine had Jason brought to an interview room. His shabby lawyer sat beside him, looking irritated.

'I take it you're still fishing for nonexistent information?' he said. 'My client is not going to confess to something he didn't do, and you have no justification for pestering him at such a difficult time. I strongly urge you to leave him to grieve in private. You can see he's in a fragile emotional state. This harassment has kept him awake for four nights.'

'I would have thought that losing his girlfriend might have something to do with that,' Geraldine murmured. She turned to Jason. 'Tell me about Rachel Clarke,' she said.

The lawyer's untidy eyebrows rose and he turned to his client for an explanation. Jason started and his face reddened.

'Who?' Jason replied, but his apparent discomfort made it clear he recognised the name.

'Rachel Clarke,' Geraldine repeated slowly. 'You can't have forgotten the girlfriend who accused you of assaulting her.' She glanced at her screen. 'According to an account at the time, you gave her a black eye. She dropped the charges against you and it seems you thought you'd got away with it?'

'Since the charges were dropped, there was evidently no case against my client. It is inappropriate to claim he "got away with" anything. My client was, and is, innocent of any wrongdoing and this line of questioning is unacceptable.'

Jason dropped his head in his hands, mumbling inaudibly, and his lawyer requested a break. Geraldine agreed to resume in the morning. Before continuing to question Jason, she wanted to track down Rachel and find out why she had accused her former boyfriend of hitting her, only to retract her statement. Jason had consistently and vehemently denied the charge, so clearly one of them had been lying.

18

GERALDINE HAD TRACED RACHEL Clarke, who had moved from York several years earlier, and was now living in Scarborough with her husband and their one-year-old daughter. Geraldine decided to pay her a visit, making the trip to Scarborough on her own. She enjoyed the solitary drive, which gave her time to think. Lately she had been feeling tired, and ready for a break, but seeing her sister in London had shaken her out of the doldrums and she was filled with a resurgence of energy. It was a sunny day, and she enjoyed the opportunity to drive away from the city where she lived and worked. Much as she loved York, she always welcomed a change of scene.

'What time will you be home?' Ian had asked her when she told him her plans. 'Shall I make dinner or will you grab something while you're out?'

'I'll probably be at least a couple of hours,' she replied, 'depending on how long it takes to find this woman. You go ahead and I'll fix myself something when I get home.'

There wasn't enough traffic on the road to Scarborough to slow Geraldine's progress. She arrived in good time and pulled up outside a terraced house in a well-maintained row of properties, each with its own individual neat little front yard. A woman opened the front door so quickly she could have been waiting for Geraldine to ring the bell. She looked surprised to see a stranger on her doorstep, and Geraldine realised that she had been expecting someone else.

'Who are you?' Rachel asked. 'What do you want?'

She was wearing a pink jogging suit, and her fair hair was tied back in a short ponytail. She was slim, with a pretty face that looked somehow faded, like an old photograph.

Geraldine introduced herself and explained she wanted to ask Rachel a few questions about someone she had once known.

'Who?' Rachel asked, glancing around warily.

'Can I come in?' Geraldine asked.

Rachel led Geraldine to a small square living room at the front of the house. The child was probably upstairs in her cot, but there was evidence of her presence in the room. A pile of brightly coloured plastic bricks was stacked up against one wall, and a high chair stood in a corner, its tray smeared with what looked like porridge. Beside the high chair a heap of fluffy toys lay in an untidy heap. Rachel cleared a few cardboard baby books off a chair and gestured at Geraldine to sit down. As she did so, a baby began to cry somewhere in the house. Rachel hurried from the room, leaving Geraldine alone. It wasn't long before she heard footsteps coming down the stairs and Rachel joined her again, this time with a baby in her arms.

'Do you mind if I feed her?'

'Of course not. Please, go ahead.'

With the baby comfortably settled in Rachel's arms, Geraldine began to question her.

'I haven't seen or heard from him in years,' Rachel replied, when Geraldine asked her when she had last seen Jason.

'But you used to know him?'

Rachel nodded, mumbling that she recognised the name.

'He was your boyfriend for a time, wasn't he?'

Rachel looked uncomfortable. 'Yes,' she muttered, 'we went out, but the relationship didn't last long. It was never anything serious. We were kids. Teenagers.'

'Jason was eighteen and you were seventeen,' Geraldine said. 'How long were you seeing one another?'

Rachel shrugged. 'I really don't remember. Like I said, we

were just kids. It was a long time ago. Why are you asking me? What's this about?'

Taking care to betray nothing about the murder investigation, Geraldine explained the police were interested in the allegation Rachel had made about Jason.

'What? Seriously?' The baby squirmed and let out a squeal of protest. Rachel turned her attention to nursing her daughter.

'You were about to tell me about you and Jason,' Geraldine prompted her when the baby had settled again.

'Oh my goodness, it was years ago. Why on earth would you want to bring that up after all this time? Don't tell me Jason's in trouble with the police?'

Geraldine persisted, determined to persuade Rachel to tell her exactly what had caused her to go to the police and accuse Jason of assaulting her.

Rachel sighed. 'Oh, very well,' she said. 'I'll tell you what happened, but it's not very interesting.'

It was a sorry enough tale, rather than a sordid one, which Geraldine finally managed to prise out of a reluctant narrator. Rachel repeated that she had been very young when she had known Jason. They had dated for several months before they split up, because they were both too young to handle a serious relationship.

'You missed something out of your account,' Geraldine said when Rachel finished.

'What do you mean?'

It was clear from Rachel's refusal to look at Geraldine that she understood exactly what Geraldine was talking about.

'I think you know,' Geraldine replied softly. 'You made an allegation which you subsequently retracted. Tell me what that was all about. Something must have led you to make the accusation in the first place. What made you do it?'

Rachel hesitated before repeating that she had been very young at the time.

'Not too young to understand the seriousness of your allegation. What happened?' Geraldine persisted.

Rachel replied that it had all been a misunderstanding.

'Why did you decide to withdraw your accusation?'

Rachel smiled uneasily and shifted the baby so that its head lay facing the other direction.

'I realised I'd made a mistake,' she replied. 'Jason hadn't done anything wrong.'

'You accused him of assaulting you.'

'Yes, well, I was mad at him for dumping me. I was only seventeen and I thought my life was over. I think I was hysterical – honestly, I don't know what I was thinking. It wasn't even my idea to accuse him of hitting me. One of my friends suggested it. She said it would serve him right. It – it seemed funny at the time.' Rachel looked away, clearly uncomfortable. 'I just wanted to get back at him. I was so mad at him. But it was a really stupid thing to do, stupid and mean. I honestly didn't realise how serious it would be. I mean, the police believed me straightaway. It was – that is, it seemed unreal at the time –' She broke off, her eyes filled with tears. 'I never thought they'd believe me. Why would they, when it wasn't true? I just wanted them to go and speak to Jason, give him a bit of a scare, show him that he couldn't mess with me and get away without a moment's unease. When he was arrested, I didn't know what to do, but I couldn't go through with it, going to court and all that, knowing I'd made it all up. I told the lawyer I wanted to drop the whole thing and he said I could drop the charges, so I did. I think the lawyer knew the accusation was made up. I never saw Jason again after that.'

'Not even to apologise?'

Rachel shook her head. 'The lawyer advised me to have no further contact with him and, to be honest, I don't think I could have faced him, not after what happened. But I withdrew the allegation and that was the end of it. He was released. I know some people thought he'd got away with it, but there was nothing I could do, not without publicly admitting I'd lied about it. You won't tell anyone, will you?'

19

IAN MAINTAINED IT WAS unlikely Jason would have been keen to draw attention to Lucy's absence straightaway if he was guilty. Listening to Ian's defence of his friend as they drove to the police station on Tuesday morning, Geraldine was inclined to agree with him. If Ian was to be believed, then something didn't quite add up, and Jason had been wrongly suspected.

'He was concerned about her on the Tuesday,' Ian insisted. 'He called me and begged me to look for her.'

Geraldine spoke tersely. 'You told me.'

'Jason's not tricky,' Ian went on. 'I don't believe he was lying to me. I realise it could have been a deliberate ploy to convince me he didn't know what had happened to her, but I think he was genuinely worried about her.'

In spite of Ian's assurances to the contrary, as Lucy's boyfriend, Jason remained the most likely suspect. The fact that she had been discovered so close to where he had been living with her didn't help his case. Yet Ian knew Jason, and was convinced he was innocent. So, there were a number of reasons why Geraldine was keen to look into Jason's movements again. According to his statement, Lucy had gone out on Sunday afternoon and had possibly not returned home on Sunday night. She had not actually been seen by anyone who knew her between Sunday afternoon and Tuesday evening. Yet she had still been alive, if unconscious, when she had been found in the street on Tuesday night. Something must have happened to her on Sunday night that had kept her from going to work on Monday, although she was still alive. The most likely explanation was that Jason had assaulted her, kept her at home for two days, and then attempted to bury her.

'It's a pity Lucy was found so close to Heath Moor Drive,' Geraldine muttered to Ian as they drew up in the police station car park. 'It really does all point to him being guilty.'

'I don't believe it,' Ian muttered crossly. 'It's ghoulish, the idea that he would try to bury her while she was still alive. It's crazy. And Jason isn't insane.'

That morning, Geraldine faced Jason once more across a table in an interview room.

'Let's go through your movements again, shall we, from Sunday afternoon to Tuesday evening?'

'I've already told you, I was at work all day on Monday. Ask anyone in the office. They'll tell you I was there, all day. On Monday evening I played five-a-side football with my mates. When I got home, Lucy wasn't there. I thought she must have gone out.'

'Was it usual for her to go out without telling you?'

Jason shook his head and pulled a face. 'I sometimes forgot she'd told me she was going out. And sometimes she went out after work without letting me know. We were living together. We weren't joined at the hip.'

'So, you were alone at home on Monday after playing football?'
Jason nodded.

'What about Tuesday evening?'

He shrugged helplessly. 'I was at home all evening. I was waiting for Lucy to come home or at least get in touch to tell me what was going on. I couldn't believe she'd walk out on me without a word, not even a note of explanation. And all her things were still at home. I checked nothing was missing, even though I never really thought she'd left me. I was worried something had happened to her, that she must have had an accident, been run over or something. I was really worried about her,' he added miserably. 'It never occurred to me that she might – that this might have happened and I might be suspected of... Don't you think I'd have planned an alibi if I was guilty of – killing her?' His voice rose in agitation.

'I don't suppose you planned for this at all,' Geraldine replied calmly. 'What happened, Jason? Tell me everything. You'll feel so much better if you come clean, and the prosecution will take your confession into account. What happened? Tell me about the argument. Was it her fault?'

'What do you mean? What argument? I don't know what you're talking about. Who told you we were arguing? They're lying. We weren't arguing about anything.' He sighed and dropped his head in his hands. 'We never argued,' he insisted, his voice muffled. 'I loved her. I wanted us to spend the rest of our lives together.' He paused. 'We talked about it, you know. About our future together. We were happy. We'd booked a holiday. Why would I have wanted to hurt her? I lived in terror of losing her.'

Everything that Jason was saying made sense, but, of course, angry lovers could resort to violence in what was sometimes called a crime of passion. The more he protested how much he had loved Lucy, the more likely it seemed that he might have killed her in a fit of temper or jealousy. Geraldine tried a different tack.

'Was Lucy faithful to you?' she asked suddenly, hoping to catch the suspect off guard. But he just smiled sadly.

'As far as I know, yes,' he replied carefully. 'If you have evidence to the contrary and think you can use that to explain why I might have killed her, you've got it wrong. I keep telling you, I loved Lucy and I wanted to spend the rest of my life with her. I can't imagine my life without her –' He broke off, his voice cracking with emotion. 'Why would I have done this to myself?' His expression hardened. 'But someone did this to her, didn't they? Was she – what kind of assault was it?'

'It wasn't a sexual assault,' Geraldine replied quietly.

In some ways it would have been better for Jason if the killer had left traces of semen on the body as evidence that another man had assaulted her. But he sighed with evident relief before continuing.

'Someone did this to her, and when you find out who it was, I want to see him suffer.' He clenched his fists and pounded them on the table. 'That's someone I could happily kill, and slowly.' He glared at Geraldine, but she could tell it was an empty threat.

In that moment, Geraldine knew that Jason wasn't capable of killing anyone.

When she spoke to Binita, the detective chief inspector was dismissive of Geraldine's opinion.

'Where's your evidence?' she asked. 'You know perfectly well that saying you don't believe he's guilty is worth nothing without evidence to back up your hunch.'

Geraldine nodded. Aware that once Binita discovered Jason was a friend of Ian's, she might be removed from the case, she resolved to keep her suspicions to herself. But she was determined to pursue the investigation further.

20

AFTER A FLURRY OF customers in the morning, the garden centre was quiet on Tuesday afternoon. It was generally only really busy at weekends, which gave them time to keep the place tidy. A middle-aged woman in a bright red coat approached George to enquire about indoor plants. He inclined his head politely, forcing a smile as her shrill voice drilled into his skull. While he struggled to focus on what the woman was saying, a young girl walked past, and he felt a sudden frisson of excitement. Out of the corner of his eye, he watched the girl walk very slowly along the aisle, scanning the shelves of succulents, seemingly unable to make a decision. Her movements were slow and appeared effortless, as though every pace was a step in a slow dance. Young and healthy, she was perfect for his purposes. Her long dark hair had a glossy sheen, and she had a flawless complexion. He shifted his gaze before she noticed his interest in her. He didn't want to scare her off before he even had a chance to approach her.

'I looked everywhere and I can't see them,' the high pitched voice whined right by his ear. 'So, can you show me? There's no point in giving me directions because I'll never be able to follow them. This place is like a maze.'

He turned back to the customer he was serving. She was wearing a garish red coat, and close up her bright red lipstick looked thick and unpleasantly greasy. When she opened her mouth to speak, he saw a smear of red lipstick on her front teeth. There was nothing else for it but to escort her outside to the flowering shrubs and wait while she fussed, unable to reach a decision.

'Which one would you recommend?' she asked him earnestly.

Barely concealing his impatience, he showed her some azaleas and said he would leave her to examine them at her leisure. Extricating himself from his customer, he set off to find the girl who had piqued his interest. Doing his best to look as though he was walking around the store for a reason, he scanned the aisles with increasing frustration. He was on the point of giving up when he thought he glimpsed her slender figure walking across the far end of an aisle. Swiftly, he strode along a parallel route. Reaching the far end, he almost ran into her. His heart seemed to skip a beat, but she didn't even look up from the decorative pots she was studying.

He glanced around. There was no one else in view. Only someone familiar with the security system would know that, if he could persuade her to take a couple of steps towards the back exit, they would be out of sight of a camera. He waited, forcing himself to be patient. At last she shifted, moving further along until they were in a position where he could speak to her unobserved. He couldn't risk leaving any evidence of their meeting. He was painfully aware that one false step might cause his carefully constructed world to fall apart. The familiar fear could be debilitating or addictive, depending on his mood. Right now, he felt a rush of exhilaration because he knew exactly what to do. With a confidence borne of experience, he stepped right up to her, certain they wouldn't be filmed.

'Good afternoon, Miss,' he said in a low voice.

She looked up at him and her black eyes gazed at him questioningly. The security cameras were not far away, and they might be able to record the sound of his voice, even if he kept out of sight.

'Can I help you?' he murmured. 'Are you looking for anything in particular? I work here,' he added, afraid his eagerness would alert her suspicions.

Her eyes flicked to his green overalls and back to his face.

'I'm sorry?' She smiled, a little hesitantly. 'What did you say?'

He took a step closer, not daring to raise his voice much. 'I asked if you're looking for anything in particular. I might be able to help you. I work here.'

'Oh no, thanks,' she replied, drawing back a little. 'I'm just having a mooch around. I probably won't be buying anything. At least, not today. Thanks all the same.'

He bit his lip as she moved off. Unknowingly, she sashayed right into the line of sight of the security camera. Cursing under his breath, he turned and nearly knocked into the woman in the red coat who had come back to tell him she had found exactly what she wanted. She was pushing an empty trolley.

'*There* you are,' she cried out, as though he was a naughty child who had run off. 'I looked for you outside, but couldn't see you anywhere. I've decided on the pink one. It's gorgeous, isn't it? Could you put it on the trolley for me? And I'll need help lifting it into the car.'

'Of course. Follow me, Madam,' he replied, staring wretchedly at her bright smiling lips. He knew when he was beaten.

It was completely by chance that he caught sight of the girl again as she was leaving the store. He was tempted to slip out of the garden centre and follow her, but the chances of finding out where she lived before his absence was noticed were almost nil, and it was essential to avoid drawing any attention to himself. He had to let her go and wait for another chance. There would be other possibilities. It didn't have to be a woman, of course, but he was afraid he might not be strong enough to overpower a sturdy young man. That girl would have suited him perfectly. With a sigh, he turned back to the shelves. As long as his wife continued to work night shifts, he could afford to be patient. He just had to make sure he was ready when the opportunity arose.

21

'How's the case going?' Ian enquired that evening.

Geraldine hesitated to admit the investigation was all but concluded. No one else seemed to entertain much doubt that Jason had killed his girlfriend. In the past, she might have been more sceptical, prepared to doubt everything until the evidence became compelling. Somehow, Ian's interest in the case, coupled with Jason's delay in reporting his girlfriend missing, was confusing her. Jason was Lucy's boyfriend, and he had no clear alibi, partly because they couldn't be sure when she had been attacked. He was the obvious suspect, and he was unable to establish his innocence. It wasn't entirely satisfactory, but Binita was confident they had enough to make an arrest.

'Did the assault take place on Sunday when she disappeared?' was the question no one could answer.

Lucy could have been attacked at any time between late Sunday afternoon and Tuesday evening. The unusually long period of time made it almost impossible to check her movements at the time she was attacked.

'She can't have been wandering the streets with a life threatening injury for two days,' Binita said. 'It looks as though someone was keeping her somewhere out of sight for around forty-eight hours. But where was she being kept all that time? And why did her assailant try to bury her? It's bizarre.'

There was a general murmur of agreement.

'He must have been keen to hide the body,' Ariadne said. 'Presumably he thought burying her was as good a way as any.'

But their discussion was built on speculation. To Binita's evident irritation, Jason remained adamant that he had last seen Lucy at home, and had tried to find her as soon as he realised she was missing. Checking with Lucy's parents and work colleagues corroborated that he had indeed been looking for her.

'But, of course, he would do that if he was guilty,' Naomi pointed out. 'Unless he's a complete idiot, he'd be wanting to cover his tracks, wouldn't he? There's no way of knowing if he's innocent, or if he's behaving like a guilty man might behave if he wanted to appear innocent.'

Geraldine was reluctant to tell Ian that the conclusion of the investigation seemed to point to Jason, but there was nothing to be gained by delaying.

'Binita's convinced this was some kind of crime of passion,' she told him. 'She's hoping he'll confess. If he does, then as long as he can convince a jury there was some provocation, he might not go down for long.'

'So, you think he did it?'

Geraldine was slightly taken aback by the aggression in Ian's voice. His normally good-natured face was tense with controlled rage.

'So, in the absence of a confession, where's the evidence?' he pressed her. 'You know, I'm just trying to understand what's going on. Because none of this makes sense.'

Geraldine sighed. 'You know it's out of my hands –'

'So, if it was up to you, Jason wouldn't be a suspect? Surely you could argue that with the DCI?'

Geraldine hesitated to admit that she had no case for defending Jason, any more than Binita had a watertight case for suspecting him. It was tricky and she was a little annoyed with Ian for placing her in such an awkward position, but seeing the misery in his eyes, she caved in. Nodding at Ian, she heard herself promising to do what she could to help Jason. The first task she set herself was to speak to everyone who had been close to him.

She started with the three other members of Ian's football team. They all lived nearby, and after an early supper she went to see them, starting with the one who lived closest to her.

Ray Masters was slightly older than the other members of the football team, and according to Ian he was the one who organised their practices. Ray lived in a flat near Micklegate. Finding a parking spot as near to the apartment block as she could, Geraldine strode along Micklegate and turned off along Barker Lane. It took Ray a few minutes to answer the bell, but he buzzed her in straightaway when she introduced herself. He ushered her into a large L-shaped living area with a kitchen area off to one side, and invited her to take a seat on a gleaming leather settee which was firm and surprisingly comfortable. Refusing a drink, she launched into the reason for her visit.

'Yes, I realised this must have something to do with Jason,' Ray replied.

'Tell me about him.'

'What is it you want to know? I can't tell you whether or not he killed his girlfriend, but I can say that I think it's highly unlikely. He never struck me as a violent type.'

'How well do you know him?'

He thought for a moment before answering. 'I've known Jason for around ten years, but I couldn't say I know him that well. We play football together once a week and he's easy to get along with, and he's got a good sense of humour.' A faint smile flitted across his face at some private memory. 'And he seemed settled with Lucy,' he added. 'He didn't really talk about their relationship, but he never complained about her. You tend to pick up hints, you know, when things aren't going well.'

Geraldine wondered uncomfortably whether Ian had ever mentioned her to his football mates. For all his evident willingness to help, Ray had very little to tell her about Jason, other than that he was a 'nice guy' and a 'good bloke', and similar phrases, none of which did anything to advance the case for or against Jason. The other two members of the team also lived nearby and Geraldine visited both of them that evening. They seemed keen to help but were equally useless in terms of moving the investigation forward. Jason seemed to be universally liked, but none of his football team could offer any particular insights into his personal life.

'It's not something we ever mention, really,' one of the other men admitted, his blue eyes sharp with anxiety for his friend. 'It's more about football, and sport in general. That's what we discuss when we go for a drink after a game. We don't tend to talk about private matters at all. Why would we? I mean, we get together to play football, not to have heart-to-hearts. That's just not something we do.'

As she drove home, she wondered if she had done enough to follow up her suspicions of Andrew. But, as with the evidence building against Jason, she had nothing definite to cling to. The only certainty was that someone had killed Lucy and, on the balance of probabilities, Jason was guilty. She wished she was confident her reservations were due to her consideration for Ian's feelings, not to her own doubts about Jason's guilt.

22

ALISON WAS TIRED, AND more than a little tipsy. It was the end of a long day. The trouble was that, every time she resolved to stop drinking, something cropped up to lead her astray. It wasn't even her fault this time. Sandy from her tutor group had invited everyone to the pub to celebrate his birthday. She could hardly refuse to go.

'You're only twenty once,' he had declared when a couple of their friends had remonstrated that it was a Tuesday evening and they had an early start the next morning.

Sandy had brushed off their scruples with a laugh. 'Just one drink won't do you any harm,' he had insisted.

Despite his urgings, a few people had cried off, but most had been happy to go out for a small celebration, and Alison had gone along with them. After all, she liked Sandy. His good humour was guaranteed to cheer everyone up, and it was his birthday. Alison's problem was that she wasn't as accustomed to drinking as she made out. All she had eaten that day was a fruit yoghurt at lunchtime and now, after two gins, she was feeling giddy and a little sick. She was relieved when a couple of Sandy's friends stood up to leave. She jumped to her feet as well, and then regretted having got up so suddenly.

'I say, are you okay, Alison?' one of the girls asked. 'You look a bit rough.'

'I'm fine,' she replied, with a smile.

Just in time, she resisted the impulse to nod her head. Keeping herself firmly upright, she made her way carefully across the bar to the exit. No one was watching her closely enough to see the room sway gently around her. She giggled to herself, because, of course, the room wasn't moving. It was her. Reaching the door, she pushed it open and a breath of chill night air whirled around her face, brushing past her cheeks. It was lovely, but she couldn't stand there all night, enjoying the cool air. The chattering of the pub customers faded as the door swung shut behind her and she felt fleetingly bereft, standing on the pavement alone, with only passing strangers for company. Her fellow students had vanished into the night, while she had been vacillating in the doorway. Drawing in a deep breath in a vain attempt to sober up, she turned and slowly began to walk along Micklegate only vaguely aware that someone else had left the pub just behind her. As long as she kept her head facing forwards, she would be fine. She only felt dizzy when she turned abruptly, or shifted the position of her head. She just had to remember not to make any sudden movements.

At first, she didn't realise the man was addressing her. He wasn't looking directly at her, and walked along beside her as though he hadn't spoken at all, but she had clearly heard him call her name. She scowled and walked more quickly, aware that her head was beginning to throb. She turned a corner, and moved briefly into the shadow of a building. This time there was no doubt the man was talking to her. Startled, she hesitated. She had a feeling she ought not to respond, but he seemed to know her and she didn't want to be rude.

'Don't you remember me?' he asked her directly, sounding amused rather than insulted.

Glancing at him, she had to admit that he looked familiar, although she couldn't remember where she had seen him before.

'Tell you what,' he went on easily, 'you're looking a little the worse for wear, if you don't mind my saying so, Alison.'

She wished he would stop repeating her name. It sounded somehow intrusive on his lips. But he seemed so relaxed, she wasn't really worried. In the shadows she could see he was smiling at her.

'Listen, why don't I drop you home?' he asked her. 'I think we ought to make sure you get home safely. If you'd like a lift, that is. I'm parked just round the corner and it's no trouble. You're really not looking that great.'

It was true, she did feel queasy. 'I think I'm going to be sick,' she muttered. It would be mortifying to throw up in his car. 'I'd better walk.'

'Don't be silly,' he said.

'But I might be sick.'

'That's okay, I can always stop and let you hop out if you need to. Come along. Follow me. I'll have you home in a jiffy.'

He turned and walked slowly away. She only hesitated for a second. She wasn't wearing a coat and it was growing chilly. It would be really nice to have a lift home. She wished she could remember where she knew him from.

'Wait for me,' she called out.

The man didn't answer. He didn't even turn round but kept walking while she trotted along behind him. Without warning, he turned into an alley. A grey van was parked near the entrance to the lane. As she reached him, he yanked open the back door of the van and shoved her forwards. She lost her footing and landed painfully on her hands and knees. She yelped loudly. The van shook as the door crashed shut behind her. To her horror, she realised the man had leaped into the back of the van with her. As she was clambering to her feet, he grabbed her by her wrists and clamped them together with makeshift wire handcuffs. She opened her mouth and drew in a breath to scream, but he slapped something across her lips and a second later a gag was tied tightly behind her head. It tasted of a combination of salt and mould, the texture like rough sacking on her tongue. She could do nothing more than let out muffled grunts, and try to kick him without losing her balance. Ducking down, the man wound something round her ankles, seized her elbows, and lowered her roughly to the floor of the van. Unable to use her hands to break her fall, she slipped and heard, rather than felt, a loud crack as her head hit the side of the van.

As she came to, a bright light seemed to fizz and flicker behind her eyes. Inside the van it was dark. She could hear the whine of the engine and feel the floor beneath her jolting and vibrating. She moaned and with difficulty turned her head to one side as her mouth filled with vomit behind her gag. She still had no idea what the man wanted. If he intended to rape her, she reasoned that he would have done it by now. He had her tied up and helpless in the back of a van where no one could see what he was doing, so he had no reason to delay. She tried to think what else he might be after. Her parents were neither rich nor famous, so there would be little point in kidnapping her for a ransom. In the end, she concluded that he had captured her in a case of mistaken identity. He seemed to know her, but he had only used her first name. He must have confused her with another Alison. That was the only explanation that made sense. She would convince him of his error at the first opportunity, and persuade him to let her go. And all the time she was speculating, the van rumbled and jolted along the streets, taking her further and further away from the pub and her fellow students who were probably still drinking, oblivious to her terrifying fate.

23

GERALDINE WAS OUTSIDE THE block of serviced offices where Jason worked, waiting for his colleagues to arrive. The purpose of her visit was to try and find out more about Jason and track down any possible source of evidence that could help to exonerate him, or if not, at least prove his guilt and so put an end to any uncertainty. She understood that Ian would be upset if Jason was guilty, but they both knew that the investigation had to follow its course, whatever the outcome.

Shortly before nine, a few people arrived and Geraldine followed them in. This time she followed the receptionist's instructions to a suite of rooms on the third floor.

'Can I help you?' a smartly dressed blonde woman enquired as Geraldine entered the outer office.

Geraldine decided she might as well start with her, and learned she was talking to the office manager, who enquired the reason for her visit. Geraldine introduced herself and held up her identity card.

'Jason? He's not in today.' The woman hesitated. 'He's on compassionate leave,' she added, looking faintly anxious but maintaining a professional composure. 'Of course, I know him. We all know Jason,' she responded to Geraldine's next question. 'There are only five of us working from this office, and we've all been here for a while.' She leaned forward slightly across her desk. 'How can I help you, Inspector?'

'What can you tell me about Jason?'

The woman frowned. 'He fits in well here. He's prompt and courteous with clients and well, what can I say? He's professional.'

Geraldine nodded. 'Did you ever meet his girlfriend?'

The woman's frown deepened. 'Yes,' she replied cautiously. 'She came to our drinks party at Christmas. It was a low-key affair. Like I said, there are only five of us here so about nine of us gathered here for a drink and then we all went home. It wasn't exactly a wild night.' She laughed a little bitterly, and Geraldine wondered if there had been some dissent over the nature of the office Christmas celebration.

'Did they look happy together?'

The blonde woman scowled at her. 'You're not expecting me to say they fought, and he lost his temper and threatened to kill her, are you?'

Geraldine smiled and shook her head 'We're investigating what happened,' she replied. 'I was wondering if you could tell me anything about Jason. Did you ever see him lose his temper?'

'No, never. In fact, I'd say the exact opposite. He's the last person I'd ever suspect of losing his cool. Jason's so laidback, he's almost horizontal. And he obviously adored his girlfriend. They seemed really happy together. It's just terrible, what's happened. Poor Jason. He must be heartbroken. I don't suppose – no... You don't know when he's coming back to work, do you? We tried calling him but he's not answering his phone. Is he all right, do you know?'

She seemed to be unaware that he had been questioned by the police several times as a suspect in the murder investigation.

'He's been helping us with our enquiries,' Geraldine said evasively.

'Oh my God,' the woman blurted out. 'You're not saying you actually think he did it? I wasn't being serious about him threatening her. He wouldn't have done that. Not Jason. I heard on the news that a suspect had been questioned. It's him, isn't it?'

'So, that would surprise you?'

'If you want my honest opinion, I think it's absolutely ridiculous if you've arrested Jason. He's not like that at all.'

'Like what?'

'Aggressive. I mean, he seems to take things in his stride. I've never seen him lose his temper or grow impatient. I've never even heard him raise his voice, at least not in the office. He'd never hurt anyone. I don't think he could. It's not in his nature to be violent. He's the gentlest person you could wish to meet.'

Geraldine thanked her and moved on to the next person in the office, a ginger-haired young man who greeted her with a broad grin. He seemed to think Geraldine was looking for a rental property. It took her a few minutes to convince him that she wasn't looking for somewhere to live.

'Well, if you or anyone you know ever is,' he sighed, 'I'll make sure you get a good deal.' He handed her a card.

'I just want to ask you a few questions,' she said. 'It's about your colleague, Jason.'

'Yes, I thought it might be,' the ginger-haired man nodded. 'His girlfriend's murder's been in the news. Must be horrible for him. Do you know when he'll be back?'

'I'm afraid I can't say.'

Geraldine spoke to everyone who worked in the office. No one was able to give her any indication that Jason might be guilty, and they all described him as cheerful and equable.

'It's not that he's never irritable and never seems frustrated, even when things go pear-shaped, I just don't think he has it in him to lose his temper. He's always the same. He just seems happy with his lot,' the office manager concluded, reiterating what all of Jason's colleagues had said. 'Even when we had to throw his girlfriend out, he just shrugged it off as though nothing had happened.'

Geraldine drew in a breath. 'Do you mean you had to ask Lucy to leave the office?'

'Oh no, not Lucy,' the manager replied. 'This was another girl, his ex-girlfriend. It seems she wanted to speak to Jason and he didn't want to talk to her.' She smiled grimly.

The manager was unable to give her any further details and claimed she had no recollection of when the encounter had taken place.

'I'm afraid I've no idea who she was,' the manager added. 'It was all over in a moment. She came in, asked for Jason, I announced her over the phone, he told me he didn't want to speak to her, and I relayed his message and asked her to leave. And that was that. She left and we never heard from her again. But that was years ago.'

The manager insisted she knew nothing more about the visit, and Geraldine had to accept that. She spoke to the cleaner last, having tracked her down in another local office.

'Jason?' the cleaner repeated. 'The guy at Weber and Collins?' Geraldine showed her a photograph of Jason and she nodded.

'Oh yes, I know who you mean. What do you want to know about him? He keeps his desk tidy enough, but they keep all the paperwork in filing cabinets and only have computers on their desks so there's nothing much for me to do but dust and polish and put the hoover round. I don't see anything. Not that I don't earn my wages,' she added quickly. 'I am extremely thorough, not like some agency workers, and I do the toilets twice a week.'

It turned out that the cleaner had never spoken to Jason, and Geraldine's visit was a complete waste of time. Frustrated, she returned to the police station and was almost late for a briefing Binita had called.

24

IT WAS IMPOSSIBLE FOR Jenny to have any idea what had happened, but she seemed to know something was wrong. After twenty-two years of marriage, she knew his different moods too well. He had given her nothing specific to point to, but she had obviously noticed something was up. Thinking back over the past week, he recognised that he had been unusually jumpy. Ever since his dreadful encounter with Lucy, he had been trapped in a web of guilt and paranoia. Later that evening, she had been found lying in the street just where he had seen her. To his horror, he had seen in the news that she hadn't died immediately. She had been discovered, apparently unconscious. He had followed the news items about her avidly, but the information was contradictory. Even discounting the reporters' attempts to sensationalise the crime, it wasn't clear whether Lucy had recovered consciousness before she died in hospital. If she had been able to talk to the police, there was no knowing what she might have revealed about his involvement in her death. He didn't even know if he had killed her, but it seemed likely. Just the thought of her bringing up his name in connection with the attack made him feel sick.

It wasn't as if he had done anything so very wrong. It had been a simple case of mistaken identity. Once he realised she had recognised him, all he had done was give her a slap to stop her screeching. With hindsight, he could see how rash he had been, but at the time he had panicked. In any case, the damage had already been done, because she had recognised him when he propositioned her. He kicked himself for not hurrying away and leaving her there. If only he hadn't been stupid enough to touch her, he could have denied any allegations she made against him as the hallucinations of an injured woman.

'Obviously she was mistaken,' he imagined telling the police. *'I never saw her there. I wish I had. I could have stopped and called for an ambulance and maybe saved her life.'*

But it was too late to extricate himself now. He had slapped her and with that contact had doubtless left his DNA on her cheek with his sweaty palm. At least the police hadn't come knocking on his door. Yet.

'Can you explain the presence of your DNA on the dead girl's face?'

The prospect of being confronted like that made him shiver. There was no answer to that question. The most skilled lawyer was unlikely to be able to argue a way out of the hole he had dug for himself. He just had to pray that Lucy's face had been thoroughly cleaned before they found his DNA on her.

As if all that wasn't enough to worry about, now Jenny was on his case, wanting to know why he was so nervy. He did his best to hide his jitters from her, but she must have noticed how he started every time the phone rang or someone knocked at the door. Sooner or later, it might be the police. In the meantime, nothing had happened. The longer it went on, the less likely it was that the police would be on to him. If they had found traces of his DNA on her face, they would have nothing to match it with because his DNA had never been entered on their database. They hadn't asked for DNA samples from her colleagues and, really, they could hardly go around taking samples from everyone who knew Lucy. All he had to do was keep his head down and wait it out, and everything would come right in the end.

Even though he had steeled himself against her curiosity, he was shocked when Jenny challenged him. Having produced his favourite supper, toad in the hole, which she had spent ages making from scratch, she poured him a third glass of beer and served him a generous portion of home-made apple pie.

'This is great,' he grinned as he tucked in, hardly daring to hope that everything was going to be all right after all. 'What's the occasion?'

'Nothing. I just had the day off so I decided to make something nice.'

He grunted. 'Makes a change.'

'Are things really that bad here?' she replied, looking strained.

'Bad? What are you talking about? We're fine, aren't we?'

Jenny cleared her throat. Although she spoke confidently, he could tell she was nervous. There was something forced about her brashness as she challenged him. 'Something's wrong, isn't it?'

Andrew stared at her with an expression intended to convey perplexity. As though she wasn't sure whether to believe he was genuinely puzzled by her question, she pressed on with a kind of desperate resolve. It struck him that she had prepared very carefully for this moment. Making his favourite dinner and pouring him an extra glass of beer had all been part of a deliberate scheme to catch him unawares. From now on he would have to be wary of her, knowing she was suspicious of him.

'Look, Andrew,' she began.

He took a gulp of beer, refusing to meet her eye, all the while trying to look unconcerned.

'I know something's wrong, or, at least, something's not right.'

He stood up and brushed her statement aside with a shake of his head. 'I don't know what you're talking about.' He turned on her suddenly. There was no mileage in being defensive when he was in the wrong. 'If you've got a problem, then why not come out with it? What have you been playing at?' Having gone on the attack, he deliberately softened his voice. 'You can tell me, Jenny. What is it? Whatever it is, you'll feel better if you get it off your chest. Talk to me. Is it money?' He paused. 'Is it me? Have

I done something wrong? I know I don't always pay you enough attention. I can do better. I will do better. Please, Jenny, tell me what's wrong.'

She faltered and he struggled to suppress a grin of triumph; he deserved an Oscar for his performance. It was a pity no one else would ever be able to appreciate his talent. All he had to do was hold his nerve, and he was in the clear. Even his wife was taken in by his impeccable façade.

25

'SO, HAVE YOU GOT any plans for a holiday?' Geraldine asked, as she and Ariadne handed their menus to the waiter.

There was no actual need for them to look at the menu, since they had fallen into the habit of going to the same Chinese restaurant every month or so, and their order never varied. They could just as easily have chatted in the canteen at the police station, but Geraldine felt more comfortable meeting her friend away from their workplace. Although neither of them had said so, Geraldine knew that Ariadne also appreciated an opportunity to gossip away from the police station where any one of their colleagues might appear in the corridor or the canteen at any time. Ensconced at a table in a booth, there was no need to keep an eye out to see who might be passing by and, in the busy hubbub of the restaurant, no one would be able to overhear their conversation.

Ariadne shrugged and pushed her long black hair back off her shoulders with both hands. 'It's not that long since our honeymoon, and we're supposed to be saving up to move, although that won't be for a while and in the meantime, well, you've got to live while you can, haven't you? So I want to go away and so does Nico.'

Geraldine nodded, gazing at her friend's subdued expression. Ariadne's usually animated black eyes were lowered, as though she wanted to avoid meeting Geraldine's gaze.

'We've both booked time off in September,' Ariadne continued, as Geraldine poured them each a glass of wine. 'But we haven't decided on anything yet,' she added, with a faint pout.

'Is that because you can't agree on where to go?' Geraldine asked, sensing there was more to Ariadne's indecision than she was admitting.

'What makes you say that?' Ariadne's serious expression broke into a grin. 'Is it that obvious?'

Geraldine smiled. 'No, not at all. But then again, yes. Sort of.'

Ariadne laughed. 'You know me too well.'

'So, what are the options?'

'Nico wants to go to Athens to see some of his cousins who didn't make it to the wedding. But I'm not sure I want to spend my holiday meeting up with family I don't even know. I mean, they're not my family. That is, I suppose they are now, in a way, but I don't know them and I can't say I'm that bothered about meeting Nico's cousins that he never even sees. He can't be that close to them. He hasn't seen some of them since he was a child.' She paused before adding darkly, 'I suspect his mother's behind the idea of our going to Greece. Next thing you know, she'll be insisting on coming with us.' She pulled a face. 'I mean, we get on all right, given that she's my mother-in-law. In fact, I'd say I get on better with her than Nico does. But I can only take her in small doses, you know? And not for my summer holiday.'

'You definitely shouldn't go anywhere near Greece. You need to discuss it all with Nico and book a holiday somewhere you both want to go. And you don't have to say anything to his mother until you've booked your holiday without her.'

Ariadne nodded and sighed. 'How about you?' she asked more brightly. 'Have you made any holiday plans?'

Geraldine shook her head. Ian had raised the subject several times, but she had been feeling too tired to think about making plans to go away.

'To be honest,' she replied miserably, 'I'd be quite happy for Ian to go away on his own and leave me in peace. He keeps on about going away, but I'd just as soon stay at home and put my feet up than go gallivanting off somewhere.'

Ariadne made no attempt to hide her concern. 'Going on holiday is hardly gallivanting. Geraldine, what are you talking about? Is everything all right? I mean, between you and Ian?'

Geraldine put down her wine glass and stared at it mournfully. 'What? Oh yes, I think so. But I've not been feeling myself lately.'

She picked up her glass and watched the plum-coloured liquid swirl around as she tipped the wine from side to side.

'What's wrong? Has Ian done something to upset you?'

'No, no, it's nothing like that.' Geraldine paused, struggling to explain how she was feeling. Ian had asked her the same question only that morning. 'He hasn't done anything. It's my fault.'

'What is?'

'I'm just tired. That's all it is,' Geraldine replied, repeating to Ariadne what she had said to Ian earlier on. 'Feeling my age, I suppose.'

'You're hardly over the hill yet,' Ariadne protested, half laughing. 'The way you're carrying on you make it sound like you're ready to retire. But seriously, is it the job? Have you had enough? People do burn out. Is that what's going on? There's no shame in it. I don't think anyone would be surprised. You do have a tendency to go at it with a ferocity that leaves the rest of us standing.'

'No, it's not that. And I'm certainly not ready to give up my career. But I am tired. I just need a break, I think.'

'From what?' Ariadne asked, with a shrewd glance. 'Are we talking about your job, or about your relationship? Here, have another drop of this fine vintage.' She smiled encouragingly. 'I'm always here if you want to talk about anything. You do know that, don't you?'

Geraldine nodded and looked away, feeling unaccountably close to tears. As she began to stammer her thanks, their food arrived, but she had lost her appetite. She picked miserably at her noodles, pushing the food around her plate in an attempt to look as though she was tucking in, but all she really wanted to do was go home and sleep. She forced a smile and turned the conversation back to Ariadne and her troublesome holiday plans.

26

HE NEEDED TO DEAL with her quickly because the van had to be returned to the fleet. He had been careful to use a different vehicle each time to minimise the risk of suspicion. The police might be searching for a van that was out on the street near the final location a missing girl had been seen, but they might not notice a few different vans and trace them all back to one garden centre. Occasionally, the manager hired a van when one of theirs was out of commission, and he always made a point of using a hired one when he could, so the vehicle wasn't directly connected to the garden centre. As long as he replaced the petrol he used, there was no fear of his trip being noticed. It was endlessly tricky, but so far he had been both careful and, if he was honest, fortunate as well. One day his luck might run out, but he hoped to complete his project before that happened. Two more bodies and he would be finished, and he had the penultimate one ready. That night he would transfer her from his garage to the garden, and she would disappear into the earth.

It had taken him a while to replace his job in the garden centre where he had worked previously. To begin with he had felt safe there, because it was an hour's bus ride away from York. But he soon realised that sneaking back to York in a van at night had been too risky, and he couldn't continue doing that for long. His dreams were haunted by the terror of a van breaking down while he was out on a night mission. He pictured a mechanic opening the back of the van to find a girl, trussed up and writhing on the floor. When the manager at his previous job had started asking questions about petrol consumption, he had quit, but he hadn't been able to stop for long, not while there remained trees in his garden in need of nourishment. Finding a job at a garden centre close to his home, he had resumed his project, and so far had added three more bodies to his private burial ground. The project was nearing completion.

He hoped she was still alive. If he buried her just before she drew her last breath, her life force would help enrich the soil surrounding her body. That way, his plants would gain the maximum benefit from her presence, and continue to flourish. When he had first begun his work, he had suspected his idea was crazy, but the results were conclusive. There was no question about it. His garden boasted the healthiest plants he had ever seen. And really, who did it hurt? Admittedly, a few young women had died before their time, but they would have died anyway and, left to themselves, they would never have found such a lovely final resting place. Everyone died in the end so, ultimately, it made no difference to the women he buried. One day he would join them. His own wishes had been delivered to his lawyer in a sealed envelope, not to be opened until after his death.

When he died, he was going to be buried in his garden at home. Concealed from view, it had become his own private graveyard. No living soul knew about it, other than him and his plants. And really, when he considered his scheme from every point of view, everyone benefited. Linda knew nothing about his secret nocturnal pastime, but she enjoyed sitting in the garden admiring the lush plants. He had even heard her boasting about how beautifully he kept the garden. She had no idea it was due to his careful implementation of an utterly brilliant plan, without which his garden would be just like everyone else's.

He waited until his wife went out for the night shift before moving the van into the garage. As soon as she had driven off, he was ready. Having moved the van with its precious cargo out of sight, he fetched his tools from the shed. This time he decided to dig the trench before carrying the body out to avoid having to hide it before he put it in the ground. That way, he would save time and it meant there would be no risk of a recurrence of what had happened on the previous occasion, when he had left a body concealed in the garden only to discover the woman had regained consciousness and crawled away. He had been stupid and reckless in the past, but he had learned his lesson. The thought of the danger he had faced still made him shudder. But, once again, luck had been on his side and he had escaped detection. He had even learned what had happened to the girl. Such a stroke of luck couldn't be mere coincidence. Some god of nature must have seen his efforts and decided to protect him. It was no more than he deserved. No one else could be taking better care of their plants.

He knew every inch of the garden and so had no need to switch on his torch as he fetched his spade from the shed. Hurrying to the site he had carmarked earlier on, he began to dig and had soon carved a neat pit. He worked in the shade of two fruit trees that were in full leaf and concealed his activity from any inquisitive neighbour who chanced to glance out of a window while he was occupied with his task. Next came the trickiest part of the operation, carrying the body from the van to the grave. He straightened up with a faint grunt and stretched his back in readiness for the imminent stress of weight-bearing. Although he would miss the satisfaction of adding to the richness of his soil, he wouldn't be sorry when his project was completed. He had been a lot younger when he had started, and he was finding the physical effort increasingly challenging. He hoped the girl wasn't going to struggle too much.

He would have liked to place her gently in the earth before she died, but as soon as he opened the van door, he realised that was impracticable. He had taken the precaution of closing the back door behind him after he entered the garage, and had already secured the up and over door at the front after driving the van inside. Despite his precautions, her muffled groans made him uneasy. If a neighbour stepped outside, it was just possible they might hear her attempts to cry out through her gag. She was wriggling and groaning, and doing her best to attract attention. As he reached for her, she began whimpering and moaning with renewed vigour, kicking out with her shackled feet. Exasperated by her fussing, he pressed down on her mouth to silence her, feeling the cold sliminess of the gag through his rubber glove. It was easier to handle things with household gloves than his leather gardening pair, and besides, he had to destroy anything that had been in contact with the bodies. It would be a waste of good gardening gloves if he had to discard them every time he carried out a burial.

In the dim light he could see her eyes, wide open and terrified, glaring at him. They made her look ugly, which was a pity. He had selected her for her good looks, which he always took as a sign of physical fitness. As with shrubs and trees, perfect blooms and fruits showed a plant was healthy. Dodging her kicks, he wrapped his free hand around her throat and pressed down with all his force, crushing her windpipe. It seemed to take a long time, but at last she stopped thrashing. Satisfied that she was dead, he set to work. There was no time to lose if she was going to be as fresh as possible when he laid her in the ground.

'It's a lovely spot, under an apple tree,' he murmured and then stopped himself, because she could no longer hear a word he said.

Talking to her was as foolish as talking to the leaf mulch he brought home from the garden centre when it was on offer. Not only was it a bargain, but purchasing bags of mulch enabled him to use a van legitimately overnight from time to time. By doing that, he was less likely to attract attention on his occasional covert operations which involved driving a van off the premises when no one was looking, and returning it very early the following morning before anyone else arrived. On such occasions, he always purchased a few bags of leaf mulch or forest bark in case anyone questioned why he had driven a van out of the garden centre. So far, no one had queried his covert activity.

Gently he patted the earth down under the apple tree, and replaced the ground cover to conceal the freshly turned soil. It would be an early start for him in the morning, but Linda would be asleep when he left and no one else would pay any attention to his movements. He was just a member of staff working at the garden centre, driving a van into the car park. There was nothing remarkable in that. Nothing at all. And he had his cover story ready, in case it was needed. He smiled as he cleaned his shovel before replacing it neatly on the rack, and went to the garage to sweep and scrub the floor of the van.

Cutting open a sack, he scattered its contents on the floor of the van, which was soon littered with a sprinkling of earth and leaf detritus from the garden centre. With a faint shock, he saw that the side of the van was pitted with dimples that he didn't recall seeing earlier. She must have kicked at the side of the van in an effort to be heard. He shrugged. Several of the vans had been dented by people transporting pots and fence posts carelessly. No one would notice and, if they did, they would not know that he had been using the van. Someone else might be blamed, but there was nothing he could do about that. With a sigh, he went indoors to shower before brewing himself a well-earned pot of tea. Despite the girl's efforts to cause a nuisance, it had been a good night's work.

27

WITH BINITA FOCUSED ON pursuing Jason, Geraldine took a rare day off to meet her adopted sister whom she hadn't seen for months. Celia lived in Kent, a long way from York, so they had arranged to meet in London for lunch. It wasn't ideal, involving them both travelling several hours, but Geraldine wasn't able to take off more than a day, and there wasn't much point in Celia going to stay in York while Geraldine was working. So, a meeting in the middle of the day, somewhere easily accessible for them both, seemed to be the best solution.

'It's been such a long time,' Celia cried out, as she flung her arms around Geraldine.

By nature more reserved, Geraldine smiled and agreed that it had been a while since they last met. Keeping her hands on Geraldine's shoulders, Celia held her at arm's length and stared at her intently.

Finally, she dropped her arms and stepped away. 'Are you all right?' she asked. 'You look pale.'

'We've been hard at work,' Geraldine replied, smiling thinly.

She didn't add that her close friend, Ariadne, had also been nagging her about looking worn out.

'I'm fine,' she insisted. 'What about you? You're looking anything but washed out. And how's the family?'

Having successfully shifted the conversation on to Celia's husband and children, Geraldine relaxed. They found a table at a small restaurant Geraldine had booked near to King's Cross station, before Celia launched into a detailed account of her family's activities.

'Honestly, Geraldine, there's so much to tell you!' she said, with a gleeful grin.

Smiling at Celia across the table, Geraldine settled down to listen to her sister's news. It wasn't actually very interesting, and most of it was predictable. Geraldine's niece was proving typically troublesome in the way teenagers often were. Celia's main gripe seemed to be that her daughter wasn't studying hard enough.

'With all the competition these days, it's really important she does well. She's bright enough but she just seems happy to coast along.' She heaved a sigh. 'If she doesn't show her potential now, she'll regret it for the rest of her life.'

'Let's not be over-dramatic about it,' Geraldine replied. 'Like you said, she's very capable and I'm sure she'll pull it out of the bag when she needs to.'

Celia shook her head. 'I'm not so sure.'

'There's worse things could happen to a young girl.'

'Like what? No, forget I asked. That was a really stupid question. Of course, you're right. It's just so frustrating. I'm sorry to burden you with all this.'

'Don't be silly. I'm your sister.'

Geraldine didn't even try to explain that she was actually finding it very comforting listening to Celia complain about such innocuous problems, very different to the kind of troubles Geraldine was used to investigating. She picked at a bowl of pasta while Celia complained that her daughter had fallen in with the wrong crowd.

'And boys,' Celia wailed. 'She's discovered boys.'

Geraldine raised her eyebrows at that.

'Oh, not like that,' Celia added, lowering her voice. 'I mean, I don't think she's had sex yet. She's barely old enough. But she tells us she has a boyfriend.'

'Have you met the boy?'

Celia nodded. 'He's older than her.'

'How much older?'

'A good six months.'

Geraldine couldn't help laughing at the answer to her question.

'Oh, I know it all sounds very tame to you,' Celia said, clearly annoyed by Geraldine's reaction.

'It sounds quite innocent and normal,' Geraldine replied gently. 'It's natural that you'd be feeling unnerved by all this, but Chloe isn't a child any more. She's beginning to grow up and really, it's not a bad thing for her to have a boyfriend her own age. Six months is nothing, is it?'

'Do you really think it's a good thing?'

Geraldine nodded. 'What's good about it is that Chloe is happy to talk about her private life to you. Because it *is* her private life, isn't it? She doesn't feel she needs to hide anything from you and I'd say that's a very good thing. As long as she knows she can confide in you if she gets in any trouble –'

'What kind of trouble?' Celia interrupted anxiously.

'Oh, you know, getting her heart broken by some callow boy. We're both familiar with the territory. We were young once, weren't we?'

Celia shrugged. 'I'm not sure I remember you ever being young,' she replied seriously. 'Not like me. You were always so conscientious and so focused on joining the police, I don't think you ever went off the rails.'

They were both silent for a moment. Geraldine wondered if Celia was thinking about Geraldine's biological sister, Helena, who had been addicted to heroin. As though sensing the alteration in Geraldine's mood, Celia asked after Ian.

'Are the two of you all right?'

'Why wouldn't we be?' Geraldine replied.

She looked down, aware that she was being defensive for no reason. Ariadne seemed convinced that Geraldine and Ian had fallen out. That wasn't the case, but Geraldine was painfully aware that she had been very snappy with Ian recently. Without doing anything particular to annoy her, he had been getting on her nerves. When he had challenged her about the change in her behaviour, she had been unable to answer him.

'If your feelings for me have altered, you could at least do me the courtesy of telling me,' he had said only that morning.

'My feelings haven't changed,' she had retorted, conscious that she sounded surly. 'I'd appreciate it if you'd stop going on at me like this.'

'I'm not going on at you,' he had replied, more gently than she had deserved. 'But something's wrong, I can tell, and you need to talk to me. What is it?'

She had shaken her head in frustration. To her dismay, she had suddenly felt as though she was going to cry. Brushing past him, she had rushed from the room before he could see the tears in her eyes.

'Seriously, Celia,' she reassured her sister, 'there's nothing wrong. I'm just tired, that's all. I haven't been sleeping well lately.'

'Is there something on your mind?' Celia asked. 'If you're stressed, please don't shut me out.'

Geraldine scowled. 'It would help if everyone stopped nagging me about looking tired,' she snapped. She immediately regretted her outburst. Now Celia was bound to suspect something was wrong.

'Listen, I'm fine, really. It's just that it sometimes seems as if the job is getting too much for me,' she suddenly blurted out, surprising herself. 'The older I get, the harder everything seems. Sometimes I feel as though I'm drowning in all the pressure. But the feeling soon passes. Now let's talk about something else, because it's nothing, really.'

'Very well, if you're sure. But you will tell me if there's anything seriously wrong, won't you? I mean, if it's just your work that's bothering you, well, it's hardly surprising you feel that way at least some of the time. It must be a really difficult job at the best of times.'

Geraldine looked away as Celia dismissed her fears about being unable to cope with her workload. It might sound unimportant to Celia, but Geraldine's career as a detective was all that had defined her for as long as she could remember.

28

MID-MORNING ON FRIDAY, BINITA summoned the team. With an exasperated sigh, Geraldine put down the report she was writing in her decision log.

'Let's hope it's good news,' Ariadne muttered as she and Geraldine walked to the incident room together. 'Something to confirm Jason's guilt will do me nicely.'

Geraldine grunted at her friend's acknowledgment that the case against Jason was not yet settled. She was still concerned that Ian's friend might turn out to be guilty, even though the account of his argument with Lucy came from a dubious source. Even if the neighbour was unreliable, Jason himself had confirmed that Lucy had been out with her ex-boyfriend not long before her death, which could give him a motive for losing his temper with her. Geraldine found it difficult to know whether she was being unduly swayed by Ian's faith in the suspect. Once she lost her objectivity, she would no longer feel able to trust her own judgement. It was a worrying prospect.

'You're looking a bit more cheerful this morning,' Ariadne murmured as they walked. 'So, everything's all right with you?'

Geraldine suppressed a flash of irritation at her friend's prying. Despite Geraldine's denials, Ariadne clung to her view that Geraldine was having problems with Ian.

'I'm fine,' she replied shortly. 'But thanks for asking. It's good to know you're there if I ever need someone to talk to.'

Geraldine hoped she hadn't sounded unintentionally sarcastic, but it was too late to say any more because they had arrived in

129

the incident room where Binita was about to begin a briefing. The news turned out to be less helpful than any of them had hoped. On the contrary, it was worrying to hear that another girl had been reported missing.

'She was last seen on Tuesday around midday,' Binita announced. 'She's a student at the university and she lives in a flat in Union Terrace.' She glanced at her notes. 'She missed a tutorial on Wednesday morning and, according to her flatmates, she hasn't been home since Tuesday. One of her friends thought it was unusual for her to stay out all night without telling anyone, and reported her missing.'

'It sounds like someone's overreacting,' Ariadne said. 'With all the hype about the recent murder of a woman who'd gone missing, and the media digging up other cases of missing women, everyone's in a panic.'

Binita frowned. 'This is a student, a young woman, who's not been home for three nights. I dare say she'll turn up. All the same, we need to look into it and see if we can trace her. I'll have a few words with her myself about wasting police time when we do find her,' she added grimly. 'But we are going to follow up the report. This comes from above. So let's get to it and knock this one on the head. The missing girl's name is Alison Truman. She's known as Ali. We have a fairly recent picture of her that one of her friends – the one who reported her missing – had on her phone.'

They all gazed at a photo Binita displayed on the screen behind her. A girl with long dark hair stared back at them. She didn't appear to be wearing make-up yet her complexion was flawless, and her glossy hair hung around a pretty face that was laughing into the camera.

With the investigation into Lucy's murder all but over, everyone was shaken by the news that another girl had allegedly gone missing. If a second victim were to be discovered, covered in earth, it would suggest that Jason was either innocent of

Lucy's murder, or else that he had attacked more than one girl. The team was already in place and it wasn't long before tasks were allocated; a search for the missing girl was due to begin. The investigation clearly lacked the impetus of a murder enquiry, and many of Geraldine's colleagues were vociferous in doubting whether they should be searching for the missing girl at all.

'So, a pretty girl goes to stay with some bloke she's picked up and she doesn't think to tell her flatmates where she's gone. Send out a search party!' a constable sneered when Binita had left the room.

'Talk about an overreaction,' someone else added. 'Just because one girl's been killed, are we to investigate any missing girl as a potential murder victim? This is ridiculous.'

'The powers that be are scared shitless the media will get hold of the story before she's found,' another voice chipped in. 'They love to blow things up and beat us over the head with rumours of a serial killer roaming the streets looking for victims.'

'That's what it is,' Naomi agreed. 'Binita wants us to track the girl down before any of her friends can speak to the press.'

'We need to impress on Alison's contacts that it's vital they don't talk to anyone but us,' Geraldine said. 'Convince her friends that it may put Alison's life in danger if the media get hold of this. That ought to do it. We have to keep it under wraps for as long as we can, or we'll be under even more pressure.'

'Good luck with keeping something like this quiet,' Ariadne muttered. 'It's just the kind of story the local press love.'

Geraldine shared her colleagues' concerns. Many of their successes were attributable, in part at least, to eyewitnesses coming forward with information. When members of the public lost confidence in the police, they were less likely to speak to them, whether on their own initiative or in response to specific appeals for information. What people failed to realise was that the police depended on their support. Binita sent a team to question the missing girl's friends discreetly. It was to be a small-scale operation as the detective chief inspector was still hoping to keep Alison's alleged disappearance under wraps. It wouldn't be easy. Her parents had already been contacted. They had not heard from their daughter for a week. The local constable who had spoken to them had done her best to assure them that the enquiry was merely routine, but she reported that they had been understandably alarmed at receiving a visit from the police.

Despite some scepticism from the detectives involved, individual searches for the missing girls were now being drawn together into one investigation. Most officers agreed that it was probably no coincidence that four girls had all gone missing from a small area within a short space of time. The conclusion that the cases might be related raised a terrifying spectre that had to be kept from the media for as long as possible. The main focus was now on the latest disappearance, where the trail might not yet have gone cold.

Geraldine set off with Ariadne to question the missing girl's flatmates, one of whom had reported her missing, while other officers were dispatched to talk to Alison's tutors at the university. They were all hoping that the girl would reappear. Geraldine could imagine the surprise she might express at the fuss her friends had made over her brief disappearance, while she had gone to stay with another friend. They could only hope for so happy an outcome to a situation which threatened to end tragically.

29

MEGAN, THE STUDENT WHO had reported Alison missing, was a short, tubby girl with very curly fair hair and a pale freckled face. She came to the door and invited Geraldine and Ariadne into the small terraced house, which Alison shared with two other students. There were two bedrooms, meaning that one of them slept downstairs in what would otherwise have been used as a dining room. In addition to that, the three girls had a small L-shaped living room and kitchen. The place was very untidy, with damp clothes draped over a metal drier, bags of shopping on the kitchen table waiting to be put away, and a sink full of dirty plates and cutlery. The kitchen bin was overflowing with paper napkins and pizza boxes. Despite all the clutter, the house was clean and had a cosy feel to it. A laptop was propped up on a coffee table in the living area beside a small pile of books, evidence that at least one of the residents was taking their studies seriously. A second girl was sitting on an old armchair in a corner of the room, staring at her feet.

'Sorry about all the mess,' Megan muttered, with an embarrassed glance around the room. 'We're in the process of tidying up,' she added.

'I hadn't noticed the mess,' Geraldine said, answering one innocuous lie with another.

Megan invited her to sit down on a sofa which felt as though all the springs had gone.

'It's about Ali, isn't it?' Megan said, her eyes filling with tears. 'I'm supposed to be going home tomorrow but I can't leave without knowing that she's all right.'

Geraldine felt an unaccountable urge to put her arms around Megan and comfort her. Stifling her inappropriate impulse, she nodded.

'Tell me about her,' she said.

'Well,' Megan replied, sniffling into a tissue, 'she's our friend and she's the nicest person. Really, she is. I mean, I know people always say that about everyone, but it's true. She always helps me with my essays. I'm dyslexic and I honestly don't know what I would have done without her this year. I mean, it's horrendous the amount of writing we're expected to do. I'm supposed to be studying drama but they expect us to *write* about everything.' She frowned indignantly. 'It's not fair. I mean, they should have warned us.'

Geraldine steered the conversation back to the missing girl. 'Did Alison have a boyfriend?'

Megan was firm in her denial. 'Not that she couldn't have had one, if she'd wanted.'

'What do you mean? Was there someone interested in her?'

'No, nothing like that.' Megan gave a twisted smile. 'No creepy stalker who was suffering from being rejected. Not like on the telly. No, I just mean that she was really pretty.'

'Why do you keep talking about her in the past tense?' the other girl in the room chimed in. 'Inspector, do you think something terrible's happened to her?' She began to cry.

Geraldine gave a vaguely reassuring response to the effect that she was sure everything was going to be fine, and missing people almost always turned up. 'When did you last see Alison?'

'She was here on Tuesday morning,' Megan said. 'We all were. We had breakfast together, me and Ali.'

'And how did she seem?'

Megan looked puzzled. 'What do you mean? She was – well, she was just Ali, you know.'

'Did she appear to be worried about anything?'

'No, she was – well, she was the same as usual. We just had breakfast and then I went out to meet up with some friends.'

'Did you leave the house together?'

Megan nodded. 'Yes. That is, we were going to leave at the same time but we both wanted to do some shopping so we were going to split up anyway.'

'Do you know which direction she took when she left the house?'

'Well, no, because she went off before me. I wasn't ready.'

'Did Alison tell you where she was going, or mention what she was shopping for?' Megan shook her head. 'I never asked,' she said, her voice wobbling. 'But we agreed we'd see each other later, so I'm sure she was planning to be home that evening. And neither of us has seen anything of her since then. She just disappeared.'

'What time was it when she went out?'

Megan frowned with the effort of recalling what had happened on the day she had last seen Alison. 'I went out after half past eleven, I think, because I remember I had just missed a bus that was due at eleven forty. I mean, just missed it. I actually saw it driving off from the bus stop and the driver didn't wait, although he must have seen me running.' She scowled.

Geraldine made a note. 'So, would it be right to say you left home at about eleven thirty-five?'

Megan nodded. 'About then, I suppose.'

'And how long before you went out did Alison leave?'

'Maybe five minutes.'

'So, she left at around half past eleven?'

Megan nodded again. Geraldine glanced at Ariadne who was trying to encourage the other girl to answer a few questions.

'Did Alison say anything to you about where she might be going?' Geraldine heard her colleague ask.

The girl shook her head and her lanky black hair swung around her thin face. 'She never said anything. But she did tell us she wanted to get something for her mother,' she added.

'For her mother?' Geraldine echoed.

'Oh yes,' Megan took up the narrative. 'That's right. She wanted to get something for her mother, to take home with her.'

'Did she say what she wanted to get?' Ariadne asked.

Megan and her flatmate, Nina, both shook their heads.

'We were planning to have a final night out tonight together,' Megan said mournfully.

'A final night?' Geraldine queried.

'Yes, before going home until term starts. Our rental agreement finishes soon and we're not moving into our new place until the beginning of September, so we can save on rent for a few weeks. We found somewhere with three bedrooms. It was Ali who found it,' she added.

Geraldine made a note of the new address. Asking Megan and Nina to contact them straightaway if they thought of anything else, they left. It didn't take long to establish that other students were still living in the address to which Alison and her flatmates were moving in September. None of them knew anything about Alison, and no dark-haired girl had turned up on their doorstep. Geraldine had no reason to doubt them. There was no point in requesting permission to search their premises. Nevertheless, she determined to make a detailed note about Alison's plans. Learning where Alison was planning to live in the following academic year was all Geraldine had managed to find out from her flatmates, and it didn't help in the search for her current whereabouts. Disgruntled at having expended so much time for so little return, she drove back to the police station to write up her notes and check whether her colleagues had fared any better.

Naomi had been checking Alison's social media profile but had discovered nothing helpful. Alison had been fairly active on Instagram with schoolfriends before starting at university, but she had attracted little attention and had acquired no new friends or followers since moving to York. She was quite quiet on other social media sites. Any hope of tracking her movements through online posts had been dashed.

30

BINITA CALLED A MEETING late that afternoon to discuss what, if anything, had been discovered so far. A couple of teams had been tasked with searching for any sighting of the missing girl after she left Union Terrace on Tuesday morning. Uniformed constables had been going door-to-door along the surrounding streets asking if anyone had seen her, but they had learned nothing. The police didn't even know which direction Alison had taken when she had gone out. A team of video images identification and detections officers had been set up to check security cameras along Union Terrace and the surrounding area, searching for a sighting of Alison. If they could establish the direction she had taken on leaving the house, with any luck they might be able to track her movements. But they had drawn a blank. It was as though Alison had vanished into a black hole.

'Or into a hole in the ground,' Ariadne muttered.

'We're throwing a lot of resources at this one missing girl,' Naomi said. 'The chances are she's staying with a boyfriend.'

'She didn't have a boyfriend,' Geraldine pointed out.

'Not that we know of,' Naomi replied.

'She might have met someone on Tuesday evening,' a constable suggested.

Binita agreed the VIIDO team should concentrate their efforts on CCTV footage from the different bars and pubs in York. In addition to the bar at the university, there were a few pubs that Megan had mentioned which were often visited by the three girls and other students. The officers focused their attention on those. It would take a few days to download all the footage that was still available from Tuesday evening, and then scan through it, hoping for a sighting of the missing girl. Even if she had gone to a pub and met someone there, the chances of spotting them were slim. Nevertheless, the search was implemented.

'We have to try everything,' Binita said. 'The boss is very concerned about this missing girl, given the current climate. He wants her found before the news gets out that another girl has gone missing.'

'He does realise that by setting up a massive hunt we are effectively advertising the fact that she's missing?' Geraldine asked. 'We're not exactly being discreet in our investigation.'

Binita shrugged as if to ask what else they could do. 'We're being as low-key as we can, and we are asking everyone to be discreet, aren't we?'

'That's hardly going to happen,' Ariadne murmured, her expression anxious.

'There are the people desperate for her to be found, like her family, and they might genuinely believe it would help us to find her if the news of her going missing is out in public. And then there are her friends, university students, teenagers, who are hardly likely to keep quiet. By now it must have spread all around the campus that a student has gone missing just when the media have been busily hyping up the story of a psychopath on the loose on the streets of York,' Geraldine said.

Binita sighed and looked uncharacteristically fraught. 'We just have to do what we can,' she said brusquely. 'Now I have to attend a meeting, so let's get to work and come up with something today.' With that, she left the room.

'That's all well and good,' Naomi muttered crossly, 'she can tell us to get results until she's blue in the face, but we can hardly search every property in York.'

'Not to mention every car boot and van,' a constable added.

'And what about digging up all the waste ground looking for shallow graves?' someone else asked, referring to the state in which Lucy had been found.

Seeing that the team were beginning to lose heart, Geraldine stepped forward. As the most experienced officer in the room, she was aware that she had some sway over her colleagues. She wasn't the senior investigating officer on the case but since Binita had left the room, someone had to take charge and make sure everyone stayed focused.

'The duty sergeant will allocate responsibilities,' she said loudly. 'So let's not waste time. We know that Alison was last seen in Union Terrace, and she left there at about half past eleven on Tuesday morning. That was the last time anyone remembers seeing her. She must have gone somewhere.'

The VIIDO team was scouting around for CCTV footage of the immediate vicinity, hoping to identify Alison and track her movements and narrow down the area to search. Security film from buses was being checked, and a constable had been despatched to the university, in case Alison had gone there and met someone on campus. The entry barriers were easy to check and it was very quickly established that Alison hadn't gone to the university at any time since Tuesday morning. In the meantime, a team was going door-to-door questioning neighbours and asking in shops, starting close to Union Terrace and moving outwards. It was hard to believe that she had vanished without a trace. Sooner or later they would find her. They just had to hope she would still be alive.

They had all known it was only a matter of time before the local media had got hold of the story, but even so, Geraldine was dismayed to encounter a group of journalists waiting outside the police station when she left the building. She recognised several of the faces as microphones were thrust towards her. Head down, she scurried away, without saying a word. No doubt 'police inactivity' and 'police ineptitude' would figure in many of their reports. She couldn't help hearing some of the questions shouted at her as she retreated. 'How long is it going to take you to catch this killer?' rang in her ears as she reached her car, and she shuddered to think what the headlines would be once they made a connection between Alison and the other women who had recently gone missing.

'Don't take any notice,' Ian counselled her that evening, when she complained to him. 'They're just looking for bad news and gossip. No one believes a word journalists say.'

But they both knew the power the media had in influencing popular opinion, and the more the police came under attack, the less support they could expect to receive from members of the public.

'You'd think they'd want to help us,' Geraldine fumed. 'Surely any right-minded person would be keen to see this maniac locked up. What the hell do they think they're playing at?'

'It's just click bait,' Ian replied. 'As soon as people read past the histrionic headlines, they soon realise the reporters have absolutely nothing to say.'

'But what about all the people who never read past the sensational headlines?' Geraldine asked.

Ian shrugged. 'There's nothing we can do about it if people are idiots.'

'That's not helpful.'

'How about a hug?' he asked, putting his arms around her and drawing her close. 'Is that helping?'

Geraldine smiled and buried her face in his shoulder, enjoying the warmth and comfort of his embrace.

'Yes,' she murmured. 'Yes, it is.'

31

GEORGE WASN'T WORKING ON Saturday, so Linda had suggested they invite their son and his family round for lunch. Robert arrived around midday with his baby, but without his wife. After greeting him, they went out to the garden.

'This little scamp kept Sharon awake most of last night,' he explained, as he laid his son down on a blanket on the grass. 'She thinks he's getting some back teeth through.'

Linda and George looked at their grandson, who was gurgling happily and waving a rattle in the air. He hit himself on the head with the toy, and they all laughed as his eyes opened wide in an expression of surprise.

'The garden's looking good, Dad,' Robert said, casting an eye around at the shrubs and fruit trees. 'I don't know how you do it. However fast I try to pull up the weeds, they only seem more determined than ever to completely take over. Sharon complains it's like a jungle out the back, but I just don't have the time to keep it under control. I could really do with some help from somewhere.'

'Not a very subtle hint,' Linda said, smiling.

'I'm afraid I don't have enough time to look after my own garden properly, let alone deal with someone else's weeds,' George said. 'I can ask around at the garden centre if you like, and see if anyone there is willing to help you out. There are a few young lads who might be interested. It'll cost you, mind.'

'You could always retire,' Linda pointed out to George. 'That way you'd have plenty of time to look after both gardens, Robert's and ours. You don't have to carry on at the garden centre, you know. It's a job, not a prison sentence.'

George shook his head. 'I like working there,' he said. 'I'm not ready to put my feet up yet.'

He didn't add that it was necessary for him to have access to a series of vans. He had earned the trust of all the staff where he worked, and no one ever questioned him when they saw him driving in or out of the car park.

'Well, I wish you would,' Robert said. 'If I could get my garden looking anything like as tidy as yours, Sharon would be very happy.'

George smiled and nodded complacently at Robert. He was used to being complimented on his gardening skills. Looking after his garden was one of the few things he knew how to do. The only thing, really. He had to agree that the garden was certainly looking spectacular this year. It seemed to improve, year on year.

'How do you manage it?' Robert asked, with what appeared to be genuine curiosity.

George shrugged. 'I just keep on doing what I'm doing,' he replied vaguely. 'I water it when it doesn't rain. You can't let your beds dry out. And I feed the flowering bushes.'

'Feed them?' Robert repeated. 'What with? Bangers and mash?' He laughed.

'Your father brings home bags of stuff from the garden centre,' Linda answered for her husband.

'What sort of stuff?'

George felt faintly irritated at his son for being so inquisitive, but at least Robert was making a serious attempt to understand how to tend to his garden, which had to be worth encouraging.

'Mainly leaf mulch,' he explained. 'It's basically just shredded leaves that have been kept moist for a couple of years. You have to be careful not to smother small plants when you lay it on the earth, but it does a good job of enriching the soil.'

'I certainly hope it does a good job, because he spends a fortune on it,' Linda interrupted. She sounded indignant, but she was smiling. 'We'll have to watch the baby when he starts to crawl,' she added. 'He puts everything in his mouth. We can't have him eating rotting leaves.'

'He'll stay on the grass,' George replied firmly.

'Yes, of course, but we'll have to keep an eye on him and make sure he does,' Linda said. 'He won't understand.'

'Well, he's not getting his hands on my flowers,' George blurted out with a sudden burst of energy.

'So, you weren't worried about your grandson eating all kinds of rotten muck, you were only thinking about your flowers,' Linda smiled. 'Don't look so cross. You know I'm teasing. Of course, we won't let him loose in the garden. We'll watch him, for his own sake, never mind the flowers.'

Robert laughed. 'Dad's more concerned about his precious plants than about his grandson.'

George grunted and Linda and Robert both laughed.

After Robert had left, Linda cleared away the tea things while George pottered about in the garden. After a while she came outside and they sat down together to enjoy the early evening light.

'You'll have to be careful if their puppy gets loose,' she commented, looking at him closely.

A sliver of fear shot through George. 'What puppy?' he asked. 'What are you talking about?'

'Oh, didn't Robert mention it? I dare say it will never happen, but it seems Sharon's set her heart on getting a puppy. Don't worry. She's researched what breeds are safe to keep around kids, and they'll only get a small dog, a placid one, maybe a Shih Tzu. But they do like to dig.'

Linda raised her eyebrows with a quizzical grin, and he had the impression she was watching his reaction very carefully. George stood up, struggling to mask his apprehension.

'Don't worry,' Linda went on breezily. 'There's no way anyone's going to leave the baby alone with a dog, however gentle it is. The chances are the baby will terrorise the puppy rather than the other way round. You'd be surprised how strong he is.'

'What would they want with a dog?' George asked, doing his best to keep his voice even and his expression equable. 'They've just had a baby for goodness sake! What the hell are they playing at?'

Linda looked at him thoughtfully. 'George,' she said, without moving her eyes from his face, 'there's absolutely no need to get so worked up about this. Robert and Sharon are responsible parents. They're not going to do anything to put our grandson in any danger. Lots of people bring children up around dogs. It's actually very good for them, and I expect they want the baby to learn to live with a dog while he's still young. It teaches children to be responsible. I'm sorry if you don't like the idea, but it's got nothing to do with us.'

'What if the baby's allergic to dogs?' he asked.

Linda narrowed her eyes, still studying him. 'They don't think he is. And, if there is a problem, obviously they'll get rid of the dog. But that's not going to happen. I don't know why you're so opposed to the idea.'

'I'm just hungry,' George muttered.

Linda's scrutiny of him was making him uneasy, but he assured himself she could have no idea of the reason for his alarm at the prospect of a dog digging around in his garden. It was well known that dogs were attracted to bones, and everything that went with them. He turned his face away and struggled to control his trembling.

32

GEORGE WANDERED OUTSIDE AND pottered around while Linda
cleared away the tea things. He checked the roses, stooping now
and then to pull out a couple of weeds, but for once he was too
preoccupied to focus on the plants. His mind was turning over
what Linda had said about his daughter-in-law wanting a puppy.
Whatever happened, he must ensure the animal never entered
his garden. He could see that was going to be a problem, and was
struggling to see how to avoid an awkward confrontation.

Before long, Linda joined him. It was a pleasant evening, and
they sat together on the narrow strip of decking to admire the
view. In front of the shrubs he had planted summer-flowering
ground cover, purple and yellow, where not long ago spring
flowers had proliferated, heralding warmer weather to come. The
first crop of roses had faded. He had dead-headed them, and the
bushes were showing buds for the second time that summer. One
bush was already in full bloom, with an abundance of yellow
and orange flowers making a sumptuous display in a corner
of the garden. The roses looked curiously old-fashioned. From
the far end of the lawn, more roses displayed startling splashes
of red and yellow and white. Interspersed between the rose
bushes hung clusters of delicate bell-shaped fuchsia flowers like
bright drops of blood. And forming a backdrop to the flowers
and shrubs, towering over them, was a row of fruit trees, their
blossom long gone. Some had already produced tiny apples and
plums, pears and even figs which some years grew large enough
to eat, sweet as jam, straight off the tree.

The garden was very nearly finished. Soon it would be perfect. Everything had been going well, but now a new danger threatened the success of his project. Gazing around at the vibrant colours of flowers set against a backdrop of lush foliage, George trembled at the prospect of a dog scrabbling around, unearthing forbidden treasures. He had to convince Linda that the presence of such an animal would be dangerous for Noah. Robert and Sharon would listen to her. After they had been sitting quietly for some time, he drew in a deep breath and tried to focus, knowing he couldn't afford to mess this up.

'You don't really think they'll be getting a dog, do you?' he asked.

'I don't see why not,' Linda replied.

'But what about the baby?' He heard his voice rise in indignation and bit his lip.

'Plenty of families have babies and dogs together,' she said cheerfully. 'It's not something I'd choose to do, but if that's what they want, then good for them. Robert's an adult now, a father. He can do what he wants.'

'But surely you must see it's not sensible,' he insisted plaintively.

Linda gave him a curious look. 'Why ever not?' she asked. 'What are you afraid of?'

'I'm afraid for Noah. What if the dog attacks him? Dogs are wild animals. However tame they appear, they're basically savage and unpredictable. You never know what they're going to do.'

'That's not what I meant,' she replied, still staring at him. 'I'm not talking about some hypothetical dog. They haven't even got one yet, and probably never will. Forget about that. I was talking in general, because I know there's something on your mind. What are you afraid of?'

'Afraid?' he scoffed, aware that his voice sounded unnaturally emphatic. 'Why would I be afraid of anything? What are you talking about?''

'I don't know,' Linda admitted, adding softly, 'but you are

afraid. I can see it in your face. Why don't you tell me what's going on, George?'

Suddenly flustered, he told her he was starving.

'After you put away all that cake with your tea?' she replied, with a grin.

Actually, she was right. He had probably never felt less inclined to eat. His stomach seemed to have tied itself in knots, and he was feeling queasy. Nevertheless, he pressed on with asking her what they were going to eat that evening, as though he genuinely wanted to know. With a sigh, Linda rose to her feet, muttering about him changing the subject. He watched her walking back to the house to prepare dinner. She still moved like a young woman, although her face had not aged well. With a pang of self-reproach, he wondered whether her erratic working hours were wearing her out, but he couldn't encourage her to give up her night shifts before his project was finished.

He sat down, feeling drained. Linda suspected he was keeping something from her, and she was right. But he had no choice. If she ever discovered his secret, there was a chance she would expose him to the world. At the very least, she might turn her back on him. He couldn't imagine life without her. Whatever else happened, he needed her to stay with him, or everything around him would lose its purpose, and his life itself would have no meaning. He sighed and gazed round the garden, his pride and his solace when he felt unhappy. He would take his secret with him to his grave, where it would lie buried with him until the end of time. Linda would continue to enjoy the garden, without ever knowing how he had nourished it. He would never reveal the secret of his gardening success to anyone, not even his wife. He only needed one or two more bodies to complete his mission. Despite his anxiety over the dog, he smiled to himself as he contemplated his brilliant plan and how well it was working out. He just had to trust in his own ingenuity, and everything would be all right.

33

FOR DAYS, ANDREW HAD hardly spoken to Jenny. It was obvious to her that something was troubling him. She was too nervous to challenge him, but his surliness was making her increasingly uncomfortable. Even the most innocuous of questions, like what he fancied for dinner, were met with silence and a blank look. When he did respond, it was only to grunt, or to dismiss her with an impatient shake of his head. On Sunday morning, he snapped at her, shouting because his breakfast wasn't ready when he came downstairs. She retorted that he could make it himself in future if her food wasn't good enough for him. He looked so crestfallen that she immediately regretted having spoken so harshly. Clearly something had upset him, yet instead of offering sympathy, she had lost her temper with him.

'What's wrong?' she asked him, suddenly reckless. 'You've been stressed about something for days. What is it? Maybe I can help. Tell me what I can do.'

Instead of confiding in her, he growled that she could piss off and stop nagging him. Turning away, he glanced at his watch, flicked on the television, and found the local news.

'Andrew,' she said, speaking more firmly, 'that's not fair. Tell me what's wrong.'

Without warning, his face turned red and he yelled at her. 'Just shut up, will you? Shut up! I'm trying to listen.'

Taking an involuntary step away from him, Jenny caught the last few sentences of a local news report about a murder.

'A man is helping police with their enquiries,' the reporter said.

The news item concluded, and a different reporter introduced another topic of local interest. Scowling, Andrew switched it off. Jenny guessed the journalist had been talking about the murder of one of Andrew's colleagues.

'You worked with her, didn't you?' she asked. 'That's who they're talking about, isn't it?'

'What are *you* talking about?'

'That girl who was murdered,' she replied. 'You must know who I mean. They were just talking about her on the news. She worked at your firm, didn't she? You must have known her.' She paused to allow him to reply.

When he didn't answer her, she repeated her question. 'I asked you if you knew the woman who was murdered.'

Andrew shrugged. Jenny had been trying to dismiss the unsettling suspicion that her husband might have been involved with the victim. The idea was almost too preposterous to entertain, but while there remained an iota of suspicion, she felt compelled to find out, however distressing the truth was. She already knew that he had been unfaithful, perhaps with prostitutes, although he had strenuously denied it when she asked him about it.

'How do you explain the make-up on your clothes, then?' she had challenged him. She didn't specifically mention the glossy red lipstick she had seen on his underpants when she was doing the washing, although she knew it wasn't hers. He denied the allegation and she had nothing to show him, having immediately thrown the pants away in disgust. A few months later, she had come across a bright pink thong under the passenger seat of his car when she was searching for her phone. That had gone straight in the bin as well. She regretted having thrown away the evidence of his philandering. He didn't even notice a pair of his underpants had gone missing, and he had no idea that she had come across any evidence of his adultery.

But being involved with a girl who had been murdered was in a different league, and she determined to question him directly.

'Were you having an affair with her?'

'What?'

Andrew looked genuinely taken aback, but that was no proof of innocence. He hadn't denied the accusation.

'Were you having an affair with the girl who was murdered?'

'That's an outrageous accusation, and a stupid one!'

He sounded indignant, but she could see he was frightened. Her words had struck a nerve. All at once, he lunged forward and slapped her face, hard. She was so startled she didn't have time to dodge the blow. The unexpected impact almost knocked her off balance and she grabbed at the table to steady herself. Her cheek stung from the blow, and she struggled not to cry out. Furiously, she blinked her tears away, determined not to break down. With a sickening jolt she understood that Andrew was capable of violence, and wondered whether he had ever assaulted anyone else.

Andrew began stammering an apology, blaming his outburst on the horrendous pressure he had been under lately.

'It's nothing to do with you,' he assured her earnestly. 'Let's just forget this, okay?'

He wanted her to ignore his vicious slap, but it was too late for that. If he had punched her with his fist he might easily have knocked her out. As it was, she had nearly lost her footing from the force of his blow. She was too shocked to remain silent. A man who could hit his wife was capable of worse. His murdered colleague might have provoked him, unaware of his proclivity for violence. Perhaps the woman had led him on and expected too much, or she might have enraged him by wanting to end their relationship. It was possible they had been having an affair, and he had wanted to silence her because she had threatened to expose the truth. Whatever the sordid reason, the change in his behaviour had started at around the time his colleague was murdered. It was hard to believe that was a coincidence. Something about the crime had unnerved her husband, and she shuddered to think what it might be.

'You were involved with her, weren't you?' she blurted out.

Her heart pounded in her chest, while her breathing was so rapid she was afraid she would become incoherent. She felt dazed, but she had to know the truth, whatever the cost.

'What are you talking about?' Andrew replied. He spoke quietly, but there was a hint of menace in his frown.

'Andrew, were you having an affair with that girl?'

Andrew hesitated before repeating his question. 'What are you talking about? I haven't been having an affair with anyone,' he added firmly, seeming to recover his composure.

His angry flush faded and he stared coldly at her. But his fleeting hesitation seemed to scream at her. He couldn't meet her eye, and she was convinced her suspicion was right. She wondered if he had met her outside York, or whether the liaison had taken place at his office.

'Where did you meet her?' she asked. 'Was it outside the office?'

He hesitated again, seemingly considering what to tell her. 'Only by chance,' he admitted at last. 'And it was only once. But nothing happened. Nothing. I swear it's not what you think.'

'Did you tell the police about your meeting?'

'There was no point,' he said. 'Now, if you've quite finished with your interrogation, I suggest we drop the subject.' He glared at her.

She felt a flicker of fear and moved out of reach of his hands. Her husband had already hit her, lashing out in anger, and she knew he had deliberately lied to the police. It was enough to convince her that he was hiding a terrible secret. Shocked to discover that her suspicions didn't surprise her, she understood that she had never fully trusted her husband. For now, all she had were nebulous suspicions. At the first opportunity, she decided she would search through his belongings, looking for evidence that would incriminate him. If she found anything at all that connected her husband with the murder victim, she would go straight to the police. With a sickening lurch, she realised that she hoped she would find proof of his guilt. Anything would be preferable to this appalling uncertainty.

34

NEARLY A FORTNIGHT HAD passed since Lucy had disappeared. Jason stared glumly at the cciling and shuddered. He closed his eyes and tried to kid himself he hadn't been interrogated about his girlfriend's whereabouts. Instead, he told himself, Lucy was upstairs where she belonged, stretched out on the bed, sleeping peacefully. In a moment, he would go upstairs and join her. He imagined hearing the sound of her breathing softly at his side and the rustle of sheets as she stirred in her sleep, until he almost convinced himself he would soon feel the warmth of her slender frame sharing his bed. But the kitchen stool on which he was sitting was hard, pressing uncomfortably against his spine, nothing like the mattress on his bed, and when he reached out, his fingers felt only the cold surface of the worktop.

It was impossible to close his mind to the truth of his situation for long. Lucy was dead. He stifled a low cry, imagining her face, and the sound of her voice calling his name. Thinking about his loss tormented him, but he couldn't put her out of his mind. After a few days, his stunned disbelief had given way to an outpouring of grief. If he had the courage, he would have ended his life. There was no point in dragging out an existence that had become no more than a disjointed series of waking moments, each one as painful as the last. For three nights he had hardly slept. When he finally did, he had slept so soundly, it was difficult to rouse himself. He hadn't wanted to wake up.

Gradually his grief hardened into a burning rage. He didn't care about his own situation, which was no worse than he deserved.

What was driving him crazy was knowing that the monster who had attacked Lucy had escaped retribution. From the little Jason had been able to gather from the media, she had been assaulted in the street after running away from her assailant. It didn't make much sense, but he had no access to reliable information. The police were tight-lipped, and he had come across all kinds of conflicting accounts about how she had been discovered. It seemed she had been rushed to A&E, only to die in hospital without recovering consciousness. He hoped she hadn't suffered for long, but the attack must have been terrifying and probably agonising. He couldn't dwell on that for long without breaking down in tears.

It was obvious the police didn't know who had killed Lucy. If they had any idea about the real culprit, they would have made an arrest by now. The knowledge that her assailant was walking around, free, was difficult to bear. What really rankled was that, as long as the police regarded him as a suspect, they were not going all out to look for the killer. Knowing that people could erase all recollection of traumatic events, he began to question whether the police might be right, and he had actually killed Lucy. Perhaps he had blocked out the memory of killing her, maybe when he was drunk. And if he was questioning whether he was guilty, how could anyone else be convinced he was innocent?

Yet there was something about the nature of the questions the police had fired at him that suggested they weren't sure of their ground. His lawyer had been quick to seize on their uncertainty and hammered the point home every time Jason was questioned.

Once again he was summoned to the police station to face the same two detectives over a table, with his lawyer beside him.

'Let's go over it once again, shall we?' the dark-haired detective said. Her penetrating gaze seemed to look right through him. 'Where were you when your girlfriend was attacked?'

He shrugged, aware that the police hadn't established the exact time of the assault. The detective was trying to trick him into admitting that he knew when the attack had taken place. Even in his distressed state of mind, he wasn't about to fall into that trap. Not that it would matter if he did. His lawyer had assured him that he could claim he was too distraught over what had happened to think coherently. He could retract anything he said on the grounds that he had been confused by overwhelming grief. But that was hardly going to be necessary. He could be obdurate, even in his present state of mind. Rigidly he stuck to the story he and his lawyer had agreed on, and refused to let the detective wear him down.

'All I know is that she was at home on Sunday and her body was found on Tuesday. I never saw her after Sunday.' He folded his arms. 'I've got nothing else to tell you. Except for this.' He leaned forward suddenly, and his voice rose as he lost his temper. 'Someone killed Lucy and you're pissing around here with me, when you should be out there looking for the monster who killed her. He's probably looking for his next victim, while you're here wasting time, doing fuck all. You're not even trying to find him. You should be out there, doing your job.' His voice rose in a furious crescendo.

While he was ranting, the detective sat watching him impassively.

'You're not human,' he shouted at her. 'You're a bloody psychopath. You might as well have killed her yourself for all the good you're doing.'

At his side, his lawyer stirred. 'My client is understandably upset,' he said, in a placatory tone. 'His girlfriend has been murdered, and he's keen to see her killer brought to justice. He's usually very equable, but he's under a great deal of stress. I suggest we stop all this right now. My client is in no fit state to continue. And in any case, he's given a statement. He has nothing to add to what he's already told you. And now, in the absence of any evidence, I suggest you leave my client alone. You have nothing to connect him with the crime scene. You have no reason to keep questioning him like this. There's no mileage in hectoring an innocent man to confess to a crime he didn't commit. You've been badgering him for days and in all that time you've come up with no evidence. Nothing at all.'

Soon after he returned home, he received a visitor. Opening the door, he was surprised to see his sister standing on the doorstep, her face scored with worry lines. For the first time it struck him that his trouble had ramifications beyond his own suffering. His family were in shock and mourning with him. They had known Lucy. And then there were her family. He stared at his sister and, as though he was looking in a mirror, he saw her eyes fill with tears.

'Oh Jason,' she murmured. 'What have you done? What have you done?'

For a second, he thought he was going to pass out and he had to hold onto the doorframe for support.

'I haven't done anything,' he cried out in a daze. 'I never – I would never have hurt her – how could you even think –'

His sister watched him as he struggled to find words to bridge the gulf that had opened up between them. He and his sister had always got on well, even though they hadn't seen much of each other in recent years.

He tried again. 'You met Lucy – you know I'd never –'

She shook her head. 'I don't know what to think. No one has told us what's going on. What are we supposed to think?'

He tried to protest, but the suspicion that she had believed him capable of killing Lucy was too much to bear. He felt as though something had broken in him and without another word he reached out and shut the door. He didn't want to see his sister any more. He didn't want to see anyone. The truth was that, without Lucy, he was always going to be alone.

35

JENNY WAITED UNTIL SHE heard the front door slam. Even then she was cautious and waited for a moment before running downstairs, calling to her husband.

'Andrew! Andrew! Are you there?'

She hadn't planned what she would say to him if he answered her, but there were plenty of innocuous questions she could ask him, like what time he would be home, or what he fancied for supper. He had told her he was off for his Sunday game of golf, but he might have changed his mind, or come back for something. What mattered was to establish whether or not he had actually left the house. If he had, she could make a start on searching his things. She called out again, but there was no answer. Just to be sure, she ran to the kitchen, calling out his name repeatedly. She was met by silence. The back door was locked so he hadn't gone out into the garden. Just as she had thought, he had gone out through the front door.

Satisfied that she was alone in the house, she turned her attention to the task that lay ahead. She needed to work fast. The weather looked changeable and, if it rained, he might be home soon. Even if the weather held, she wouldn't have time to search the whole house, or even all the likely places where he might have left evidence, but she could make a start. Convinced he had been having an affair with the murdered girl, she just needed to find proof so she could confront him and force him to confess the truth. The thought that he might have been unfaithful angered her. Worse than that, it made her afraid of what he might have done. But she had to know the truth.

On reflection, she changed her mind about confronting him. It would make more sense for her to take her findings to the police, and leave it to them to interrogate Andrew. They would do a better job of it and anyway, she wasn't sure there was much point in her hearing his confession herself. Whatever he told her, he could easily deny it afterwards. Her attempt to force a confession from him could backfire. If it came down to his word against hers, he might retaliate and accuse her of having attacked Lucy in the mistaken belief that he was having an affair. She could imagine him arguing that he was completely innocent of any wrongdoing, including adultery, and blaming his innocent wife for the murder. He could be very persuasive. If the police were to take him seriously, that might put her in a precarious position. Besides, if she was right and Andrew *had* attacked Lucy, there was no guarantee he wouldn't turn on her next. She might be his wife, but he had made it clear that he no longer cared for her.

She would be sensible and keep her suspicions to herself, only taking them to the police once she found proof of her husband's infidelity with the murdered girl. It wasn't going to look good for him, she thought with grim satisfaction. But first she had to find proof the affair was more than mere speculation on her part, the crazy fantasy of a jealous wife. She decided to start in the bedroom. She wasn't really sure what she was looking for but, if she came across anything suspicious, she hoped she would know when she saw it. A note from Lucy or an unexplained receipt would be enough. With luck, she might stumble on a hotel bill and the staff would recognise Andrew and Lucy as guests. That kind of discovery happened in films. Her thoughts raced as she hurried upstairs and began rummaging through the pockets of his trousers.

'Come on,' she muttered to herself as she searched, 'there must be something here. Something. There has to be.'

It occurred to her that he might have kept a receipt in his desk in his study. Abandoning her search of the wardrobe, she ran downstairs. Andrew's jacket was hanging on the newel post at the foot of the banister. She seized on it, and began rifling through the pockets where she found bits of fluff, a few elastic bands, a penny and some crumpled receipts. As she was taking the receipts out, one by one, and scrutinising them in turn, a noise behind her made her spin round. She hadn't heard him come home. With a cry of alarm, she dropped the receipts and the elastic bands on the floor.

'What the hell do you think you're doing, going through my pockets?' he snarled.

Reaching out, he grabbed both her arms and pinned her against the wall, facing him. She stared back at him as though mesmerised, unable to move.

'I asked you a question,' he hissed, thrusting his face forward until their foreheads were almost touching. 'What were you doing, going through my pockets?'

She drew back, shaking her head. 'Nothing,' she stammered. 'Nothing. I wasn't doing anything.'

'You were going through my pockets,' he said. 'What did you expect to find? Credit cards? Cash? Or was it something else?'

He was holding her by both arms, shaking her and pushing her back against the wall.

She wriggled frantically, and tried to squirm out of his grasp. 'Let me go,' she cried out. 'You're hurting me. I was emptying your jacket pockets so I could put it in the wash. Andrew, what's happening? What's got into you? Why are you being like this?'

'I don't need to explain myself to you. I've not been caught out going through your things.'

'I don't know what you want. Your jacket's dirty,' she stammered, hoping that he wouldn't remember she had only recently taken that same jacket to the dry cleaners.

With a grunt of annoyance, he let go of one of her arms without releasing his grip on her other arm. Before she realised what he was doing, he raised his free hand and slapped her face, hard, yelling that she never washed his jacket at home. Too surprised to protest, she stared at him. Her silence seemed to incense him further. He began to yell at her for lying to him, following up his verbal assault with his fists. Whimpering, she slid down the wall to the floor where she crouched, cowering. Covering her face with her arms, she did her best to protect herself from the furious onslaught. It seemed to go on for hours, although he couldn't have been hitting her for more than a few seconds. At last, he stopped and she heard his feet pounding up the stairs.

Sobbing softly, she hauled herself to her feet. Every part of her seemed to be aching. Glancing in the mirror in the hall, she was shocked at her appearance. Her eyes were bloodshot and puffy from crying, and one of them was half-closed. It looked as though a bruise was developing around it. Other than that, she had managed to cover her face quickly enough to shield it from further injury, but her upper arms and her chest throbbed from where he had struck her repeatedly. This had been no one-off blow, flung at her in fury, but a sustained attack. Next time he might kill her. Her fear crystallised into cold hard fury.

36

GERALDINE WAS ENGROSSED IN studying Jason's statement. The vague and confusing information available about the nature and timing of the attack on Lucy made it impossible to be sure she had not seen her boyfriend between the time he claimed to have seen her on Sunday afternoon and the discovery of her lying unconscious in the street, on Tuesday evening. If the post mortem could have been more specific about the time of the fatal assault, not to mention what appeared to be an abortive attempt to bury her body, it would have made more sense to try and track Jason's movements over the two days and three nights when he alleged Lucy had been missing. As it was, the truth remained impossible to establish with any certainty. All they had was hazy supposition. As for the macabre attempt at burying her, that made no sense at all. The general consensus was that the killer had panicked and tried to hide the body. Possibly he or she must have intended to retrieve the body at a later date and dispose of it properly. But the police still had no idea where she had been so perfunctorily buried, or how she had escaped her living grave only to collapse in the street. All the team could agree on was that it was all very odd.

'I've never seen anything like it,' was the refrain that went around.

'He must have got a shock when he went back and found the girl he buried had climbed out of her grave and walked away,' one of the constables had commented, laughing, and several of his colleagues had chuckled.

'It's just a shame she didn't recover,' Geraldine had added solemnly.

Having spent most of the morning poring over statements, she decided to take a quick break to clear her head, and went for a coffee. In the canteen, she was pleased to be joined at the counter by a young detective constable, Sam Curren, who had recently joined the force after training at Hendon. With his blond hair and bright blue eyes, he reminded Geraldine of Ian when they had first worked together. Ian had been a keen young sergeant back then, and they had instantly felt a connection. He had been with his ex-wife at that time, and there had been no hint of romance between him and Geraldine, but she had always been attracted to him. She felt a faint pang of nostalgia when Sam smiled at her. His youth was a reminder of how much Ian had changed over the years. Time, and the demands of the job, had turned his hair white over his temples and given him slightly bowed shoulders and a spreading paunch which he worked hard to keep in check. Until Lucy's death, Ian had trained and played five-a-side football several times a week with his friends, but now the football team had been decimated and Ian wasn't sure if they would ever recover.

'I'm sure this will all blow over,' Geraldine had said, in a futile endeavour to comfort him.

Now she turned her attention to her young colleague as they waited for their orders.

'How's everything going, Sam?' she asked him.

'You know,' he answered vaguely. 'Can't complain.'

'You don't sound very enthusiastic.'

He shrugged. 'I'm enjoying the job, most of the time anyway.'

'I've been hearing good things about you.' She hesitated, not wanting to pry. 'No job is a hundred per cent perfect.'

'You're right. Like I said, I'm enjoying it. But I could do without all the paperwork.' He grinned. 'Still, it has its moments.'

'What have you been up to this morning?'

'I sat in when DS Arnold took a statement from a woman who came to the station complaining she had been assaulted.'

Geraldine was instantly alert. 'Who was the victim? Where was she attacked?'

'Her name's Jennifer Whittington. She says her husband beat her up.'

Geraldine's surge of interest faded as rapidly as it had arrived. 'Oh,' she replied. 'A domestic. I was afraid it might have been another attack on the street.' She turned to collect her coffee, but something was niggling at her. 'Hang on, Sam,' she called out to the constable's retreating back as they were both walking away. 'What did you say the woman's name was?'

He turned back to her and swallowed a bite of doughnut. 'Jennifer,' he replied, wiping his mouth on a serviette. 'Jennifer Whittington.'

Geraldine frowned. 'Send me a copy of her statement.'

He nodded, looking faintly surprised by the hint of urgency in her voice.

'And do it now,' Geraldine added. 'There's something I want to check.'

Back at her desk, she waited impatiently for Jennifer's statement to arrive. Having read through it, Geraldine carried out a quick check that confirmed her suspicion; the husband accused of assault was called Andrew Whittington. His wife claimed he used prostitutes and had beaten her, giving her multiple bruises to her arms and torso, and a black eye.

'Andrew Whittington is one of Lucy's colleagues,' she told Binita. 'His wife alleges he's been seeing prostitutes and beating her up. Enough to give her a few nasty bruises anyway. Naomi sent her to hospital to get them checked out. They were probably just superficial. We've got images from when she came in, but it's just as well to have them examined by a doctor.'

Binita scrolled through several images of Jennifer's injuries and nodded, her black eyes animated. 'So, Lucy had a violent

163

promiscuous colleague. Good work, Geraldine. Let's put some pressure on him. Bring him in and see what he has to say for himself. And get a sample of his DNA. If he's involved, he won't get past us a second time.' She scowled.

Geraldine nodded. They both knew this could lead nowhere, but there was a chance Jennifer's accusation might be the break they needed in investigating Lucy's death.

'I'm on my way,' she said.

'Geraldine,' Binita detained her as she reached the door.

'Yes?'

'Don't forget to take someone with you. We're talking about a man who could be dangerous.'

Geraldine nodded, thinking of a young detective constable who, she knew, would be pleased to accompany her on a trip away from the police station. As she had expected, Sam responded to her request eagerly, jumping to his feet and announcing that he was ready to leave right away.

'Is this about the allegation of domestic violence?' he enquired as they strode out of the building together.

Geraldine explained the reason for her interest in Andrew as they drove to his office.

'So, he could be a suspect in the murder enquiry?' he said thoughtfully. 'That'll teach him to hit his wife. Without her allegation, he might have slipped under the radar.'

'We'd have caught up with him eventually,' Geraldine replied. 'One way or another we'll get this bastard. Once we spread the net, we'd have taken DNA from everyone who worked with Lucy.'

She didn't add that, if Binita hadn't been convinced Jason was guilty, they might have done that by now. Having missed out on her own chance of promotion by acting unprofessionally to protect her twin sister, she was in no position to disparage a senior officer. Even Ian might attribute her criticism to envy. If she was honest, she wasn't sure her own thwarted ambition wasn't part of the reason she tended to question Binita's decisions. She spent most of her working life puzzling over other people's motives, but she found it hard to analyse her own.

37

FOR THE SECOND TIME in less than two weeks, Geraldine set out for the offices where Lucy had worked. This time she was going to bring Andrew to the police station for questioning. As she had anticipated, Sam Curren was really pleased when she asked him to accompany her.

'So, we're off hunting down a wife beater who might turn out to be a killer,' he exclaimed as they left the police station compound. 'This is more like it!'

Geraldine chuckled, recalling her own excitement when she had first been going out to question suspects in a murder investigation.

'No matter how many hours I spend questioning potential witnesses who turn out to have nothing at all useful to tell us, the thrill never fades,' she told him. 'There's always a chance the next person we speak to will crack the case. You never know, someone who seems completely harmless could turn out to be a vicious killer.'

'But Andrew Whittington's far from harmless. His own wife came forward to accuse him of violence. Now we need him to confess to the attack on Lucy.'

Geraldine nodded. 'Yes, together with some conclusive DNA evidence, a confession would do very nicely.' She smiled. 'Confessions aren't always reliable, but there's no arguing with evidence.'

'Do you never trust what people say?'

Geraldine sighed. 'It can be tricky. Dealing with people is

tricky. The most amoral felons can come across as very credible. The point is, you never know who you're dealing with. If you want my advice, take no one at face value, and suspect everyone.'

'So, can I believe what you just said?' Sam laughed.

They both fell silent as they drew up outside Andrew's building. The secretary at the law firm's offices buzzed them in and looked distinctly irritated to see them.

'How can I help you?' she asked, tapping the fingers of one perfectly manicured hand on a folder she was holding, as though she was itching to begin typing.

After putting the question, she pressed her lips together in blatant disapproval.

Geraldine saw no point in hiding the reason for their visit, and asked to speak to Andrew.

'I'll check when he's free,' the secretary replied. She sounded composed, but Geraldine noticed her hand was trembling as she reached for her phone. 'There's a detective inspector here to see you,' she said, staring blankly over Geraldine's shoulder. 'I don't know,' she replied after listening for a few seconds. She listened again before her eyes flicked to Geraldine. 'Mr Whittington is very busy. He suggests you make an appointment. I have his diary –'

'Good, so he's here,' Geraldine interrupted her. 'Which is his office?'

As the secretary hesitated, Sam turned and walked off along the corridor leading to the solicitors' rooms. He returned a moment later and nodded. Without another word, Geraldine followed him to an office with Andrew's name on the door.

'Wait,' the secretary called out behind them, sounding alarmed. 'You can't just walk in –'

Sam rapped sharply on the door before pushing it open. They entered the office, and the door closed behind them, shutting out the secretary's shrill protest. Even seated, Andrew dominated the room. His bald head and broad face looked enormous. With his legs spread wide and his fingers splayed out on the large wooden desk in front of him, he seemed to occupy all the space in the office. A window behind him was concealed behind a slatted blind. It was flanked by metal filing cabinets, each drawer neatly labelled, and a buff folder lay open on the desk in front of him. Seeing Geraldine's eyes hover on the desk, he slapped the file shut with a sullen glare. She was in no hurry to open the conversation, hoping that the longer he was kept waiting, the more unnerved he would become. He continued to glare at her. His face and bald pate, already florid, turned a deeper shade of red, and she had the impression he was struggling to contain his anger.

'How can I help you, Inspector?'

Andrew spoke through gritted teeth, making his question sound more like a threat than an offer of support. Having broken the silence, he leaned back in his leather chair and raised one eyebrow in an expression of barely concealed insolence. Lifting the edge of the front cover of the file with one finger, he glanced down at the topmost document, deliberately indicating that she did not have his full attention.

Geraldine suppressed an urge to reach out and slam his file shut. 'We'd like to ask you a few questions.'

'I'm an extremely busy man,' Andrew replied, with a dismissive shrug of his broad shoulders. 'I can only give you a moment before my next client arrives. If you'd like to make an appointment with my secretary, I'm sure we can fit you in soon.' His lips stretched in a placatory grin, but his eyes remained wary.

'I don't think you heard me,' Geraldine said. 'We'd like to ask you a few questions, so I'm afraid you're going to have to reschedule your client's appointment, and accompany us. Now.'

Sam moved quietly to stand in front of the door where he stood, gazing dispassionately at Andrew.

'You really expect me to drop everything and come with you?' Andrew asked with fake surprise.

Geraldine had the impression he was playing for time while he planned his response.

'Do I need a lawyer?' he asked, without stirring from his seat.

'Mr Whittington, you're not under arrest. We haven't come here to caution you. We merely want to ask you a few questions.'

'Go ahead.' Andrew leaned back in his chair and gazed insolently at her.

But Geraldine wasn't prepared to question the suspect in his own office. Despite the fact that he would doubtless see straight through any attempt to intimidate him, she wanted to take him to the police station for questioning. He would feel secure seated at his usual desk, and she was keen to rattle him. Confronting a man accustomed to feeling powerful, she was determined to use every means at her disposal to undermine his confidence. Sam had been right, she thought wryly. She was going to try and persuade Andrew to confess to assaulting Lucy. She knew it wouldn't be easy. Not only was the suspect strong-willed, but he was clever enough to see through her manoeuvres. But he couldn't deny having beaten his wife, and that was a start.

38

As GERALDINE WAS ON the point of insisting Andrew accompany her to the police station for questioning, her phone rang. Seeing it was Ariadne, she hoped new evidence had come to light to implicate Andrew in Lucy's death.

'One moment.'

She stepped into the hall, leaving Sam to guard Andrew.

Behind her, she heard Andrew laugh. 'Do you think I'm going to do a runner?' he called out.

The news was disappointing. Jennifer had withdrawn her statement accusing Andrew of physical abuse, claiming her original complaint had been a mistake. She said she had been angry with her husband after an argument, and had made a false accusation to cause him trouble.

'So, she now says her report was vexatious and there was no justification for it.'

'But what about the bruising?' Geraldine asked. 'We have images.'

'I know, but she's now claiming he wasn't responsible for her injuries. She said they're nothing to do with him. According to her latest statement, she fell down the stairs and "bumped herself", her words, and that's what caused the bruises. But she's clearly frightened of him,' Ariadne added. 'She insists we don't tell Andrew about her original allegation, which she now says was false.'

In the light of his wife's retraction, Geraldine felt it might be difficult to find a reason to insist on driving Andrew to the police station. Instead, she had to resort to putting pressure on him to admit there had been a close connection between him and Lucy. But Andrew stuck doggedly to his earlier statement, and denied having had a relationship of any kind with Lucy.

'She was a kid,' he protested, raising his hands with a dismissive shrug.

'Some men find that attractive,' Sam pointed out.

'So now I'm a paedophile?' Andrew retorted coldly. He glowered at Sam. 'Have a care what accusations you fling around, Constable. There's a danger they might come back to plague you.' He leaned forward and spoke with an air of authority. 'I strongly advise you to retract your comment, or I might be seriously tempted to take issue with your slanderous insinuation.'

'My colleague wasn't talking about you,' Geraldine interceded, with a warning glance at Sam. 'He apologises if his words caused offence. That wasn't his intention. There is no question here of any paedophilia. Now, let's get back to talking about your relationship with Lucy Henderson.'

'What relationship might that be? The one that exists in your imagination?'

Now that Jennifer had withdrawn her statement, they no longer had any evidence of Andrew's violent behaviour. Admittedly, they had seen Jennifer's bruises, but there was no proof her injuries had been inflicted by her husband.

'We have reason to suspect you were having an affair with your colleague,' Geraldine said, aware that she was grasping at straws.

Andrew sneered openly at the suggestion. 'So, now I'm an adulterer?' he said, adding indignantly that he was a married man.

'Oh yes, and how's that going?' Sam asked.

Geraldine looked at Sam who cast his gaze down, realising he had spoken out of turn again. Andrew looked momentarily nonplussed, but they had no official reason to enquire into his marital relations. He was ignorant of the complaint his wife had made against him earlier, which she had since withdrawn.

Geraldine tried a different tack and enquired about Andrew's movements from Sunday to Wednesday, the period when, according to Jason, Lucy had been missing.

'That weekend,' Andrew replied, glancing at his wall planner, 'I was playing golf from first thing Saturday right through to Monday evening. I caught the train there on Friday after work and was back at work on Tuesday morning. I'm sure you can verify all of that without any problem.'

He gave them the name of the golf course, which was over a hundred miles away, along with the times of his train journeys.

'I left the car at York station and came straight to work on Tuesday without even stopping off at home on the way. Now, if that's all?'

'What did you do after leaving work on Tuesday?'

'I drove home, as my wife will verify if you ask her nicely.'

Having prolonged the questioning for as long as she could, Geraldine admitted defeat. Andrew was never going to incriminate himself. They couldn't continue interrogating him indefinitely. Geraldine was already beginning to feel awkward, while her suspect lounged in his large leather chair, watching her with a faint smile on his lips, as though he wasn't at all worried by her questions. It was a pity he was accustomed to dealing with the police, and to maintaining his composure in stressful situations.

'We'll need a sample of your DNA, for the purposes of elimination,' Geraldine said.

Andrew's relaxed demeanour didn't alter, but he licked his lips in what could have been a sign of nerves. 'Is that really necessary?' he enquired with a derisive sniff. 'I think you've wasted enough of my time as it is.' He stood up.

'To eliminate you from the enquiry, yes, I'm afraid it is necessary,' Geraldine replied.

He shrugged and sat down again. 'Very well, then, let's get on with it. As if you haven't wasted enough of my time already,' he added, suddenly tetchy.

'We'll send an officer round straightaway.'

Later that morning, Binita gathered the team together to discuss how the investigation was progressing.

'Andrew's story checks out,' Sam said. 'I've spoken to the golf club and they had a tournament that weekend. The station CCTV backs him up, and his car was at York station from Friday evening to early Tuesday morning, just like he told us.'

'So, he wasn't the reason she was missing on Monday and Tuesday,' Geraldine said.

'He could still have attacked her on Tuesday evening, on his way home from work,' Naomi suggested.

Binita shook her head. 'No, her disappearance was down to someone else, who must have been keeping her out of sight. Someone other than Andrew was responsible for her fatal injuries. Andrew would have had no time to attack Lucy and attempt to bury her on his way home. Realistically, Jason remains our only suspect. Unless some other suspect crawls out of the woodwork to challenge our theory, we concentrate on Jason. He remains our only suspect,' she added, looking directly at Geraldine as she continued. 'No matter what our personal preferences might be, we continue to focus our attention on Jason. It's only a matter of time before the VIIDO finish tracking his movements, and we complete the door-to-door questioning. I know it's taking a while, but this is a painstaking process. We just need to confirm he was spotted with Lucy at any point between Sunday and Tuesday evening, whether on film or through an eyewitness statement, and we'll have him. Once we catch him out in a lie, his protestations of innocence will all start to unravel. You'll see. We just have to be patient.'

'And if we don't find any evidence that he saw Lucy during the period she was missing, what then?' Geraldine asked.

Binita frowned. 'We'll cross that bridge if we come to it,' she replied. 'Now, less negativity and more work. Let's get going and find the evidence.'

At lunchtime, Sam caught up with Geraldine and Naomi in the canteen.

'What makes you so sure Jason's innocent?' he asked, pulling up a chair between them.

'You know Jason's mates with Ian?' Naomi said.

'It's not that,' Geraldine replied irritably, although she wasn't sure she was being entirely truthful. 'We should be working outwards from what we know, not searching for evidence of a hypothesis, however probable it is. Jason was Lucy's boyfriend. We all agree that makes him the most likely suspect, but it doesn't prove he's guilty. And without any proof, we don't have a case. Binita knows that as well as anyone.'

'Which is why she's determined to find evidence Jason did it,' Naomi said.

'However determined you are to find evidence has no bearing on whether or not you're going to find it,' Geraldine said. 'We have to work from what we've got.'

Sam put his mug down. 'What if we haven't got anything?'

'Then we keep looking.' Geraldine sighed. 'We can't come up with a convenient suspect first, and then decide we're going to find evidence to convict him.'

'Why not, if throwing everything we've got at it means we find the proof we need?'

'Because we might not find that elusive proof, and then we're back where we started, only worse off because by that point the trail has gone cold. The killer has had time to cover his tracks and maybe even leave the area altogether, while we've been wasting time and resources chasing around after the wrong suspect.'

'You don't know he's the wrong suspect,' Naomi pointed out. 'That's just supposition.'

'As is the idea that Jason's guilty,' Geraldine retorted sharply.

39

NOW THAT THE POLICE were investigating him, there was no time to waste. He wasn't going to sit around waiting to hand them a sample of his DNA. Telling his secretary he was popping out, he sprinted to his car and drove straight home. The police would be able to find a sample of his DNA in the house, or at his office, but he wasn't going to make it easy for them to prove he had been in contact with Lucy before she died. He rehearsed possible scenarios in his mind as he followed the familiar route back to his house, along Fulford Road, turning off into Heslington Lane, then on to Main Street and Field Lane where he lived.

He remembered slapping Lucy. As far as he could recall, the flat of his right hand had struck the left side of her face. That contact meant it was possible his DNA would have been detected on her cheek. He might come up with a perfectly reasonable explanation as to why his DNA was present, given that Lucy had worked for the same firm as him. He pondered various explanations, and thought carefully about which one might best explain why his DNA had been detected on the mud on the dead girl's face. But he knew his position would be precarious. His best course of action was to delay the discovery of his involvement until he was out of the country.

His thoughts began to spin uncontrollably. Taking a deep breath, he tried to calm himself down by focusing on his driving. As soon as he reached home, he gave up trying to control his panicky feelings and ran to his desk. He couldn't understand why the police suspected him, but the fact remained that they wanted his DNA and he wasn't going to take any chances. Grabbing a notepad and biro, he began frantically scribbling a list of things he was going to need. He was in a desperate hurry, but it was still best to plan his next move instead of rushing off in blind panic. He guessed that, once the police got hold of his DNA, the results would take at least a few hours to obtain, even if they insisted the test be expedited for some reason. By the time the police had evidence that might point to him, he would be long gone. 'Passport', he jotted down, and 'cash'. With enough ready money, those were really all he was going to need, but he made a further note of things he might pack for a holiday, adding 'disguise' as an afterthought. It would do no harm to take his hooded jacket and sunglasses. There was no point in going away empty-handed.

He hurried upstairs to pack a small case, determined to leave home unobserved. He had initially decided to leave the car at home and escape on foot, but now he decided that would slow him down. It would be better to leave the car somewhere close to the station. He would pay cash for a ticket to London, and then make his way to Heathrow and catch a plane from there. It would mean wasting the cost of a train ticket, but if that succeeded in throwing the police off his scent for long enough to allow him to get away, it would be worth it. At a busy airport, he could quite easily disappear in the crowds, especially with a minimal disguise. Having finished packing, he sat down on the bed to check his list. He couldn't wait around for long, because Jenny might come home at any time. It would be easier to leave while she was still out.

It was a pity he couldn't enlist her help, but she wasn't to be trusted. Hitting her had been a reckless blunder. Without her support, he had no one to rely on to help him out of this mess. He hadn't even really hurt the girl. All he had done was give her a slap. It wasn't his fault she was dead. But with his DNA potentially left on the body, he wasn't going to hang around to argue. He supposed he ought to have felt something as he prepared to leave his wife after more than twenty years of marriage, but he seemed to be numb inside. If anything, he felt she had let him down, and he was grimly pleased to be seeing the last of her. No doubt she had done her best, he thought, with a sudden stab of pity for the dull life she had led as his wife. He had never made much of an effort to please her, but she had seemed happy enough being a mother, and had never paid him much attention once their son had come along.

Preoccupied with his work, he hadn't minded that her thoughts had always been elsewhere. They had both known for a long time that neither of their worlds revolved around each other. Only now he was forced to abandon the career he had worked so hard to build. It was galling. And all because some stupid girl had crossed his path by an unlucky fluke. With a sigh, he closed his case. His passport and keys, and what cash he had available, were safely stowed in his pockets. He would pick up some more cash at a dispenser in town before he left York. He was apprehensive but, at the same time, curiously elated at the prospect of entering a new phase of life, one in which he would be absolutely free. He would change his name once he had left the UK. He wondered what to call himself in his new incarnation. Something unremarkable. As long as the police were looking for him, he was going to have to blend into the background. They might spend years looking for him, but he refused to dwell on the negative aspect of his position. He was going to walk out of his house and never return and, once he was safely away from York, he would be free. They were never going to catch him. And that, he assured himself, was just as it should be.

It was a wrench leaving his whole life behind him as he fled the city. But in many ways it was a glorious situation for a strong, intelligent man like him.

'Why then the world's mine oyster,' he murmured under his breath, as he carried his suitcase down the stairs, 'which I with sword will open.' He felt invincible, hugging his secret departure to himself as if it were a fabulous secret which, in a way, it was. He was passing through a portal to a new life. There was a weird disconnect between this intrepid psyche he had adopted and his former life as a reliable lawyer, a family man, sensible and steady. Fetching a handful of cash from a drawer of his desk, he caught sight of a family photograph which Jenny kept proudly displayed in the living room. For a second, he paused, staring into his son's eyes, permanently frozen in time by the click of a phone camera. The breath seemed to catch in his throat as he looked at it, but he shook off his fleeting regret with a shrug. Once he was settled out of reach of UK law enforcement, he would send for his son. *Use this ticket and fly out to join me. Make sure you tell no one where you're going. Only a fool would stay in the UK, where your earnings will never amount to more than a pittance. Come and settle with me, and we'll live like kings.* His son wouldn't be able to resist the lure of a life filled with luxury and compliant women.

As he reached the foot of the stairs, the doorbell rang. He froze, afraid that it was the police, wanting to collect his DNA. The inspector had said she would send someone to his office straightaway. If she had done so, unable to find him at work they might well have come looking for him at home. He kept perfectly still, praying that Jenny wouldn't choose this precise moment to return home. It would be just like her to mess everything up for him. The bell rang again and he waited, terrified. There was no other sound from outside, but he had no way of knowing if they were still there, waiting. The longer he delayed, the more likely it was that Jenny would return. He had no choice. Taking a deep breath, he crossed the kitchen and opened the back door.

No one came running up to him, and there was no sign of anyone watching for him. Quietly, he made his way along the side of the house. Reaching the front yard, he pressed himself close to the hedge and scanned the street in both directions. As far as he could see, it was empty apart from his neighbour's car. He was safe. He felt a surge of confidence. Luck was on his side. More than that, the police were incompetent and he was one step ahead of them. Everything was going to turn out well. A man of his intellect and discernment was unassailable. He smiled, thinking of the police diligently plodding around, sniffing for clues. He had observed their laboured procedures in the past. They would take a week for a process that could easily be completed in a day. Thorough though they were in collecting evidence, they were painfully slow to reach any kind of conclusion. He had only to move swiftly, and they would never catch him.

40

'WHAT DO YOU MEAN, he wasn't there?' Geraldine demanded.

There was a hollow feeling in the pit of her stomach, and for a second she thought she might throw up. She could so easily have insisted on taking Andrew to the police station and keeping him there while they ran a test to see if his DNA matched the unidentified sample found on Lucy's face.

'Are you all right?' Sam asked.

'Yes, yes, I'm fine,' she replied crossly. 'Where is he?'

Sam shrugged. 'He told his secretary he was just popping out, but that was over two hours ago, and he still hasn't returned. She tried to call him, but he wasn't answering his phone. She was worried something might have happened to him. I checked his home, but there was no one in. Should I check the hospital?'

Geraldine frowned. 'The station more likely,' she muttered. 'We need to get hold of that DNA urgently. Check his desk – no, call his wife and see if she's home. She can give you his toothbrush or something. And then we need to expedite a test to see if it matches what we've got. If she doesn't answer her phone, go straight back to his office and see what you can find there. Go!'

Geraldine went to speak to Binita to let her know the latest development.

'If he's not at home or at his office, we should send out an alert to search for his car, and circulate his details to stations and airports. We don't want him to leave the country.'

Binita looked worried. 'Do you really think that's likely?'

Geraldine nodded. 'We're dealing with a criminal lawyer,' she said. 'He knows what goes on. And he disappeared just after we requested a DNA sample. It could be coincidence, but I think we ought to err on the side of caution. If he's innocent, why is he avoiding a DNA test?'

Binita grunted. 'Yes. We've already let him slip through our fingers once.'

'I don't know how I managed to misjudge the situation so badly,' Geraldine admitted.

'It happens,' Binita said kindly.

Even if it turned out Andrew's DNA didn't match the one they already had, the possibility had been there, and they shouldn't have allowed him to escape.

'He won't get far,' Binita added, seeing Geraldine's stricken expression. 'We'll pick him up if he's trying to leave the country.'

'He might not have left his house,' Ariadne suggested when she heard what had happened.

'The DCI's applying for a search warrant,' Geraldine told her. 'But without any evidence to tie Andrew to the crime, all we can really say is that he worked with her and we haven't been able to find him since this morning.'

'He vanished when he was told we wanted to take his DNA,' Ariadne pointed out. 'It definitely looks suspicious.'

They had no proof Andrew was guilty of any crime, but that might change very soon. Summoning Sam to accompany her in case Andrew was at home, Geraldine drove to his house and found Jenny there on her own. After conducting a quick search of the property, Geraldine went to the kitchen to speak to Jenny, leaving Sam waiting in the hall. Jenny claimed she hadn't seen her husband since that morning when he went out to work.

'He often works late,' Jenny said. 'It's only half past six. He could be home any time before eight, or later if he's out for the evening. I don't always know when he's not coming home for supper. He doesn't always remember to tell me.' She sighed. 'I'm not going to change my mind again. It was stupid of me to accuse him of battering me, when all that happened was I fell down the stairs.' She smiled anxiously. 'I am sorry for wasting police time but, like I told the constable, I was angry because we'd had a row. Andrew said some very hurtful things. He could be nasty like that. But he never hit me. He would never do anything like that. Really, you have to believe me.'

'I didn't come here to discuss your allegation of domestic violence,' Geraldine assured her. 'Now you've withdrawn your statement, that's over.'

'What are you doing here then?'

'We are trying to find Andrew to question him in connection with a different matter altogether. He left work at around eleven this morning, and hasn't been seen since. His secretary has no record of any appointments. We've checked with his doctor and dentist, and with local opticians, and no one seems to have heard from him today. Do you know where he is? If you do, it's very important you tell us so we can find him without delay. Do you understand?'

Jennifer nodded, looking dazed. 'You're saying you can't find Andrew,' she muttered uneasily.

'We're beginning to wonder if he's come to some harm,' Geraldine added untruthfully.

Geraldine still believed Andrew had beaten his wife, but they had been married for over twenty years, and Jennifer might not want to see him arrested, however angry she was with him.

'Oh no,' Jenny replied. 'Andrew knows how to take care of himself.'

'It might help us if we had a sample of his DNA,' Geraldine said gently. 'We're going to need to take something away with us.'

She called to Sam and instructed him to go ahead. Jenny looked worried, but she didn't remonstrate when they heard Sam's feet pounding up the stairs.

'No toothbrush,' he reported when he joined them. 'But I found this in the bin.' He held up an evidence bag and showed Geraldine a used razor blade. 'And I've taken these pyjamas from a laundry bin.'

Jenny opened her mouth as if to protest, but then closed it without a word.

'I want you to contact us the instant he comes home,' Geraldine said. 'Here's my number. Put it on speed dial on your phone and make sure to call me straightaway. Don't delay even for a second. Do you understand?'

Jenny nodded. 'Yes,' she whispered. 'He's in trouble, isn't he? Tell me, what did he do?'

Geraldine drew in a deep breath. 'We're doing our best to keep your husband out of trouble,' she said. 'Unfortunately, he's reacted very stupidly to our request to speak to him in relation to a serious crime. For all we know, he's innocent of any wrongdoing, but we need to speak to him because we think he might be able to help us. But first we have to find him. Either way, it's imperative you call us as soon as you hear the front door open. Don't say anything, just click on my number and I'll know it's you.'

Jenny nodded. 'I'll do it,' she said. 'I'll let you know.'

'If he's innocent, then it can't hurt him,' Geraldine said. 'And if he's not–' She sighed and shook her head.

Jenny's eyes widened in alarm. 'I'll be sure to call you,' she said.

'It doesn't matter what time it is,' Geraldine said. 'However late it is, call me.'

'I'll let you know as soon as he comes in. I promise.'

41

THEY WERE SITTING WATCHING television together, as they usually did when Linda was home in the evening. Every time George glanced in her direction, her eyes seemed to flick away from him as though she had been watching him. He stared at her for a moment, but she appeared to be engrossed in the programme. Reassured, he turned his attention back to the screen but when he glanced at her again a few moments later, her eyes shifted rapidly away from him back to the television. A prickly feeling crept down his spine. Her furtive manner was disconcerting, but somehow he dared not accuse her openly of spying on him.

He shifted uncomfortably in his seat, wondering if she could have spotted him at work in the garden. He had been careful not to bury anyone out there when she was home, so she couldn't possibly have observed him at it. He did all the gardening, so it was hard to see how she could have discovered the bodies he had buried. But he couldn't be sure what she got up to when she was at home by herself. He wondered if she had been ferreting around under the trees for some reason, and had stumbled on his secret. She clearly suspected something was going on. It wasn't just this one evening. Recently, he had noticed a watchfulness in the way she treated him. There was nothing specific he could identify, but she was different. Eventually, her furtive scrutiny unnerved him so much that he blurted out a clumsy challenge.

'What is it?' he demanded, twisting round on the sofa to look at her directly. 'Why are you looking at me like that?'

Her eyebrows shot up in surprise as she asked him what he was talking about.

'You keep looking at me,' he replied sullenly.

'I'm watching the telly,' she protested.

He settled back down, satisfied that she had stopped staring at him. Her reaction to his accusation had seemed genuine. Probably he was just being paranoid. Ever since Linda had mentioned that Robert and Sharon were considering getting a puppy, he had been feeling anxious. A dog would be catastrophic, especially one that liked to dig. He had to scupper their plans, but how? He would have to find a way to put them off the idea of getting a dog. Robert and his wife were bringing the baby over at the weekend. That gave George a few days to make his plans. He was going to have to be subtle in his approach. If Robert learned that George was opposed to him getting a dog, it might prove counterproductive. Robert had always been contrary. George sometimes thought his son enjoyed deliberately winding him up. No, he was going to have to come up with a persuasive argument against introducing a puppy into a household where there was a baby.

It was a pity Linda wasn't worried by the idea. As a nurse, her opinion might have held some sway. He decided to try and enlist her support, but he would have to proceed cautiously, and guard against alerting her to the real reason for his concern. He had to convince her this was about protecting their grandson, and nothing to do with the potential damage a puppy could cause in the garden. Once she understood his true motive, she would dismiss his reservations with a laugh. 'You and your precious garden,' he could imagine her saying. 'Not everything revolves around the garden,' and he would protest that he was only thinking of the baby.

If he could have confided the real reason why he couldn't countenance the prospect of a dog digging in his carefully tended earth, Linda would have understood why Robert couldn't be allowed to bring a dog into their garden. But George could never reveal his secret to another living soul. Not even Linda would understand. There were moments when he himself questioned the sanity of his actions. He couldn't expect anyone else to appreciate the need to bury healthy young bodies in the soil, sharing their life energy with his trees and shrubs. Even the grass flourished in his garden. He claimed that was only because he watered it regularly; he alone knew how it benefited from being fed as well as watered.

He broached the subject tentatively when Linda muted the television during the adverts. 'You don't really think Robert and Sharon should get a dog, do you?'

'Why not? Don't you think it would be a good idea?'

He took a deep breath. 'I think it's a terrible idea. What if it attacks Noah?'

'Don't be daft. George, we've talked about this before. They're not going to get an aggressive breed and, in any case, they won't leave the baby alone with the dog.'

He could tell from the tone of her voice that she was growing impatient with him, but he felt compelled to keep trying to convince her. 'You can't be sure of that.'

The adverts finished, and she turned the sound back on, drowning out his feeble protestations. Clearly, he couldn't rely on his wife to help him prevent Robert getting a dog.

As the television played out its story, his thoughts whirled. He couldn't pretend to be allergic to dogs because Linda knew his parents had one when he was a child. People did develop allergies, but it would be almost impossible to dupe his wife. She was a nurse. Besides, claiming to be allergic to dogs risked making the situation worse, because his family might suggest leaving the dog outside in the garden so it didn't shed any hair indoors. No, he would have to convince them that a dog could endanger his grandson's life.

With Linda now engrossed in the television, he switched on his phone and began trawling the internet for articles about babies and dogs, saving links to a few that seemed to support his cause. Many of the articles claimed that owning a pet could actually be good for a baby's health. There was some evidence to suggest that exposure to household pets, particularly dogs, during pregnancy and infancy was believed to increase immunity and help lower a baby's risk of health problems such as allergies and asthma. Impatiently, he moved on from those, searching for others that were more helpful, suggesting that all dogs had the potential to injure children. Admittedly, that could be said of all humans as well, but dogs had the potential to bite or maul small children, sometimes without any provocation. Several articles said that no dog should be left alone with small children. That would have to do. Making sure he had saved the links, he switched off his phone just as the television programme finished.

'Do you think he killed her?' Linda asked.

Momentarily startled, he could only stammer, 'What? What?'

'Do you think it was him?'

Realising she was talking about the television series, he shrugged, half laughing in relief.

'Well?' she prompted him.

'I don't know.'

'Obviously you can't *know*,' she replied. 'They're deliberately making it confusing so we can't really be sure of anything. I'm just asking what you think.'

'I don't know,' he repeated, and Linda sighed, muttering something about him being 'hopeless'.

If she knew the care he had taken to work out how best to look after the garden, and how cleverly he had concealed his activities from everyone, she wouldn't dismiss him as hopeless. He was almost sorry he couldn't reveal the extent of his brilliance, but, of course, he couldn't say anything.

'Never mind,' she went on, with a smile. 'You're not a bad old chump, all things considered. I'll make us a cup of tea, shall I?'

He jumped to his feet. 'I'll make it.' As the kettle boiled, he thought about what he might say that could possibly persuade Linda to support him when he challenged his son and daughter-in-law about their plans. He sighed. It was going to take more than a cup of tea to convince her to back him up.

42

TOO WOUND UP TO relax, Jenny stayed downstairs, waiting for Andrew to come home. She wasn't looking forward to seeing him again after their last encounter. She had retracted her accusation for the sake of the family, but she was still angry with him. The injury to her eye had developed from an angry red patch to a massive black bruise, slightly purple around the edges. The skin surrounding it appeared to be turning yellow. It was very sore when she touched it, but otherwise wasn't causing her much pain. The hospital had checked her over carefully, with X-rays as well as a physical examination of her head and chest. Waiting for the results of the examination had been terrifying, but the doctor had assured her that her injuries were superficial and had discharged her with a prescription for painkillers in case she needed them. Wary of taking any kind of drugs, she had left the prescription unused. A doctor had questioned her about how she had sustained her bruises, but she had declined to talk about it, telling the doctor that she had already given a statement to the police.

Having promised to call the police inspector when Andrew returned home, no matter how late it was, she kept her phone within reach on the arm of the settee. After nine attempts throughout the evening, she had given up trying to call him. A Jason Bourne film distracted her for a while, but as she was scrolling through the channels, it occurred to her that Andrew might think it strange if he came home to find her still up and watching television after midnight. Not wanting to alert him to the fact that anything unusual was happening, she went up to bed where she lay awake for hours, listening out for him. Eventually, she slipped into an uneasy doze, still clutching her phone. She woke with a start and glanced at the time. It was twenty past three, too late to call Andrew to ask him where he was.

She wondered how she would have reacted to his absence if she hadn't suspected he was involved in a dodgy affair that had ended with a woman's death. The more she thought about it, the more ridiculous it seemed to suspect Andrew of committing murder, but he might know more than he was telling the police. She assumed it was not a coincidence that he had disappeared shortly before the police came to the house looking for him. But, on reflection, she realised she had no proof he had committed any crime, and she might have been jumping to the wrong conclusion. For the first time, it struck her that Andrew might have met with an accident. Instead of being a vicious criminal, as she had suspected, it was possible he had witnessed a crime and had been silenced by a killer. The police had never accused him of being guilty of any wrongdoing. They had only said they wanted to question him. She had drawn her own conclusions about why he might be wanted by the police. But she could be mistaken. Worn out with all the confusion, she burst into tears.

Now that he was not at home, Jenny began to wonder whether she mightn't have misjudged him. She could no longer remember why she had been so quick to assume he had done something terrible to that poor girl whose fate had been splashed all over the news. It was a devastating story, and perhaps her own shock on reading about it had led her to draw false conclusions. There was really no reason why she should suspect Andrew of being involved in a murder. The more she thought about it, the more far-fetched the idea seemed. He had a temper, it was true, and she knew only too well how violently he could react when provoked. But murder was another matter altogether. According to the news reports, the poor girl had been strangled and half buried. The reports described it as a cold-blooded and carefully planned murder, very different to Andrew when he hit out in sudden temper. He had never raised his hand against her before, and he must have been under almost unbearable pressure to mistreat her like that.

The longer she lay awake in the house on her own, not knowing where her husband was, the more worried she became for his safety. Even the police had been concerned for his wellbeing. He had been understandably upset by his colleague's death. No doubt everyone who knew the victim had been similarly disturbed. As his wife, Jenny ought to have shown more sympathy, not gone searching through his belongings looking for evidence of some wrongdoing. She was suddenly overwhelmed by a wave of guilt. Andrew had mistreated her, but she had hardly been a model wife. If he would only come home, and reassure the police he was fine, she would never mistrust him again. She began to cry, and the tears stung her bruised eye. Confused and miserable, she tried to call Andrew but he still wasn't answering his phone. This time, it didn't even ring but a stranger's voice told her that the number had not been recognised and she should try again. She knew she had the correct number, because she had Andrew's mobile on speed dial. All the same, she clambered out of bed and hurried down to the kitchen. Switching on the light, she scrabbled around in her drawer of documents and checked her list of phone numbers before trying again. The same message greeted her. Andrew's phone had been disconnected.

Either he didn't want to speak to her, or anyone else, or his phone had been stolen and destroyed. All kinds of terrible scenarios flashed through her mind. It was possible Andrew had witnessed his colleague's murder, and the killer had found out and eliminated him. Perhaps the girl had confided in Andrew who had lost his temper and confronted her killer. She pictured her husband lying at the bottom of the river, his pockets filled with stones, pieces of his smashed phone floating away down to sea. The inspector's words rang in her head. 'We're beginning to wonder if he's come to some harm.' The police must have realised he was in danger, or they wouldn't have told Jenny they were concerned for his safety. First thing in the morning, she would phone the inspector and insist they tell her exactly what was going on.

There was nothing she could do but return to bed and try to get some sleep. Holding her phone to her chest, she drifted into an uneasy doze.

43

A TEAM OF CONSTABLES had been searching for a link between Alison and Lucy, but so far they had not found anything to connect them. Meanwhile, a report came in from the lab the following morning to say that a trace of Andrew's DNA had been detected in the mud scraped from Lucy's left cheek. This evidence indicated that he had touched her either during or after the abortive attempt to bury her. The evidence was confusing, seeming to refute the theory that Andrew had actually manhandled Lucy, and attempted to bury her. Tests had been carried out on her clothing and hair, and only that one trace of his DNA on her cheek had so far been detected. The lab insisted they had been thorough.

'If he left his DNA on one cheek,' Binita repeated, frowning, 'what exactly does that tell us?'

'The other traces must have been wiped away or contaminated when she was buried,' Naomi suggested. 'There must have been more.'

'One cheek,' Geraldine said thoughtfully. 'Perhaps he slapped her face? It was her left cheek, so if he's right handed, that would make sense.'

A quick check with the secretary at the law firm confirmed that Andrew was right handed.

'Nothing about this DNA sample makes sense,' Binita grumbled. 'Let's return to his alibi.'

Having spent a long weekend playing golf, Andrew had not returned to work until early Tuesday morning. As a consequence of his absence on Monday, he had worked late on Tuesday. According to him, and the secretary, that was not unusual. He had left the office at eight o'clock on Tuesday evening, and driven straight home. CCTV from the car park at the office bore out his statement, as his car had been recorded leaving shortly before five past eight. His journey home would typically take between ten and fifteen minutes, depending on traffic. He said he had arrived home before eight fifteen, and a CCTV camera outside a pub on the way to his house had recorded him passing at ten past eight.

'We have confirmation of the time he left the office, and the evidence that he went straight home is pretty clear.'

'He might have had time to stop off somewhere if he was speeding?' Ariadne suggested.

'Which might have given him time to attack Lucy, but not to bury her,' Binita replied. 'No, it doesn't add up.'

'It can't all have been down to him,' Geraldine said, and Binita nodded. 'He can't have attacked and buried her in a matter of a few minutes. So, it can't have been him.'

'Then what the hell was his DNA doing on her face, if he didn't kill her?' Binita asked irritably.

'He could have been present,' Geraldine suggested. 'Maybe he wasn't working alone.'

'And if he's innocent, why hide what he knows?' Binita asked. 'Who is he protecting?'

'We know it wasn't his wife,' Ariadne said. 'We've checked her movements and she was at home all evening and nowhere near the scene of the attack.'

'We don't actually know where the attack took place,' Binita reminded her irritably.

'But we know it can't have been far from where Lucy was found,' Geraldine said. 'And Jennifer wasn't in that area on Tuesday. She doesn't drive so she couldn't have been involved and got back home without being picked up on CCTV somewhere.

In any case, I'm not sure Andrew would perjure himself for his wife. I get the impression it's not the happiest of marriages, and he would stand to lose his whole career if he obstructed our enquiry, not to mention the possibility of a custodial sentence.'

'So, if he's not protecting his wife, who is he protecting, assuming he had some contact with the girl during or after her burial?' Binita asked.

'His reputation?' Geraldine suggested. 'If he was in some way involved, he might well be keen to keep his name out of the investigation.'

'So, if he didn't assault Lucy, but was somehow there as a witness or accomplice, who was he working with?' Binita asked. 'Could Andrew and Jason have both been involved in this?' She looked around with sudden decisiveness. 'We need to find out whether those two could have known each other. Let's get going. We have a lot to do.'

A team was set up to question neighbours about the time Andrew had arrived home on the evening Lucy was discovered, unconscious. Several neighbours had private security cameras and it wasn't long before the film from the local pub was corroborated by CCTV film from two more sources. At the same time, security cameras near Andrew's office were checked. There could be no question that Andrew would not have had time to carry out an attack, and an attempted burial, on his way home that evening. There remained the possibility that the attack had been carried out before Tuesday evening, but once again Andrew's movements seemed to allow no time for him to have been involved. He had been away for a golf weekend from Saturday to Tuesday morning and at work all day Tuesday. A constable was sent to question the golf hotel and check CCTV but the message came back that Andrew's car had been in the car park all weekend, and he had not left the hotel until he checked out early Tuesday morning. They all agreed it seemed like a convenient alibi. Nevertheless, it proved he could not have driven home at any point on Sunday or Monday and attacked Lucy and tried to bury her. Nor had he travelled by taxi. But there remained the conundrum of his DNA found on her face.

Armed with all the information they had so far gleaned, Geraldine prepared to question Andrew yet again. She took Sam with her, explaining that it was a useful exercise for him to see an investigation through.

'Assuming we are going to get to the end of it,' he said. 'We don't seem to be making much progress at the moment, and we don't even know if we're going to be able to find Andrew.'

'Every detail draws us one step closer to seeing the whole,' Geraldine assured him. 'Some investigations are like a complicated jigsaw puzzle. We might have some of the pieces, but they don't fit together yet, and while other pieces are still missing it's impossible to slot them into the right places. We have to keep looking, checking CCTV, asking questions, and generally ferreting around, until we have enough information for it all to make sense. It can be a protracted process, but it's worthwhile if we get a result in the end.'

'What if we don't?'

'We will,' she assured him.

'You can't know that.'

Geraldine didn't answer. Sam was going to have to find out for himself how important it was to maintain a positive approach to their work. She resisted admitting to him that blind belief was sometimes the only thing that kept her from giving up.

44

GERALDINE WAS TROUBLED THAT she hadn't heard from Jenny. Andrew's wife had agreed to let the police know as soon as he returned home, but she had been silent. As Geraldine was leaving the building, accompanied by Sam, Jenny rang her. Geraldine nodded to Sam to wait, and took the call.

'Is he there?' Geraldine asked, mouthing to Sam that Andrew's wife was on the line.

'No,' came the shrill reply. 'And I insist you tell me what's happening. Is Andrew in danger? I have a right to know what's going on.'

Geraldine sighed. 'We don't know where your husband is. We're trying to find him.'

'Why? What's going on?'

Geraldine hesitated. 'Are you at home?'

'Yes.'

'Stay there. We're coming to see you.'

Geraldine hung up and told Sam their first visit would be to Andrew's home, where his wife might be able to give them some clue as to where he might be. At the same time, she dispatched Ariadne to Andrew's office, accompanied by a detective constable, in case Andrew was there.

'What's this about?' Jenny demanded, without inviting them in.

She looked as though she hadn't slept, and her bruised eye was black and dark purple.

197

'We're looking for Andrew,' Geraldine repeated. 'May we come in?'

'What for?'

Jenny's belligerence was new, and Geraldine wasn't quite sure what had caused the change in her manner. What was clear was that she was very frightened.

'Has your husband been in touch with you?' she asked gently. 'Don't be afraid. We're trying to help him.'

'I haven't heard from him and he's not answering his phone. Where is he? Has something happened to him?'

Her anguish seemed genuine and Geraldine was disappointed to realise that Jenny probably had no idea where her husband was.

'What makes you think something's happened to him?' Sam asked.

'Why else would you be here?' Jenny countered. 'Something's going on and I insist you tell me what it is.'

With a show of reluctance, she let them into the house. Geraldine explained that they believed Andrew was in some way connected with the death of his colleague. Jenny didn't seem surprised, but nodded as though she already knew that. It didn't mean she had spoken to Andrew. She could have worked it out for herself. What Geraldine wanted to focus on now was finding Andrew. She didn't add that the police were concerned he might be involved in another girl's disappearance. It was now nearly a week since Alison had gone missing and neither her friends nor her family had heard from her.

'Can you think of anywhere he might have gone?' she asked. 'We need to find him. We really want to clear this up so you can get back to your lives,' she added, once again glossing over their suspicions.

Jenny seemed to be sticking by Andrew, and Geraldine was reluctant to reveal the real reason for the police interest in him. Jenny might continue to be loyal to her husband, despite the physical abuse she had suffered at his hands. Geraldine had seen too many people cowed by violent partners, or else simply devoted to them, to feel confident that Jenny would abandon Andrew.

'We'd like a list of his friends and associates, and any clubs or organisations he belongs to. We'll take his laptop,' she added, nodding at Sam who stepped over to the desk in the corner of the room.

'You can't do that,' Jenny protested. 'Take your hands off it. That laptop's not yours. It's not Andrew's either,' she added quickly. 'It's mine.'

'You'll be able to give us the password then,' Geraldine replied, with a smile.

Jenny shook her head. 'I can't remember it,' she mumbled.

'We'll take it to the station,' Sam said. 'The IT geeks will have it unlocked in no time.'

They waited for a second, but Jenny didn't reply.

'Very well,' Geraldine said, 'we'll take it with us. And check to see if there are any other electronic devices in the house.'

Sam nodded and left the room and a few seconds later they heard him going upstairs.

'Now,' Geraldine went on, 'about that list. I take it you have no reason for wanting to obstruct us in our investigation?'

With a scowl, Jenny took the pen and notepad Geraldine was holding out. 'I just want my husband back,' she muttered. 'I want to know what's going on.'

'What's going on is that your husband appears to know something about a recent murder victim, and we want to ask him to share that information with us. But in order to ask him, we first have to find him, and he seems to have disappeared. So, when you've finished that list, we'll go upstairs and you can tell me if anything's missing.'

'What do you mean?'

'Money, passport, suitcase,' Geraldine suggested, watching Jenny closely.

Jenny looked down quickly, but not before Geraldine had seen an expression of dismay on her face.

'You think he's run off?' she whispered. 'You think he's gone and left me here?' She looked up, her eyes filled with tears. 'But he'll come back for me, won't he? He'll send for me?'

'Like I said, at the moment we don't know where he's gone, or why, but we think he may be a very frightened man. Once we find him, we'll be able to discover who he's running from. But until we find him, we can't do anything to help him. You do understand that, don't you?'

Jenny nodded uncertainly, and began to scribble down names. Jenny wasn't sure if anything was missing, and shortly after that Geraldine and Sam left with two laptops, Jenny's phone, and a list of names and telephone numbers. As soon as they were back at the police station, a team was tasked with tracing addresses for everyone on Jenny's list and local constables were despatched to speak to all of them. The two laptops were taken to the IT officers to search for other possible locations where Andrew might be. While Geraldine and Sam had been visiting Jenny, Ariadne had gone to Andrew's office to question his colleagues, and an alert had been sent out to all train stations, bus networks and airports.

As Geraldine left the police station that evening, she was dismayed to encounter a group of reporters, jostling each other to thrust microphones at her. There was an air of frenzied excitement surrounding them as they shouted out their questions.

'Is there any news of the missing girl?'

'Was it Lucy Henderson's killer?'

'Do you have a suspect?'

'How many arrests have you made?'

'Do you expect more murders?'

Pushing her way past them, she hurried to her car. 'No comment,' she muttered, 'No comment.'

Clearly, the reporters were also speculating that there could be a connection between Lucy's death and Alison's disappearance.

45

OTHER THAN THEIR ADDRESSES being close to each other, nothing had been found to connect the missing girls, but the search continued. The team tasked with this aspect of the investigation were now looking for any links between the girls' parents, in case their families had known each other. Again, so far nothing had been discovered. Binita was also keen to explore the possibility of a possible link between Andrew and Jason. She became quite animated as she discussed her conjecture.

'But why?' Geraldine asked. 'I mean, I don't understand. Are you suggesting they worked together to abduct and kill young women?'

'We don't know Alison's been killed,' someone pointed out.

'Lucy could have been a blunder,' Binita said. 'We know that five young women have gone missing recently, all from the same area around Heslington Lane. That's a small area, too small for this to be a coincidence. Lucy's the only one whose body has been found. There are four others still unaccounted for.' She listed the names. 'They all disappeared in York over the past few months and no one has any idea what happened to them. It's as though they just vanished without trace. What if they are being held captive somewhere, and Lucy managed to burrow her way out?'

'Young women go missing all the time,' Naomi said. 'There isn't necessarily any connection between them. They might just have wanted to move somewhere else, run away from home, gone to find their fame and fortune on the streets of London, who knows?'

'That's just it,' Binita said. 'No one knows what happened to them. Granted girls often run away from home, but isn't it unusual for so many to have gone off, leaving no trace behind, and never contacting their families again? As far as we know, none of them had fallen out with their parents or friends, and no one else had any inkling they were going to leave.'

The other members of the team agreed that four girls disappearing within a few months was unlikely to be a coincidence, five if Lucy was a victim of the same attacker. Geraldine agreed to look into a potential connection between Jason and Andrew, other than them both knowing Lucy. She didn't believe they had been accomplices in kidnapping women. The theory struck her as far-fetched. But she was happy to have a reason to explore Andrew's contacts. Someone had to throw up a lead as to Andrew's location. She was feeling tired and so, unusually for her, she wasn't averse to sitting at her desk for a while, researching names and histories.

After a morning spent on her computer, she had failed to find any connection between the two men. Other than both living in York, and knowing Lucy, they did not appear to have met in the past. While Geraldine was researching Andrew and Jason, Ariadne had been looking into Lucy and Alison, along with the other three women who had recently been reported missing. All five women had lived within a few minutes' walk of each other, but Ariadne had found nothing else to link them to one another. They had not attended the same school or university, nor did they seem to have any interests in common, and there was no evidence to suggest they had joined the same gym or club.

'There's no obvious point of contact between them all,' Ariadne said, as she had lunch with Geraldine in the canteen. 'I can't find anything to suggest Alison ever met Lucy or the other three girls. Of course, she might have known her. They did live near one another.'

'Same with Jason and Andrew,' Geraldine said. 'Maybe we're looking in the wrong place. We know Lucy knew Jason and Andrew, but I can't see where Alison or the others fit in. And in any case, if Lucy is the common link between Jason and Andrew, how would that fit in with the idea that Jason and Andrew were working together to kidnap those other women?'

'Unless Lucy found out about it and they decided to silence her?' Ariadne suggested.

But they both agreed that sounded ridiculous. Apart from anything else, Jason had by all accounts been devoted to Lucy. Geraldine decided to focus on Alison, as she had been reported missing the most recently. In an attempt to persuade a witness to come forward, Geraldine made arrangements for an appeal to be broadcast the following day. With luck, at least one person would come forward to report a sighting of Alison over the past week, which might give the police a lead as to where she had gone.

'She can't have simply disappeared,' Geraldine muttered.

But three other young women had done just that in the past few months. Ian had been right in thinking that something odd was happening in York, and Geraldine was determined to discover what was behind it. While the search was continuing for Andrew, Geraldine wanted to find out more about Alison. After going missing only a week before, there was a chance that she might still be alive. Her disappearance had not yet been investigated as a serious crime since, in the absence of a body, there was no evidence any crime had been committed. But with every passing day, it was looking increasingly unlikely that Alison was going to reappear, unharmed.

Geraldine returned to Alison's lodgings, accompanied by a search team. The university term was over and one of Alison's flatmates, Nina, had gone home for the summer. Only curly-haired Megan was still there. Her expression changed from hopeful to worried when she saw the officers on her doorstep.

Geraldine explained that the police were looking into Alison's whereabouts, and following several leads. To assist them in their search, they were going to take the missing girl's laptop away. Megan nodded anxiously.

'I suppose that's okay,' she said. 'You're doing it to help her.'

When Geraldine asked for a hairbrush or a toothbrush that belonged to Alison, Megan let out a low cry of alarm and her face, already pale, turned almost white.

'Does that mean you've found her?' she stammered. 'Is she – is she dead?' Tears filled her eyes. 'It's been so horrible here without her. Nina's been all over the place, so stressed out and crying all the time. I've been doing my best to keep it all together because – well, I thought she might phone. She still might. Do you think she might? I thought one of us ought to stick around, in case, you know –' She paused to wipe her eyes. 'In case she comes back.'

'We don't yet know what happened to her,' Geraldine said gently. 'And you could be right. She might well turn up, safe and sound.' She frowned. 'Did she often stay out overnight? I'm wondering whether she might be staying with a friend?'

Megan shook her head vigorously, making her fair curls jiggle about, then scowled. 'You think she met some guy and went off with him, without saying a word. No, absolutely not. Alison's not like that. She wouldn't go out on the pull like that. In any case, if she did randomly happen to meet someone, she wouldn't just disappear for a week without at least telling us she was okay. Alison would never do that. She's too sensible, and really thoughtful. She'd know we'd be worried.'

'Have you ever seen her behave impulsively?'

'No. Alison's not like that. She's really steady.'

Gently, Geraldine reminded Megan that she was waiting for a brush of some kind. She said it was to help them track Alison's movements, although Megan clearly realised that wasn't the reason behind Geraldine's request. Taking the toothbrush and hairbrush, Geraldine carefully stowed each in its own evidence bag to minimise any further contamination.

'You will find her, won't you?' Megan blurted out tearfully, as Geraldine was leaving.

Geraldine barely hesitated before reassuring Megan that they would find her friend. She left, uneasily aware that there was no basis for her confident claim.

46

HAVING IDENTIFIED ALISON'S DNA, Geraldine sent specialist officers to scour Andrew's house to search for any evidence that the missing girl had ever been there. They had found nothing so far. His car, which they also wanted to examine, was missing. The registration number had been sent out across the country but, like its owner, the vehicle had not yet been located. The situation was frustrating. Like the missing girls, Andrew seemed to have vanished without trace. Jenny was adamant she had no idea where he was, and Geraldine believed her. If even his wife was unable to locate him, tracking him down was going to be difficult. The only connection the police had discovered between him and the missing girls was the fact that he had worked with Lucy and, significantly, his DNA had been discovered on her face. Not only that, but he had run off as soon as the police requested a sample of his DNA. That was not the action of an innocent man.

Binita was increasingly frustrated that they hadn't brought Andrew to the police station for questioning when they had the chance.

'We could have found some reason to keep him in custody while we were waiting for the results of the DNA test on Lucy,' she muttered. 'We let him slip through our fingers.'

The responsibility for failing to hold Andrew in custody lay with Binita. She was clearly angry with herself more than anyone else on the team, but that did nothing to improve her mood. She scowled as she insisted Andrew be found quickly.

Geraldine didn't need the detective chief inspector to tell her how important it was they find Andrew. No amount of talking was helping. All Andrew's known contacts had been questioned, but if anyone knew where he was, they weren't admitting it, and there had been no sightings of him anywhere.

While the search was continuing, Geraldine was preparing to run an appeal. Alison's mother and sister arrived at the police station mid-morning, as arranged, and Geraldine went to meet them. She had seen images of Alison, a pretty girl with long dark hair and black eyes that seemed to glow in the pictures. Geraldine could see an obvious resemblance between the missing girl and her mother and sister. Mrs Truman was dressed in a beige shirt that seemed to drain the colour from her gaunt face. She was too pallid and haggard to be attractive, but Geraldine could imagine she had been stunning when she was younger. Miranda, her daughter who accompanied her, was four years older than Alison. She was beautiful, with delicate features and the same lustrous eyes as Alison. She was wearing jeans and a grey T-shirt with a motto, 'Choose Kindness', emblazoned on the front in gold lettering. If the police only knew where Alison had last been seen, her sister would have been an ideal substitute in a reconstruction.

Sitting down with the two women, Geraldine explained how a televised appeal might prompt a witness to come forward.

'Have you been able to think of anywhere Alison might be?' she asked.

The two women both shook their heads and Geraldine proceeded to talk them through what to say.

'Can't you do this for us?' Mrs Truman asked. 'I just don't think I can.'

Carefully, Geraldine explained the benefit of family members giving a personal feel to an appeal. She didn't add that Alison's similarity to her sister might also be helpful in jogging someone's memory, if someone had chanced to spot Alison over the previous week. With a sigh, Alison's mother agreed. Miranda said nothing but looked uncomfortable.

'Miranda,' Geraldine addressed the girl. 'Do you have any idea where your sister might be?'

Flicking her long hair off her face, Miranda shook her head. 'If I knew, do you think I'd have kept my mother in the dark?' she replied, a little testily.

'If your sister has given you any information in confidence,' Geraldine said gently, 'you need to tell us. If you don't think you can share her location, at least tell us if you know she's safe.'

Miranda shook her head and mumbled that she didn't know anything.

Thinking it might be time to put pressure on Miranda to share anything she knew, Geraldine replied quietly. 'If you know where Alison is, keeping any information from us is not only irresponsible, it's a criminal offence. So, I'm going to ask you one more time, do you have any idea where Alison could be or who she might be with?'

This time, both women shook their heads.

'We appreciate you're only doing your job,' Miranda said. 'But we genuinely have no idea where Alison is. She wouldn't just go off without telling anyone. She'd know how much we would all worry.'

Mrs Truman sniffed and nodded. 'We just want to know she's safe,' she muttered. 'Where is she? You have to help us.'

Geraldine reiterated that the police were doing everything in their power to trace the missing girl and went over what Mrs Truman and Miranda were going to say in front of the television camera. They nodded to show they understood, and then Geraldine led them into the room where the film crew were setting up.

Mrs Truman's voice trembled as she spoke, after Geraldine's introduction. 'Please,' she said, 'we just want to know our daughter is safe. Please, if you know where she is, tell us. We can't live with this uncertainty any longer. It's tormenting us. Alison, if you can hear us, come home. And if anyone has taken her, please just let her go. We just want her to be safe.'

Time was running short so Geraldine thanked Mrs Truman and repeated the telephone number where the search team could be reached. 'Or you can contact any police station if you have any information at all that might help us find Alison. You can phone us anonymously with your information. But do call if you have seen this missing person.'

An image of Alison was displayed on the screen and Geraldine heard Mrs Truman gasp on seeing her missing daughter's face. With a sob, she broke down in tears. Geraldine noticed the camera focus on the crying woman for a second before the filming was concluded. The sight of the grief-stricken mother hardened Geraldine's resolve to track down whoever was responsible for the girl's disappearance. Whatever it took, she was determined to bring the perpetrator to justice. Turning to Alison's mother and sister, she thanked them.

'Will it help?' Mrs Truman asked. 'Do you think we'll ever see her again?' Her voice broke.

Geraldine sighed. There was no point in lying, and the truth was she had no idea. 'I hope so,' she replied. 'I really hope so.'

She escorted the two women from the room and issued a final reminder that they should contact her the moment they heard anything, or if they remembered any information that could possibly help the enquiry into Alison's disappearance.

'We're doing everything we can,' she repeated.

'What if it's not enough?' Mrs Truman replied, reflecting Geraldine's own fears back at her.

47

JASON WOKE WITH A jolt. One of his shoulders ached from where he had been lying on it in an uncomfortable position. He remembered he had been drinking the previous evening, and he must have fallen asleep on the floor of his living room. He was shivering, although that wasn't what had woken him up. For a few seconds he felt disoriented. When he reached out, his fingers encountered only empty air. Wearily, he blinked away his sleepiness. He had been dreaming that Lucy was teasing him, laughing and running away from him. He had tried to hold on to her, but she had slipped through his fingers like water. The scent of her hair seemed to infuse the room, and he could almost feel the elastic softness of her flesh with his fingertips. But he was awake, lying sprawled on the floor, and Lucy had gone forever. The memory of his dream made his eyes water. He pressed a clenched fist against his lips, as though silence could quell the grief that swamped his thoughts.

Heaving himself to his feet, he began doggedly pacing across the room, backwards and forwards, backwards and forwards, pushing himself to keep going, faster and faster. It was important to keep moving to prevent his joints from seizing up. He realised he was grunting as he made his way across the floor. With an effort, he forced himself to focus on counting his steps. He tried counting aloud, anything to push thoughts of Lucy out of his mind. It worked for a moment, and then memories came rushing back: Lucy's slender pale feet in pink summer sandals; her face grinning at him from the folds of a fluffy winter jacket; her intense concentration as she created a cocktail especially for him at Christmas. It was horribly sweet, although he had lied and told her it was lovely. Memory after memory played through his mind like some crazy video of their life together.

And all through the jumble of his recollections ran a thread of guilt. It had been his responsibility to take care of her. She was dead, and it was his fault for failing to protect her. They had argued about her seeing her ex, and shortly after that she had vanished. He was afraid his temper had driven her away. The bell rang, making him tremble with a sudden hope that Lucy had come home, but it was only his lawyer wanting him to write down everything he had done in the days leading up to Lucy's death, from when he had last spoken to her on Sunday to the exact time on Tuesday evening when she had been discovered, unconscious. His recollection of his movements was hazy at best. He recalled being preoccupied with searching for her, but he struggled to bring to mind exactly what he had done and where he had gone.

'What do you mean by that?' his lawyer demanded. 'It's a simple question requiring a straightforward answer. I'm sorry to be blunt, but you surely don't expect to convince anyone you're innocent if you keep bleating that you can't remember where you were or what you did when your girlfriend went missing. Now, shall we start again? And this time, you're going to tell me exactly what you were doing.'

Jason shrugged helplessly. 'It's the truth,' he told the lawyer. 'I was worried about Lucy and I wasn't thinking clearly.'

'What about now? Are you able to think clearly now?'

Jason nodded uncertainly.

'Good. Now cast your mind back and tell me where you were on the Monday and Tuesday.'

Jason looked uneasy. 'I was at work,' he replied. 'And then I drove around for a bit, looking for Lucy.'

'Did you know where she was?'

'Of course not,' Jason burst out. 'Why would I be looking for her if I knew where she was?'

'You need to focus. If this goes to court, you can expect far more searching questions. Now, is there anything you're not telling me?'

Jason shook his head and the lawyer sighed in exasperation. 'We don't have much of a case but there's no actual evidence to tie you to her disappearance and there are the other women who have gone missing. Let's go through what you were doing at the time each of them disappeared.'

Miserably, Jason told him that only Lucy would have been able to vouch for his movements in the evening. Whether they had gone out or stayed in, they had been together. When the lawyer had chided him for not helping himself, he declared that he no longer cared what happened to him. Without Lucy, his life was over.

The lawyer scowled. 'You'll feel very differently after a spell behind bars,' he said.

But Jason was already locked in a cell of despair. He had nothing to live for any more.

'Jason, you have to fight this,' the lawyer urged him, but there was no conviction in his voice. 'We have to come up with a defence that will convince a jury you're innocent.'

'You think I did it, don't you?' Jason asked, with a sickening realisation that even his own defence lawyer believed he was guilty.

'What I believe or don't believe is beside the point,' the lawyer responded wearily. 'What matters is that we come up with –'

'I know, you just told me,' Jason interrupted him. 'You want to come up with a defence that will stand up in court. But what's the point?'

'Do you want to make a confession?' the lawyer enquired, suddenly alert. 'There could be a case for this being a crime of passion. Were you angry with Lucy? Jealous? Did she do something that provoked you to violence?'

Jason shook his head. 'No, no, nothing like that. We were –'
His voice broke. 'We were happy together. We were so happy…
Lucy was – perfect… She was everything to me. I don't know
what I'm going to do now.'

'What do any of us do?' the lawyer asked irately. 'We just
keep going. What else is there to do?'

48

LEAVING YORK PROVED MORE difficult than he had anticipated. Avoiding main roads, he set off along Main Street to Field Lane, and turned off onto Osbaldwick Link Road with a vague idea of crossing the A64 and continuing along Moor Lane to take local roads out in the direction of Stockton. He wasn't quite sure where he would go from there. His one idea was to distance himself from York, where the police would soon be looking for him. Away from the city, he would be able to catch a train without anyone watching out for him. But it was imperative he escape from York without leaving any trace. It seemed like really bad luck when he had a burst tyre, although the incident was entirely his own fault and not really a question of bad luck at all. He couldn't believe he had misjudged the corner so badly. Admittedly, he was driving too fast, but that wasn't the reason he had lost control of the steering. The truth was that in his agitation he had been driving like a lunatic, with no clear idea of what he was doing. There was a loud clunk and a violent jolt as one tyre hit the kerb. He slammed his foot on the brake, shocked, and the car skidded to a halt. He sat for a moment, clutching the steering wheel and shaking, and realised he didn't have a clue what he was doing or where he was going. All he knew was that he had to get away.

For the first time, the enormity of what he had done began to sink in. He would never see his home again. He would never see Jenny again. He wasn't sure how he felt about that. But there was no going back on his decision. If he stayed in York, the police were bound to match his DNA to traces on the body. Once that happened, he would have no hope of avoiding a long prison sentence. At least if he could get far enough away, he had a chance of a future outside a prison cell. He might be able to send a message to Jenny, in time. But he couldn't stop to consider that now. He had to focus on his escape. Even before his tyre burst, he had known he couldn't hope to travel very far in his car. The police would be searching for it as soon as they discovered he had fled. His intention had been to drive right out of the city and hide the car as well as he could, off the road, somewhere remote. Now, it was almost out of the question to drive around scouting for a hiding place. In any case he couldn't go very fast, and it wouldn't be long before the police discovered he had run off, and started looking for his car. Ignoring the scraping and screeching of the wheel rim scraping on the ground, he drove on slowly, fighting to control his panic.

On another day he might have dawdled along, enjoying the sight of wide grass verges and green hedges, and admiring the well-tended gardens. But today, his slow speed had nothing to do with his surroundings as he jolted along with a burst tyre. At the back of his mind, he had a hazy recollection of seeing a garage somewhere along there. That could be just the opportunity he needed. He was looking out for it, but even so he might have driven straight past if he hadn't been crawling at such a slow pace. At the last minute, he noticed the sign and pulled in. Satisfied that no one had followed him, he checked his pockets quickly before leaving the car. Entering a grubby office, he shut the flimsy door behind him. A man in oily blue overalls nodded without looking up.

'I need my car fixed,' Andrew said.

'You made an appointment?' the man asked. 'It's lunchtime and there's no one here but me,' he added by way of explanation.

'No, no appointment,' Andrew replied, waving a fistful of notes. 'It's just a burst tyre. I'd like it fixed quickly.'

The mechanic eyed the money warily. 'You said it's a tyre?'

'The thing is,' Andrew blustered, 'it's not my car. It belongs to my wife, soon to be my ex-wife, to be exact. I don't want her getting her hands on it. It sounds petty, I know, but I just don't want her getting her hands on the car. I'd rather give it away.'

He wasn't sure he was making any sense, but the mechanic gave a sly grin, his eyes still fixed on the money Andrew was brandishing.

'You want me to keep the car out of sight, that it?'

Andrew nodded, relieved at the turn the conversation had taken. 'I'll pay you,' he said.

The mechanic glanced around thoughtfully. 'I can take the car,' he said at last, 'change the plates and–'

'Yes, yes, you can do that, and keep it or sell it, whatever. I don't care. I just want you to take it off my hands and make it disappear.'

Understanding that Andrew was desperate, the mechanic hesitated.

'If it's a problem, I can take it somewhere else –' Andrew fibbed. He had no idea where else he could go. 'Tell you what, just fix the tyre.' He shoved the money back in his pocket.

The mechanic frowned, seeming to make up his mind, and they agreed. Andrew accepted that he was paying the man two hundred pounds to take a car which was worth a few thousand. Under any other circumstances he would have scoffed at the idea. But he had no choice.

'You will change the number plates, won't you?' he asked, with a sudden stab of doubt, although by the time the police found the car, he would hopefully be long gone.

'Look, I get it,' the mechanic said. 'You think I want to be caught with a stolen car?'

On the point of protesting that the car was legally his, Andrew stopped short. If the mechanic believed there was an urgent need to change the number plates, so much the better.

'I'll get on to it straightaway,' the man said, thrusting his hand out for the cash.

'Drop me somewhere first,' Andrew said, as the finality of what he was doing hit home.

'Where?'

Andrew hesitated. 'I need to get to a station,' he replied.

'York?'

'No, no, not York.' Andrew thought quickly. 'Wait.' He checked his phone.

From Malton station he could pick up the TransPennine line which would take him across country. No one would be looking for him in Manchester. He could slip away from such a busy station and travel south to lose himself in London, where he could catch a train to Heathrow. Or he might make his way to the south coast and board a ferry before the port authorities had been alerted. He might even be able to leave the country from Manchester Airport. But whatever route he took, he had to hurry.

'I need you to drop me at Malton station.'

The mechanic raised his eyebrows. 'That's half an hour away,' he protested. 'What's wrong with York station?'

For answer, Andrew felt in his pocket and drew out another two hundred pounds. 'This is for your trouble,' he said.

He decided to wait until they reached Malton before revealing that the mechanic had become an accomplice to a wanted criminal. If he told anyone where he had taken Andrew, the police would arrest him as an accessory to a crime far more serious than merely changing the number plates on a stolen car. That ought to convince the man to hold his tongue.

49

RONNIE DROVE FAST. HIS exhilaration at this unexpected windfall was tempered by apprehension, and he wondered if he had done the right thing in agreeing to give his dodgy customer a lift.

'You got an urgent appointment?' he asked, cautiously fishing for an explanation.

'Shut up and drive,' the man snapped.

It was one thing for a bloke to be asking for a hot car to disappear, but another matter entirely for him to be fleeing York, which seemed to be what he was doing. Ronnie supposed the police were after his passenger, but he didn't dare ask. The less he knew the better. He told himself he was giving a customer a lift, that was all. Nothing wrong with that. Quite the opposite in fact. He was doing a good deed. But his passenger wasn't officially a customer at all. Ronnie couldn't claim he was, because there was no paperwork, no car booked in and no payment through the books. His hands felt sweaty on the steering wheel and he gripped it more tightly. The sooner he returned to the garage and changed those plates the better. If one of the other mechanics came back and spotted the car, and started asking questions, there could be trouble.

He put his foot down. At his side his passenger stirred but didn't protest as their speed increased. Ronnie relaxed the pressure on the accelerator. It wouldn't do to be stopped by the police for speeding. The half-hour journey seemed to take days but at last they reached the village of Malton without incident and drew up in the station forecourt. The passenger turned to him with a menacing scowl.

'If you breathe a word of this to anyone, you'll be in deep shit. Once the police hear about it, you'll be arrested for helping a wanted man to escape,' he hissed. 'They'll treat you as an accessory to murder.'

'Murder?' Ronnie stammered. 'You never said anything about murder.' Terrified the man was about to attack him, he tensed, reaching for the handle to throw his door open. 'Don't worry,' he stammered, holding the man's gaze so he wouldn't notice when Ronnie gripped the door handle. 'I won't say a word.'

'Not to anyone,' the man insisted.

'Not a word to anyone,' Ronnie agreed. 'Trust me. I don't want any trouble with the law.'

The man smiled, and Ronnie relaxed a little and held out his hand for the money. The man grunted, and thrust a wad of cash at him. There was no time to count it as the man flung his door open.

'Remember,' he said, looking back over his shoulder as he climbed out of the car, 'not a word or you'll end up behind bars.'

Ronnie laughed nervously. 'Don't worry,' he repeated. 'You can trust me.'

'If I go down, you go down.' With that final parting shot, the man ran off.

Ronnie didn't wait to see him enter the station. With a screech of tyres he spun the wheel and drove off. As he drove, he thought about what had just happened, and the potential consequences. The money would come in handy, that was for sure. Pulling into the side of the road, he glanced in his mirror. There was no one coming up behind him and the road ahead was clear. His fingers shook as he took out the money and counted it: two hundred pounds. He checked it and swore. He had been promised four hundred, two hundred for taking the car and another two hundred for driving the bloke to Malton. He swore again. He could hardly turn round and drive back to Malton and demand the missing cash. The bloke was probably on a train by now, and good riddance. It would serve him right if Ronnie told the police what had happened.

On balance, he decided to keep out of it. He would change the registration number, sell the car on, and say nothing about it, not even to his girlfriend. She would only nag him to tell the police and she'd probably want him to hand over the money as well, in which case he would have suffered all this aggravation for nothing. Having reached a decision, he drove off. By the time he reached the garage, a fellow mechanic was already at work.

'Just been taking this for a bit of a run,' he called out.

His colleague grunted without looking up.

It was going to be impossible to change the plates without anyone noticing so Ronnie would have to work on other jobs, leaving the stolen car out of sight in a corner of the forecourt until he had time to deal with it. He had a set of number plates ready, and decided to go in early the next morning to change them over when no one else was about.

'You seen this?' his governor demanded as Ronnie went into the office to fetch the details of his next job.

'What's that?' the other mechanic asked, following Ronnie in.

'It's an urgent addition to the list of stolen vehicles. The cops are looking for this one in particular, so keep your eyes peeled.'

'Was it a getaway vehicle in a bank robbery?' the other mechanic asked. 'Could be a wad of cash in the boot.' He winked and laughed.

'It's more than just any old stolen car, it's been involved in something serious for the cops to send out a special notice like this,' the manager said.

Ronnie glanced at the screen and froze.

'Blimey, they don't hang around,' he blurted out before he could stop himself.

'What's that supposed to mean? Ronnie?'

Without answering, Ronnie dashed out of the office to check the registration number of the car that had arrived earlier. He took a quick shot of it on his phone and ran back to the office to show it to his manager.

'Where the fuck did you get that?' the manager asked, sounding shocked. 'It looks like –'

'Yes,' Ronnie replied breathlessly. He could feel the blood pounding in his ears. 'It's here. On the forecourt. Some geezer brought it in earlier with a bust tyre.'

'Jesus,' the manager gasped.

'Best tell the cops,' Ronnie said.

He was relieved to pass that responsibility on. There was nothing else he could do. One of his colleagues at the garage might notice the car, or it would be spotted on the CCTV. If it ever came out that Ronnie had known it was there and had kept quiet, he would be in trouble, and for what? To protect some tight arsehole who had cheated him of two hundred quid he had been promised. He hadn't even touched the car, but its arrival would have been registered on the security cameras. It wouldn't be hard to establish that Ronnie had been there alone at that time.

There was no reason why he should hand over the two hundred quid. All he had to do was tell the police he had dropped the man at Malton station, thinking nothing of it at the time. How was he supposed to know the car had been nicked, and the police were looking for the driver? The man had told him the car belonged to his wife and he had brought it in with a burst tyre. That was all Ronnie needed to say. If the police were suspicious of him for giving the driver a lift to Malton, that was too bad. They couldn't arrest him for doing a customer a good turn.

50

As soon as a call came through to the police station that Andrew's car had been seen at a car repair shop less than three miles from the police station, Geraldine set out to question the manager who had phoned. Within minutes she was driving onto a tarmacked forecourt where half a dozen cars were tightly packed together. A few had magnetic weights on their roofs, displaying a job number. Leaving her car near the entrance, she scanned the vehicles and soon found what she was looking for: a gleaming silver BMW. Walking closer, she saw that one tyre was completely flat. Having taken a photo on her phone, she summoned a vehicle recovery team to remove the car to a police compound for a thorough forensic examination. Only then did she walk over to the shoddily-built hut that served as an office. The workshops were more substantially constructed, and she could see a couple of cars up on ramps inside them. Two mechanics in oily overalls were working on the vehicles. They barely glanced in Geraldine's direction as she watched them for a second before walking over to the office. The door quivered on being opened, and when she shut it behind her, the walls trembled.

'We received a call about a car we've been looking for,' she announced by way of introduction, brandishing her identity card as she spoke.

'Yes, that was me,' the man behind the desk replied. 'I called you.'

He launched into an animated account of his feelings on realising the wanted car was standing outside on the forecourt.

'Tell me how it came to be here,' Geraldine said.

Somewhat pompously, the manager told her how he had come back from lunch to find the car parked on the forecourt. He had recognised it from the description, and a quick check of the registration number had confirmed his suspicions. That was when he had called the police.

'Soon as I knew, I picked up the phone,' he assured her, with an ingratiating smile.

'Did you speak to whoever left it here?'

The man shook his head, mumbling apologetically that he had popped home for lunch when the car was brought in.

'Was any of your staff here when the BMW was brought in?'

'Only Ronnie.'

Geraldine asked to speak to Ronnie but was told he was working.

'You can speak to me,' the manager insisted. 'You won't get much sense out of Ronnie. To be honest, he's not the sharpest tool in the toolbox. Top notch under the bonnet,' he added quickly, 'but not much good for anything else.'

Geraldine thanked him and repeated her request. With a grunt, the manager strode away to find Ronnie. He returned a moment later, with a mechanic in tow. Ronnie was short and wiry, with anxious eyes that darted everywhere but Geraldine's face. Fiddling with a greasy rag he was clutching, he cleared his throat nervously and stared down at his feet. Gazing at his untidy black hair, Geraldine wondered whether he was hiding something as she questioned him. In contrast to his manager, she had to winkle every detail out of the mechanic who was laconic in his responses.

'And that was all?' she asked. 'He just wanted you to change the tyre?'

He nodded.

'Very well. I'd like to see the paperwork,' she said, suspecting there was no mention of the stolen vehicle in the schedule of repairs.

Ronnie shrugged, muttering that it was only a burst tyre.

'But he left the car here.'

Ronnie nodded without looking up.

'Where did he go when he left?'

Ronnie mumbled that he had given the customer a lift.

'Where to?' Geraldine enquired sharply.

She was impatient to find out what had happened, but suspected Ronnie might clam up altogether if she was too aggressive in her questioning. He hadn't been accused of any wrongdoing, so far, and she suspected she would make faster progress if she treated him gently.

'Malton. The station.'

'That's about half an hour's drive from here.'

He nodded and shuffled his feet.

'What time was that?'

Ronnie shrugged, but one of the constables answered for him.

'The CCTV shows them leaving at one fifty-five.'

Geraldine hesitated, aware that Ronnie could have lied about Andrew's destination, but he appeared to have been truthful. Although she was curious to find out how much Ronnie knew, she couldn't afford to spend any more time questioning him while Andrew was still at large. Advising Ronnie that she would need to speak to him again, she hurried away and called Ariadne. A search was set up to track Ronnie's journey after he left the vehicle repair shop. In the meantime, they could only hope to reach Malton station before Andrew boarded a train.

'Alert the nearest patrol car,' Geraldine said. 'I'll go straight to Malton from here and meet the team at Malton station. There's a chance we might intercept him, although he's probably long gone. But we should be able to find out what train he boarded and pick him up when he alights. I wonder where he's headed? Probably Manchester. He'll want to lose himself in a crowd,' she continued, speculating as she ran to her car.

'He doesn't know we're on to him,' Ariadne pointed out before Geraldine rang off.

Geraldine drove fast, but it still took her over half an hour to reach Malton. It was a quiet little town, and she passed few people as she drove through the streets to the station. Two patrol cars had already arrived and a constable in uniform scurried to meet her. After brief introductions, they confirmed that there was no sign of Andrew. The only passenger waiting for a train was a middle-aged man who hadn't seen anyone else at the station. There were no railway staff in evidence, as the station was only manned part-time, and a message had been sent for someone to come and make the CCTV footage available as soon as possible. They waited impatiently and, ten minutes later, a disgruntled looking official arrived. His expression altered when he saw the two police cars parked on the station forecourt, and four uniformed officers waiting for him. The security film showed Ronnie's car drawing up at two twenty-five and they watched a blurry image of Andrew hurrying into the station. He had purchased a ticket which the machine registered as being for Manchester Victoria. The patrol car had missed him by a few minutes.

'He's going to the airport,' Geraldine said. She turned to the railway official. 'Where does the train stop?'

'Well, it's a fast train to York,' he replied.

Geraldine called Ariadne and brought her up to speed. 'He's on the train, heading for Manchester Victoria, and presumably to the airport. He should be arriving in York in less than ten minutes. Make sure he doesn't get away.'

Geraldine wanted to be there when Andrew was apprehended, but she didn't have time to reach York station before the train arrived. All the same, she drove there as fast as she safely could, in convoy with the two patrol cars, hoping to arrive before Andrew left the train station in police custody. If she missed that, she would see him at the police station.

'Have a full team ready,' she told Ariadne over the phone as she drove with her escort. 'We don't want him to leave York.'

A large crowd had gathered outside the station. Geraldine hurried in to find all the platforms empty of passengers. One train was standing idle on the tracks. A line of officers in uniform were guarding the barriers, and several railway officials were standing around looking worried. Binita was talking animatedly to a group of plainclothes officers, none of whom Geraldine recognised. Spotting Naomi in the group, she hurried over to speak to her.

'Where is he?' she demanded.

Naomi shook her head. 'We can't get at him, not yet. We're waiting for a negotiator.'

'Why? What's happened? He's not armed is he?' Geraldine asked, looking around. There was no sign of an armed response unit but they could be on their way.

'It's not that,' Naomi replied, her voice taut with anxiety. 'He's taken a hostage.'

51

ON WEDNESDAY AFTERNOON, SHARON called round with the baby, as she often did on her way home from her weekly visit to a toddler group in a local church hall.

'It's never too early to get Noah used to other children,' she said.

'And all the germs they carry,' George had added soberly.

But Linda had agreed with her daughter-in-law and George knew better than to challenge his wife on medical matters.

'I'm sure Linda knows what she's talking about,' he had said, eliciting a scowl from Sharon. 'That's not to say that Sharon isn't equally knowledgeable about anything concerning the baby,' he added quickly.

So, every Wednesday, Sharon took Noah to the toddler group which he didn't seem to mind, and she enjoyed.

'It's nice to have a chance to sit and chat with other mums,' she said on this particular afternoon when George and she were sitting in the garden watching Noah.

'Linda will be back any minute,' George had told her when she arrived. 'She was hoping you'd be round and just popped out to get some biscuits.'

Noah was lying on his mat in the shade, gurgling and reaching out to pull at the grass. Sharon kept darting forward to remove blades of it from his chubby grasp before he could stuff it in his mouth.

'Everything goes in his mouth at the moment,' she said, laughing.

'Actually,' George began diffidently and paused. 'I've been wanting to speak to you about something.'

Sharon sat back on her heels and looked up at him, waiting.

'I've been doing some research,' he said, and stopped, fiddling awkwardly with his belt. 'Yes, I've been looking into something.'

'What?' Sharon prompted him after another pause. 'What have you been looking into?' she asked with an air of resignation.

Clearly, she was fed up with other people telling her how to take care of Noah, but she didn't want to appear rude to her father-in-law. She looked hopefully towards the house but Linda had not yet appeared.

'It's about dogs,' George admitted. 'And getting them.'

'Dogs?' Sharon repeated, looking puzzled. 'What about dogs? You're not thinking of getting a dog, are you? I wouldn't have thought it was something Linda would want.'

'Oh no,' George said. 'Not me. You.'

Sharon shook her head, looking, if anything, even more puzzled. Idly, she reached down and scraped a few blades of grass off Noah's chubby upturned palm.

'What do you mean?' she asked.

George hesitated, uncertain how to express himself. 'I heard,' he said at last, 'I heard that you're going to get a dog and well, I'm not sure that's a good idea, with Noah being the age he is and grabbing hold of everything he can get his hands on.' He gazed anxiously at Sharon who barely seemed to be listening to him. 'He might pull the dog's fur and provoke it. Don't you think a dog might be a bit risky with a little child? At his age?'

'Oh yes, I quite agree. I don't understand why so many people want to get puppies when they've just had a baby. It seems quite extraordinary to me. But then it takes all sorts, I suppose, and there are plenty of people who absolutely adore their pets.'

George felt as though a weight had lifted from his shoulders, but he remained bemused and wasn't quite sure whether to believe what he was hearing.

'So, you're not planning on getting a dog?' he asked, just to be clear.

'No way. One baby is quite enough for me for the moment. Two, if you count Robert.' She laughed.

Reassured, George leaned back in his chair contentedly and watched the young mother tending to her baby, while a sense of wellbeing suffused his thoughts. But there remained the mystery of Linda's claim that Robert and Sharon had told her they were set on getting a dog.

'What about Robert?' he enquired, with a resurgence of his former apprehension. 'Does he want to get a dog?'

'Good lord, no. Why would he when he's out at work all day? I'd be the one having to take care of it and I've got my hands full with this little mischief.'

She leaned forward to tickle the baby who gurgled appreciatively and waved his fat little arms in the air. Just then they heard Linda calling from the house. After tea, Sharon announced she had to get Noah home for his afternoon nap.

'You can put him down here,' Linda suggested.

Sharon thanked her but said she had chores to do at home while Noah was asleep and, soon after that, she took her leave. As soon as she had gone, George turned to Linda, determined to confront her straightaway.

'You told me Robert and Sharon were getting a dog,' he burst out.

'Did I?' Linda replied, scarcely reacting to his accusation. 'I don't remember but, if you say I did then I'm sure I did.' She smiled. 'What did Sharon have to say?'

'Nothing. She wasn't saying anything. That is, she told me there was no question of them getting a dog, at least not while Noah's so young.' He stared closely at Linda. 'So, what I want to know is, why did you tell me they are getting a dog when it's not true.'

Linda shook her head, smiling. 'I must have misunderstood something Robert said,' she replied mildly.

'What?' George demanded. 'What exactly did he say to you?'

Linda shook her head, looking faintly bemused. 'Well, I can't remember. I really can't be expected to recall everything he says to me, can I? Now, would you like another cup or shall I clear away?'

George watched his wife thoughtfully as she carried the tea tray into the house. He had a feeling she was keeping something from him, but he was damned if he knew what it was. Dismissing his suspicions as paranoia, he gazed complacently around the garden, noticing how the fruit trees were thriving despite the dry weather. More buds had appeared on the rose bushes since he had pruned them; they could look forward to another display before the summer was over.

52

IT HAD PROBABLY BEEN a mistake to mention the murder charge at all to the car mechanic, but he couldn't turn the clock back. His intention had been sensible enough: to scare the man into silence. The risk was that the seriousness of the charge might send him running to the police. There was no way of knowing whether he would keep his mouth shut. Andrew could only hope that the money he had handed over would be sufficient to buy the man's silence. When it came down to it, no one could be trusted. He couldn't even rely on his own wife.

All that mattered now was that he reach the airport before the police caught up with him. After a seemingly endless wait at Malton station, he had finally caught a train and should be arriving in York any minute now. Changing trains was going to be dangerous, but at least he could do so without leaving the station. They wouldn't be looking for him on a train arriving in York. All he needed to do was keep his head down. He was pleased he had thought to bring his sunglasses. On reaching Manchester, he had resolved to catch the first plane out of the country. He didn't care where it went, as long as he got away. He would have to be careful not to arouse suspicion by seeming too eager to board the first plane available, but once he was at the airport, he would keep his wits about him and find an escape route. It made sense to board an international flight as soon as he could, rather than making his way to London, and leaving the country from there. He had come this far, but the police would be on his tail by now, and he needed to be in the air before they realised where he had gone.

Despite his anxiety, he smiled to himself. With a combination of intelligence and nerve, he had outwitted them all.

As the train slowed down on its approach into York station, he lowered his head to avoid being spotted from the platform, even though he was seated at the very end of the front of the carriage, with only part of a window beside his seat. As far as the police knew, he had never left York, and they might be looking out for him in case he tried to board a train. Having escaped detection thus far, he wasn't going to throw himself to the wolves by being careless now. Until he was safely out of the country, he would remain constantly on his guard. He was only sitting on a train, but the stress was exhausting and he leaned back and closed his eyes for a moment. Time seemed to drag as he waited for the aisle to clear so he could leave the train quickly. Opening his eyes, he glanced through the window and froze. For a few seconds he couldn't breathe.

A line of uniformed police officers stood on the platform, which was otherwise empty. He felt a cold shiver, because he couldn't see anyone boarding the train which remained stationary. As he watched, he saw passengers stepping off the train from the carriage behind his. He was in the front carriage and it seemed the police had been working their way along the train, evacuating it. Before he could decide what to do, the connecting door opened at the far end of his carriage, and a familiar woman stepped through. Two uniformed policemen followed close behind her. Swiftly, they ushered other passengers out through the far door, until he was alone in the carriage with three police officers.

They had not yet spotted him, but were moving inexorably closer, checking seats on both sides. He had to seize the initiative before they reached him. Flicking open his knife, he leapt to his feet and dashed forward. Swiftly, before the detective could react, he grasped both of her wrists in one of his fists, at the same time pressing his blade against her throat.

'Get back!' he roared to her uniformed colleagues who stood, poised to run towards him. 'Get back or she'll never get off this train alive!'

The two officers scrambled backwards and he watched them vanish through the open door. He was alone in the carriage with his hostage. Breathing deeply, he tried to marshal his thoughts. Beads of sweat began dripping down his forehead. He blinked furiously, unable to release his grip on the woman's wrists or the handle of his knife. Carefully, he lowered his head and wiped his face on his sleeve, inadvertently jogging the blade. His captive let out a low cry of pain.

'Shut up,' he hissed at her.

'You won't get away with this,' she murmured, her eyes wide with fear, yet watchful. 'I know you're frightened, but you need to think what you're doing –'

'I told you to shut up,' he repeated, his voice rising in agitation. 'Shut up and let me think.'

She was wrong, because he *was* going to get away with it, and he knew how. Far from scuppering his plans, her arrival had been a stroke of luck, because he was no longer a helpless fugitive. She had provided him with a valuable bargaining chip that would enable him to negotiate his way out of this trap. As long as she was alive, he had the upper hand, but he had to remain on his guard. She was a trained detective and he couldn't risk letting her wriggle free. He pressed the flat of the blade against her throat. One twist of his wrist, and it would be over. He smiled, knowing the police had to comply with his demands if they wanted their colleague to survive.

53

GERALDINE MADE HER WAY over to Binita, who was standing on the platform surrounded by solemn officers. No one was speaking and everyone looked tense. Geraldine manoeuvred her way through the group until she was standing right in front of Binita, who greeted her with an enquiring frown.

'I want to speak to Andrew,' Geraldine said, without pausing for any preliminaries.

'We'd all like to get our hands on him,' one of the officers remarked grimly.

'You don't understand,' Geraldine said. 'I need to get in there right away. I know Andrew, and I'm sure I can persuade him to trust me.'

'We're waiting for the negotiator,' Binita replied curtly. 'This is no time to start trying to run the show with our own initiatives. We need to follow strict protocol without allowing our emotions to sway our decisions. We can't rush this. Listen, Geraldine,' she added more gently, 'Ariadne's a valued colleague, and that makes it even more important –'

'No,' Geraldine blurted out, shocked to learn the hostage was her friend. 'We need to act now. The longer this goes on, the more desperate he's going to become. I have to go in there and speak to him before he gets even more wound up.'

Without waiting for a response, Geraldine turned and dashed towards the train. Ignoring the shouts of protest behind her, ordering her to stop, she climbed aboard and made her way cautiously along the train, towards the carriage where Andrew was holding Ariadne hostage.

The first thing Geraldine noticed on reaching them was her colleague's eyes, stretched wide in terror. The second thing she noticed was that Andrew's face was sweaty, and he was trembling. He had grasped both of Ariadne's wrists in one of his fists, and was holding them behind her back. She would no doubt have struggled free from his grip, had his other hand not been pressing a knife against her throat.

'Get away from here!' Andrew shouted, as Geraldine entered the carriage. 'Don't come any closer or she gets it.'

He jogged the knife and a thin dribble of blood trickled down Ariadne's neck. It wasn't clear whether that was a deliberate act of aggression or an accidental consequence of his shaking. Controlling her panic, Geraldine ignored the warning and took a step closer, speaking very softly.

'Andrew, you must realise you're not helping yourself, behaving like this. I can see why you might be in a tizz and try to run off, but it was a spur of the moment decision, wasn't it? You thought everyone suspected you of doing something wrong.' She forced herself to speak very slowly and clearly, in as calm a voice as she could muster. 'We know it wasn't you who hurt Lucy. You had nothing to do with the attack on her. We've confirmed that now, because we've arrested the man who attacked her. There's no need for you to be afraid any longer. You can leave here and go home without any fuss. That's what you want, isn't it? To go home and forget any of this ever happened?'

Ariadne let out a faint squeal.

'We've worked out what happened,' Geraldine pressed on. 'It's obvious you were trying to help Lucy when you found her on the street. That's right, isn't it? You wanted to help her.'

Andrew nodded. 'Wanted to help her,' he mumbled. 'Yes. I wanted to help her.'

'So, you must see there's no need for any of this.' Geraldine gestured at the train carriage. 'You don't have to run any more. Come with me, and we can sort this out quietly. No one else even needs to know you tried to run away.' She held out her hands in an expansive gesture. 'I'm not even going to put you in handcuffs. As far as anyone watching will know, you're just leaving the train to go home. We're still in York,' she added. 'I'll let you get off the train first, so no one will know you've been speaking to me. This can remain between us. No one else need know about it. I'll call and tell all those officials out there to disperse and let you go home. I'll explain this was all a misunderstanding. The reality is, they were only sent here to find you, so we could tell you that we've arrested the man who killed Lucy and there's no need for you to run.'

With a sigh that shook his whole body, Andrew let go of Ariadne who collapsed on a seat, shaking. Taking no notice of her, Geraldine made a show of talking into her phone, issuing instructions to no one, before ushering Andrew towards the open door of the carriage, ready to subdue him if he realised her real intention. As soon as he clambered off the train, two burly constables pounced on him and handcuffed him. As he attempted in vain to resist his captors, Geraldine was momentarily dazzled by flashing cameras. In the distance, there was a muffled cheer from a throng of reporters who had gathered beyond the barriers, along with members of the public who were eager to capture the arrest on their phones.

'You told me no one else knew about this,' Andrew cried out in dismay. 'You said I could go home – you said –'

Geraldine moved to stand right behind him and spoke very softly. 'I would have said day was night to save my colleague's life. You can argue your case in front of a jury.' She went on in a louder voice. 'Come along, sir, there's no point in resisting arrest.'

'You lied to me,' Andrew screeched. 'You tricked me.'

'Take him away,' Geraldine told a burly constable. 'We'll interview him when he has a lawyer. Mind how you go,' she added to Andrew.

Turning, she watched Ariadne supported off the train by two constables. The scratch on her neck would need medical attention, but she appeared otherwise unharmed, if shaken.

'Ariadne's going to be fine,' Naomi said, coming to stand beside Geraldine and following the direction of her gaze. 'But what about you? Are *you* all right? You look like a ghost.'

Geraldine nodded. Only then did she realise that she too was shaking uncontrollably.

'I'm fine,' she fibbed. 'I just need to avoid the DCI for a while,' she added, smiling weakly.

'What are you talking about? She'll be recommending you for a commendation after what you did today.' Naomi beamed at her.

'More likely reprimanding me for insubordination,' Geraldine replied. 'I disobeyed orders and flouted protocol.' She sighed.

'Forget about the DCI,' Naomi said firmly. 'Sometimes you have to do what needs to be done. Binita will get over it. Now, can we focus on what actually matters? Because it seems to me that you very probably just saved Ariadne's life.'

Geraldine turned and hurried away before Naomi saw she was almost in tears. She had come so close to losing Ariadne, a colleague, and her closest friend. She drove to an empty street. Pulling into the kerb, she dropped her head in her hands and wept. She was still sobbing when her phone rang, a few moments later.

'Geraldine, where are you?' It was Ian. 'It's all right. Naomi told me what happened. I've spoken to Binita and you're not in any trouble. Well,' he added, 'not much, anyway. Andrew's cooling off in a cell for the night, and he's going to be interviewed tomorrow. She's considering giving that pleasure to you and Ariadne, if she feels up to it. There's no immediate rush, and Binita thought we might all need time to gather our thoughts.'

'How is Ariadne?'

'She's fine, thanks to you. Just a bit shaken, which is understandable. Now, what time are you coming home? Only I'm thinking of getting a couple of steaks ready.'

With those words, the horror of the last few hours seemed to vanish, and Geraldine remembered she had missed lunch.

'I'm on my way,' she said. 'I'm starving.'

54

ANDREW STARED AT GERALDINE, his expression filled with rancour.

'I've no idea what I'm doing here,' he burst out. 'And I don't appreciate being locked up all night like a common criminal.'

His lawyer frowned at him, and cleared his throat in warning. Clearly, he had advised his client to keep quiet.

'My client is satisfied he has done nothing to warrant being kept in custody,' the lawyer said smoothly, his smile sliding from Geraldine to Ariadne. 'His alleged acts of aggression were carried out in self-defence.'

While Ariadne stared at him indignantly, Geraldine had to suppress a bubble of laughter that threatened her composure. Recovering quickly, she read out a series of charges which included assault, and taking a police officer hostage.

'Let's deal with the last charge first, shall we?' she enquired pleasantly, once she had finished reading out the list. 'That seems to be the most straightforward one, and there can be no disagreement over what happened.' She glanced at Ariadne, who was sitting beside her, poker-faced.

'My client was acting in self-defence,' the lawyer repeated with dogged determination. 'He was under the impression that the police officer who accosted him on the train was a member of the public who intended to assault him. He had done nothing to provoke such an attack. Assuming she was on drugs, he panicked. She wasn't in uniform,' he added firmly. 'How was he supposed to know she was a police officer?'

'Because I was holding up my identity card and was accompanied by two uniformed constables,' Ariadne replied.

Andrew scoffed but said nothing.

'Ah, you say that now,' the lawyer replied smoothly. 'At the time of your assault on him, my client states that you did no such thing. He acted in good faith in a case of what was clearly mistaken identity. He believed he was resisting the advances of a maniac. Had that indeed been the case, everyone would now be congratulating him for his bravery. He believed he was protecting a trainload of passengers from a potentially dangerous lunatic.' He turned to Geraldine. 'She could have been armed, for all he knew.'

Ignoring the lawyer, Geraldine turned to Andrew. 'You were trying to leave York,' she said. Andrew grunted and refused to meet her eye. 'You fled to avoid giving a sample of your DNA. You bought a ticket for Manchester from Malton station. If you'd made it to the airport without being apprehended, who knows how far you might have gone?' She paused but he didn't respond. 'How far were you planning to travel?'

The lawyer took up the implied accusation. 'You seem to be suggesting that my client wanted to leave the country.' He smiled coldly. 'Really, Inspector, that's a ridiculous idea. My client is a happily married man, with a house and a successful career, here in York. What on earth do you suppose might possess him to suddenly take it into his head to leave the country without telling anyone, including his wife? Since you don't have a shred of evidence to support your far-fetched theory, I insist we end this interview now. You can hardly charge my client with seeking to flee the country just because he booked a seat on a train to Manchester!' He laughed and Andrew grinned.

'He doesn't need his passport to go to Manchester,' Ariadne pointed out. 'He was travelling with his passport and several thousand pounds – in cash.'

'It's no crime to catch a train, which is all my client has done, any more than it would be a crime to go abroad, had that been his intention. But my client has stated that he had no such purpose in travelling to Manchester.'

'We found your client's DNA on a woman who was the victim of a fatal assault,' Geraldine said quietly. 'It was no coincidence that Andrew abandoned his car and attempted to leave York – and yes, possibly the country – as soon as we requested a sample of his DNA. The threat of a murder charge hanging over him might certainly have prompted him to try and leave the country.'

Andrew stirred uncomfortably in his seat. 'But you didn't get my DNA, so you have no proof I went anywhere near Lucy,' he retorted. He turned to his lawyer. 'They can't force me to give them a sample, can they? There must be something you can do to stop them.'

His face twisted with apprehension, and he was sweating. He knew the answer to his question, but was evidently too alarmed to think clearly.

The lawyer sighed. 'I need to take a moment with my client.'

'There's no need for us to request a sample,' Geraldine told him. 'We found more than enough in your house to establish that you had contact with Lucy, shortly before her death.'

'You can't prove that was mine,' Andrew blurted out, but his voice was flat with despair and there was a bleakness about him that Geraldine hadn't seen before.

'Your lawyer has requested a short break,' she said, stating the time before switching off the tape. 'We're in no hurry. Take all the time you want.'

She and Ariadne left the room together and went for a coffee.

'Are you sure you're feeling all right?' Geraldine asked, as they sat down.

Ariadne was still looking pale, but otherwise seemed fine. Apart from a small plaster on her neck, she might never have been taken hostage at all.

'I actually slept pretty well last night,' Ariadne admitted. 'Thanks to you, it was all over so quickly, it passed in a blur.

I'm not even sure I can remember exactly what happened any more. Don't worry, I gave a full statement once I'd been taken off the train. But now, after a night's sleep, it no longer feels real. It's hard to believe any of it actually happened.' She paused. 'He could easily have killed me, you know.' She paused again, before mumbling that she had felt helpless. 'I should have been able to handle the situation, but I was absolutely useless. Fear can do that to a person, you know. Even after all our training, I went to pieces.' She paused again. 'You won't tell anyone, will you?'

'What? That you were frightened out of your wits when a suspected murderer held a knife to your throat?' Geraldine smiled. 'You wouldn't be human if you weren't terrified under those circumstances. However well trained we are, they can't take our humanity away from us. We wouldn't be much use to anyone if we lost all feeling. Society might as well be policed by robots.'

Ariadne nodded. 'I can see that coming before too long.'

'I hope not. We may be flawed and yes, terrified when our lives are in danger, but surely it's our humanity that enables us to serve justice with the right balance of compassion and ruthlessness.'

Ariadne laughed. 'You ought to be working in PR. You sound like a spin doctor.'

'Talking of doctors, how's your neck?' Geraldine asked.

'It's fine. It's just a superficial cut. The only query was over how hygienic the blade was, but they cleaned me up and checked I was up-to-date with my tetanus jabs and all that. As long as I keep it covered up it shouldn't get infected. Seriously, Geraldine, it's only a scratch. I don't think he actually meant to do it. If he had wanted to harm me, he could have done a lot worse. That blade was sharp!' She forced a smile. 'If you hadn't come along when you did...'

'Well, I did, so that's that,' Geraldine said.

She wondered whether Ariadne's husband would try to use the incident to persuade her to leave the police, and asked how he had reacted on hearing what had happened.

'He was surprisingly okay about it,' Ariadne replied. 'I think he didn't want to say anything that might upset me. Once it's all over, he'll probably try to convince me that the job is too dangerous. I know he's hoping I'll lose my nerve.'

'And have you?'

'Have I what?'

'I mean, do you think you've lost your nerve? It would be perfectly understandable.'

'Of course, I haven't lost my nerve,' Ariadne replied firmly. 'They'll have to kick me out if they want to get rid of me.'

Geraldine smiled. 'Well, that's all right then.'

55

WHILE GERALDINE AND ARIADNE were on their break, a message
came in about a potential sighting of Alison Truman, who had
been missing for ten days. The search had been continuing,
but all efforts to trace her had so far proved frustrating. Like
the three other girls who had gone missing from the vicinity of
her digs, she had vanished without trace. Finding her was more
urgent than questioning Andrew, who was being held securely
in custody, so Geraldine went to speak to the constable who had
logged the information.

'She's here,' he said. 'Waiting in an interview room.'

'Alison Truman's here?' Geraldine asked in surprise.

'No,' the constable replied, looking slightly flustered. 'There's
a woman come in who thinks she saw Alison and I thought you
might want to speak to her yourself.'

'Very well,' Geraldine agreed. It wouldn't do Andrew any
harm to have to wait for her to continue the interview.

There had been numerous calls from people claiming to have
seen one or other of the missing girls, all of which had led nowhere.
Each report had to be acknowledged and processed. So far, none
had led to an even vaguely credible lead to the whereabouts
of one of the girls. The longer they remained missing, the less
likely it was they would turn up. Without much hope that the
latest witness would prove anything other than a waste of time,
Geraldine went to speak to her. A slightly overweight middle-
aged woman stood up when Geraldine entered the room, and
introduced herself as Gloria Sands, a local district nurse. She

seemed to be sensible enough, and Geraldine invited her to share what she had witnessed.

'It could well be nothing,' the woman said, 'but I'm almost certain I saw Alison Truman, the girl you were looking for. I recognised her face on the television appeal, the one with the families, and I thought that was her.'

'When did you see her?'

'Well, it was a few days ago.' She fished in her bag and drew out a slip of paper. 'It was when I was at the garden centre. Here you are. I had to go through my kitchen drawer to find the receipt so I could be sure of the date. I went through the checkout at three on Tuesday, that's ten days ago, isn't it?'

Geraldine frowned. The woman had named the day on which Alison had allegedly disappeared, having failed to return home that evening.

'Tell me exactly what you saw,' Geraldine said, taking the flimsy receipt and slipping it into an evidence bag to keep it safe. 'Try not to leave anything out.'

'I know,' the nurse nodded. 'Any apparently trivial detail could turn out to be crucial.' She smiled. 'It's the same in my profession. Patients don't always know what is significant and what isn't. Very well. So, I was at the garden centre and I noticed this girl. She was tall and very pretty. I wouldn't have really noticed her except that there was a man who I thought was pestering her.' She paused. 'I could have been wrong. It was just an impression. He spoke to the girl.'

'Did you hear what he said?'

The woman shook her head. 'They were too far away. Anyway, after a moment she moved away but I saw him hovering and he could have been following her at a distance. He might have been walking quite innocently around the store, but I just felt he seemed to be interested in her, watching her. It wasn't necessarily anything dodgy. He might have been interested in making a sale –'

'Do you mean he worked at the garden centre?' Geraldine asked, hardly daring to put the question.

'Oh yes, didn't I mention that? Sorry. Of course, that could be important. Yes, he was wearing the green overalls they all wear there. I just thought it was worth mentioning, because you never know, do you?'

'Can you describe the man you saw?'

Gloria sighed. 'I wish I'd thought to take a picture of him on my phone, but you don't think of doing that, do you? I mean, it's not as if anything happened. If I hadn't seen that girl's image on the television, I honestly wouldn't have thought anything more of it. Right, well, I think he was tall and thin, and he had dark hair.' She broke off and sighed. 'To be honest, I'm not even sure that's right. I could be confusing him with the man who served me. It was a while ago.'

'Would you recognise him if we showed you photos of everyone who works there?'

Gloria shook her head. 'I don't know. All I can say is that it was definitely a man, because I remember wondering what he was up to, the way you do sometimes, you know?'

Geraldine thanked Gloria and asked her to make a formal statement. Armed with that, she went to speak to Binita.

'How are you getting on with Andrew?' the DCI enquired.

'Andrew can wait for a while,' Geraldine replied, as she drew Binita's attention to Gloria's statement. 'If her impression was correct, and this man works at the garden centre –' she said.

Binita nodded. 'He shouldn't be too difficult to find.' She gave a guarded smile. 'Let's not get ahead of ourselves.'

Geraldine nodded. They needed to gather as much information as they could before questioning the staff at the garden centre. If the man they were looking for was working there, they couldn't afford to alert him to police interest in his activities. Geraldine sent Naomi to speak discreetly to the manager of the garden centre and download all their CCTV footage from the past month. The manager was told that the police were carrying out a routine check, looking for a gang of shoplifters known to be operating in the area. The sighting had been less than two weeks earlier, and there was no problem with having the film sent to the police station. A VIIDO team were tasked with examining it on the day of the alleged sighting. It didn't take them long to confirm that a girl who looked just like Alison had entered the garden centre and walked around the aisles on the day she had disappeared. By comparing the images with the picture they already had of Alison, the IT officers were able to confirm the sighting. Alison had visited the garden centre on the day she disappeared. The footage of her walking around the store was possibly the last image of her before she was abducted or killed.

The VIIDO team studied the film but couldn't see a man following her. She had seemed to be speaking a couple of times, when no one else was in the shot. Although there was nothing to indicate that she was being stalked, her presence there confirmed that they finally had a lead and there were a couple of frames where a dark-haired man appeared to be walking towards her. Possibly deliberately, he had kept his back to the camera, but it looked as though the same man had approached her twice. Not only was his face hidden, but he was standing hunched over so it was difficult to judge his height. Geraldine stared at the image but, like her colleagues, she was unable to identify the man. In any case, his approach to Alison might have been perfectly innocent.

The next task was to establish where Alison had gone once she left the garden centre. The film showed her leaving just over half an hour after her arrival, but they could find no sign of her after that. The search would have to focus on the garden centre for now. There was no point in trying to conceal a police presence at the garden centre, so Geraldine arranged for a full search team to go in and look for evidence of Alison's abduction. More importantly, she was going to head up a team investigating all the staff who worked there. Gloria's description of the man she had seen would be treated as unreliable; no one who worked there would escape close scrutiny.

56

'CHARGE MY CLIENT OR release him,' the lawyer insisted.

'Very well,' Geraldine agreed.

Facing Andrew across a table in an interview room, with a tape running, she charged him with the murder of Lucy Henderson.

'What?' Andrew stuttered. 'I never killed her. I – look, I know it looks bad, but I found her. I never killed her. You said it yourself, I was trying to help her.'

'I think you'd better tell us exactly what you did.'

Andrew sighed and described how he had been driving home from the office. 'And I admit it, I'd had a drink before I left. I wasn't over the limit. I could still drive, no problem. But I was –' He hesitated. 'I was feeling relaxed, when I saw this girl and –' He broke off, shaking slightly. 'Look, I'm not proud of what I did, all right? And I'd rather my wife didn't find out. But I saw this girl all on her own and I thought she might be up for it, you know?'

'I'm not sure I do know,' Geraldine replied coldly. 'What exactly was on your mind when you saw her?'

'Sex. Sex was on my mind, all right? Sex. Like I said, I'm not proud of it. I had no idea who she was, or that she was in such a state. All I saw was a woman out on her own and I thought she might be willing to have a quickie.' He paused. 'It's not a crime to have sex with a consenting adult, is it?'

'What happened?'

'I stopped the car and went over to her, and asked her how much she charged. Only then I saw she was covered in mud. It was horrible, hideous. I was backing off, when she shrieked my name and I panicked because she recognised me. I barely had time to react before she hurled herself at me, screeching that I was a dirty pervert. I tried to push her away.' He broke off and wiped his brow with his sleeve.

'You pushed her?' Geraldine promoted him.

'Well, not exactly.' He hesitated and glanced at his lawyer before continuing. 'I slapped her face to shut her up, you know, like they do in films when a woman becomes hysterical. I just slapped her, that's all, but she fell over, sort of collapsed, blind drunk, and I left.'

'She collapsed and you abandoned her on the street.'

Andrew shook his head. 'I had to get away from there. I couldn't be found with her. I thought if I went straight home, I could deny ever having seen her. To be honest, I never thought she'd remember seeing me, she was so out of it. I couldn't believe it when I heard she was dead. She was alive when I left her. She was lying on the pavement, groaning and mumbling to herself. She was still talking, I swear it.'

'And you left her like that?' Ariadne asked sternly. 'You didn't try to help her?'

'She wasn't dead. She was alive. I thought she was drunk, or on drugs. I wouldn't have left her like that if I'd known she was hurt. I would have called an ambulance. I wish I had now, but how could I have known she was going to die?' He broke down in tears, mumbling that he had been scared.

'The point is that the girl was very much alive when my client left her. To charge him with murder is a waste of everyone's time,' the lawyer said.

Geraldine was inclined to believe what Andrew had just told them. He would only have had time for a very brief encounter with Lucy. But if he hadn't covered her in earth, who had?

By the time she had finished processing Andrew's statement, Geraldine received a message that all the staff at the garden centre had been brought to the police station for questioning.

The manager was furious at having to close the store but he was given no choice, since all the staff were being questioned, regardless of gender. Although the police were looking for a man, the female staff couldn't be left out, since they might be aware of a male colleague who seemed shady. Geraldine made her way past rows of men and women. Most were wearing green overalls which displayed the logo of the garden centre: a simplified representation of a tree with the letters YGC incorporated into the image. They were quiet enough, despite the uneasy atmosphere as they waited. Geraldine looked down the list and asked to speak to the manager.

Arthur Winston was a pompous man. Short and broad shouldered, he seemed to have adopted some of the characteristics of the garden gnomes on sale at the garden centre where he was employed.

'Now then,' he said fussily, as he took a seat opposite Geraldine, 'I think it's time you told me what this is all about.' He spoke with an air of authority, as though he didn't doubt she would do exactly what she was told.

'I'm afraid I can't share details of an ongoing investigation,' Geraldine replied mildly.

'Now you look here. When your people came in with some cock and bull story about shoplifters, I complied with all your requests, without demur I might add, but this – this is going too far. Closing down the entire garden centre like this! I demand to be told exactly what is going on.' Arthur glared at her and his shoulders rose with tension.

'I'd like to ask you a few questions,' Geraldine replied, ignoring the outburst. 'This won't take long.'

'I demand to see a lawyer,' the little man said.

Geraldine made no attempt to conceal her surprise. 'We only want to ask you a few questions,' she said. 'Are you sure that's necessary? Unless you have something to hide,' she added in a low murmur.

Arthur jolted as though she had slapped him in the face, and he began to complain about a preposterous state of affairs, when the police could haul innocent people off the street and start accusing them of he didn't know what, exactly, but it certainly wasn't something he would ever be mixed up in.

'That's a pity,' Geraldine said. 'As manager of the garden centre, I was hoping you would be our most valuable source of information. Mr Winston,' she went on, leaning forward and speaking quietly, 'can I rely on your absolute discretion?'

He nodded, looking slightly mollified.

'Very well, then. I'm telling you this in absolute confidence.'

He nodded again, involuntarily lowering his hunched shoulders.

'You must have gathered by now that we are investigating a serious crime. I can't stress how important it is that you tell no one what I am about to say. I'm not at liberty to give you any further details, but we suspect a wanted criminal may have visited the garden centre, and we need to find out where he went after he left your premises.'

Arthur smiled grimly. 'I thought as much. I could tell there was something going on.'

Geraldine gazed at him with a serious expression. 'I knew you were an intelligent man.'

She hoped her flattery wasn't too blatant, but she needn't have worried. Arthur visibly relaxed.

'You don't get to be manager by being an idiot,' he said, with an air of complacency.

Geraldine smiled in acknowledgement of his remark.

'Now then, what is it you want to know? I'm ready to cooperate fully in your investigation. Just tell me what it is you want me to do. Is there any individual in particular you'd like me to keep an eye out for?'

His resistance forgotten, Arthur was eager to be involved in the investigation. As she struggled to dampen his enthusiasm,

Geraldine wasn't sure she hadn't preferred him when he was refusing to cooperate.

'That won't be necessary,' she insisted, when he repeated his offer to take on a role as an undercover cop, gathering intelligence about his colleagues. 'I merely want to ask you a few questions for now, and then you can leave. But if we ever do need to carry out covert surveillance at the garden centre, I'll be sure to call on you.'

Arthur beamed and seemed content with that. It was possible he was bluffing to distract attention from some guilty secret he was keeping from the police, but Geraldine doubted he was that conniving.

He didn't react when she showed him a series of pictures of young women, one of whom was Alison.

'You're sure you haven't seen any of these women before?'

'Positive. I never forget a pretty face.'

Geraldine decided it was definitely time to let him go.

57

THE NEXT PERSON GERALDINE spoke to was young and quite tall, with black hair and a cadaverous face. He glared nervously at her as he lowered himself onto a chair and confirmed his name was Benjamin Wesley.

'It's Ben,' he muttered sullenly.

Geraldine learned that Ben had been working at the garden centre for six months, and before that he had been at college, studying horticulture.

'That must be an interesting course,' Geraldine said, keen to put him at his ease.

He shrugged. 'It was okay,' he conceded diffidently. 'Not everyone was interested.'

'It can't have been easy finding a job with that training.'

He nodded, fleetingly animated as he talked about his plans. 'I want to work outdoors, properly outside, I mean. Ideally, in a National Trust property, or somewhere like that, with acres of landscaped gardens. This job's okay. I mean, it's a job. But I'd be lying if I said it was my dream job.'

When Geraldine showed him a photograph of Alison he gave no guilty start, nor any sign of recognition, but merely stared at the picture.

'She's a looker,' he commented without much enthusiasm.

'Have you seen her before?'

Ben shook his head. 'I don't remember seeing her, but, you know, we see a lot of people in our job. I think I might remember her,' he added, narrowing his eyes appreciatively. 'Is she in trouble? Is she the person you're looking for? Is she the reason we had to close? Only, no one's said anything about docking our pay so I'm assuming we'll be paid for today?'

Ignoring his questions, Geraldine followed up with a few more of her own, but Ben had nothing to add. The next staff member to face her also matched Gloria's description, being tall and dark-haired. His movements were those of a young man, lithe and quick, with more than a hint of latent strength. As he took a seat opposite her, close up she saw that his dark hair was speckled with white and his face was that of a man older than his physique suggested. He was probably in his sixties. She wondered whether he worked out, or if his level of physical fitness was solely due to his work at the garden centre. He confirmed his name was George Young, and he had been working at the garden centre for nearly seven years. Before that, he had been unemployed for a while, after several years working in a different garden centre, on the Tadcaster Road.

'Why did you leave your previous job?' she enquired.

George shrugged. 'Just didn't suit,' he replied.

'But you decided to work in a garden centre again?'

He nodded. Since he wasn't forthcoming, Geraldine questioned him further about why he left his former job for a similar one.

'What, specifically, did you dislike about your previous job?'

He thought for a moment. 'Not enough hands-on with the plants.'

'You must enjoy working with plants,' she said pleasantly, 'if you moved from one garden centre to another.'

'I love it,' he replied fervently.

Geraldine smiled at his enthusiasm. This time, when she showed him half a dozen pictures of different girls, he gave an involuntary start on seeing Alison's face. The change in his demeanour was almost imperceptible. Had Geraldine not been studying him very closely, she would have missed it. Careful not to react, she laid out some images of other girls, and he shook his head.

'Do you recognise any of these faces?' Geraldine asked carefully.

George shook his head. 'I don't recognise any of them. Sorry. Always happy to help the police, but I don't know them.' A smile sat awkwardly on his wary face.

'And do you ever drive any of the vans at the garden centre?' Geraldine asked casually, as she removed all the pictures.

George nodded uneasily. 'Yes,' he said. 'I have done. Most of us do, from time to time, if they need us to.'

Geraldine tried to put him at his ease by seeming to focus her attention on the garden centre. 'Would you say the vans were properly maintained by your employers?'

The question seemed to reassure him, as she had intended.

'As far as I know,' he said. 'At least, I've never heard of anyone having a problem with the vans. I'm sure they get serviced regularly. But I hardly ever drive them. That's not part of my job. I just help out when I'm needed. There are drivers who usually make the deliveries.'

Geraldine thanked him and told him he could go before she recorded her notes on their conversation, flagging him as a person of interest.

'He has access to the vans,' she concluded her report.

58

'YOU'RE BACK LATE,' LINDA said, coming into the hall as he closed the front door. 'How was your day?'

George scowled, struggling to conceal his fear. There was no point in pretending everything was fine. 'It was a really shit day, since you ask.' He passed her and flung himself down in a chair in the living room, where he stretched his long legs out in front of him, half hiding his face behind one hand. 'The police were on at us all bloody day.'

'The police?' Linda repeated, sounding alarmed, as she followed him into the living room. 'What did they want?'

She perched on the chair beside him, staring at him with a shocked expression that seemed to emphasise the lines that criss-crossed her face.

'Oh, there's no need to look so worried. It wasn't anything to do with me.' Peering at her through his fingers, he decided to disguise his fear behind a show of anger. 'The bastards shut us down. Can you believe it? We were closed all day. The entire bloody day. No one was allowed to go back and turn the water on in the afternoon.'

He leaned back and closed his eyes. Worn out with the stress of the day, he was too tired to keep up his pretence. He hoped Linda would drop it, but she persisted with her questions.

'So, what did the police want?'

George shrugged without opening his eyes. 'Search me. They just swooped in and closed the garden centre for the whole day.'

'But why? I mean, they must have had a reason.'

'They just arrived in a couple of vans and questioned us, like we were a bunch of common criminals.'

'Did you have to go along with it?'

'Of course. It was the police. They can do whatever the hell they like. A few of the guys tried to challenge them, but they didn't take a blind bit of notice. The women were the worst,' he added, opening his eyes and glancing at her with a twisted smile. 'They didn't like it one bit. Some of them threatened to contact the local paper, and make a fuss on social media. But there was nothing any of us could actually do about it. Arthur tried to get them to listen to reason. I mean, you can't abandon all those plants without making sure they're going to be all right. But they just didn't care. Bastards.'

Linda could have pointed out that no one watered the plants when the garden centre was shut, but she seemed more interested in what the police were doing.

'What sort of questions did they ask you?' She hesitated. 'You didn't say anything – anything that might attract their attention, did you?'

He stared at her, fleetingly wondering what lay behind her words. But she didn't know anything about his project, and he dismissed her interest as superficial. The police had never visited the garden centre before, and naturally she was curious.

'They asked about what we did and that. And while we were all being questioned, they sent in a team to search the garden centre. Can you imagine? I don't think they were being that careful either.' At the thought of clumsy hands disturbing the shrubs he had been so carefully nurturing, he felt a surge of hatred for the men and women who had been allowed to march into the garden centre and tamper with the stock. 'If they've damaged any of those plants, there'll be hell to pay,' he muttered, his anger no longer an act. 'They won't get away with it. That's criminal damage, even if they are in bloody uniform and following orders.'

'I still don't understand. What were they looking for?'

'They didn't say.'

Linda gazed solemnly at him. 'Don't worry,' she said, almost under her breath. 'I'll protect you.'

George stared at her in surprise. 'What are you talking about? Protect me from what, exactly?'

She turned her head away and he studied her hair, which was turning quite white.

'I just want you to know that, whatever happens, I'm going to make sure nothing bad ever happens to you,' she murmured.

'Now it's you that's making no sense,' he replied. 'Has the whole world gone stark raving mad? First, the police march in and take the place apart, and now you're talking in riddles.'

Linda went off to put the kettle on, leaving him bemused and frightened. Linda seemed to think he needed protecting from the police, but that made no sense. He wished he could understand what was on her mind, and he was tempted to challenge her about her comment when she returned with the tea. But something held him back. If she had cracked under the strain, he wasn't sure he could cope with what might follow. Besides, although she couldn't possibly know about it, there was a very good reason why the police might be very interested in what he had been doing in his own garden. He had been careful not to do anything to arouse suspicion, but Linda's reaction to the police visit unnerved him. It was almost as though she knew what he had been doing while she was away working at night.

Before long she was back, suggesting they share a pot of tea in the garden. With a sigh, George heaved himself to his feet and followed her outside. Sitting in the fresh air, cooling after a hot summer day, he began to relax. The police had only been at the garden centre for one day, and now they had gone. The drama of their visit was over. No doubt the staff would be talking about it for a long time, but other than his colleagues' gossip and chatter, it was all in the past.

'Are you all right?' Linda enquired as they sat sipping their tea.

He looked around the garden, satisfied with his handiwork. The work was never finished, but everything was certainly looking vibrant and glorious.

'Me?' he replied. 'Yes. Why wouldn't I be?'

She sighed. 'You've just been a little – preoccupied lately. Are you sure there's nothing on your mind?'

He thought carefully. He had been careful not to do anything that might lead her to suspect what was taking place in the garden, but Linda was a clever woman and he might have slipped up. Putting his cup down, he sighed.

'I'm a bit worried about police searching the garden centre,' he admitted. 'Handling plants carelessly could cause all kinds of damage.'

'It seems odd, doesn't it?' she replied. 'What could they be looking for? Drugs, maybe? But I didn't just mean today,' she said. 'You seemed bothered before today. Is there something on your mind?'

He shook his head. 'No. Nothing at all. I mean, there are always issues at work, but nothing out of the ordinary, and nothing I can't deal with.' He hesitated. 'But there is something I've been meaning to ask you.'

'Well? Ask away.' She gave him an encouraging smile, but he sensed she was worried.

He took a deep breath and plunged in. 'Why did you tell me Robert and Sharon were getting a dog?'

She looked startled. 'What?'

'You told me they were getting a dog,' he repeated testily.

'Yes,' she agreed uncertainly. 'I thought they were.'

'Well, you were wrong. Sharon told me they're not. She flatly denied it.'

'Well, I'm relieved to hear that,' Linda replied, smiling uneasily.

'So, why did you tell me they were getting a dog?' he persisted.

'I must have misunderstood,' Linda murmured. 'Sharon said something, and I took it at face value, but it seems I was wrong. I thought she was being serious, that's all.'

She shifted in her chair and looked away. George had the uncomfortable impression that she was lying.

59

ANDREW REMAINED IN CUSTODY. His insistence that Lucy was still alive when he had left her was borne out by statements given by the couple who had come across her lying unconscious in the street. In addition, since she had died several hours later under medical supervision, there was irrefutable evidence from the hospital that she hadn't died in the street. Andrew had injured her, but it wasn't clear whether his assault had been a contributory cause of her death or irrelevant to it. What *was* clear was that someone else had carried out a macabre attack on Lucy before Andrew had encountered her in the street.

As to why she had been covered in a film of earth, that remained an enigma which was prompting a great deal of speculation. Eventually, everyone had agreed the most logical explanation was that someone had tried to bury her. The general consensus was that whoever had attempted to bury her had made a complete hash of it. The worrying aspect of the theory was the possibility it raised that the other girls who had vanished might have suffered a similar fate. Only in their cases, the burial might have been more successful. That would certainly explain why they had vanished without trace. It might also make the bodies impossible to find.

In the meantime, they were holding Andrew in a cell on grounds which were beginning to appear shaky. His lawyer had not yet been agitating seriously for his release, but it was only a matter of time before they would have to alter the charge against him and let him go. Several officers were discussing the situation while they were waiting for a briefing on Friday afternoon.

'Even if she was still alive when he left her,' Naomi began but Ariadne interrupted her.

'There's no "if" about it. We've got hospital records, in case you don't believe the witnesses who found her, although why they should lie about it is anybody's guess. We know Lucy died hours after Andrew left her.'

'Even if she was still alive when he left her,' Naomi repeated, 'she fell over when he hit her and he just buggered off and left her there to die. It makes no difference if she died hours later or straightaway. For all he knew, she was already dying. The fact is, she was seriously injured, fatally injured as it turned out, and he abandoned her in the street. If she'd received medical attention sooner, she might have survived.'

'And she would have been able to tell us what had happened to her,' Geraldine added wistfully.

'I appreciate he didn't want to risk being found there, after the disgraceful way he behaved, but he could have called an ambulance before he left,' Naomi insisted. 'He could have claimed to have noticed her lying unconscious when he was driving by. He could easily have come up with an account which left out his real reason for approaching her. He could have touched her face in an attempt to help her.' She shrugged. 'The man's not merely a moron, he's a menace. If he didn't murder her, he might as well have done.'

'But as far as we know, he didn't,' Ariadne said.

'He could have saved her life and he chose to ignore that chance,' Naomi insisted.

'All the same, a murder charge won't stick,' Geraldine said. 'We know someone else is responsible for her injuries. Let's hope the garden centre throws up a lead to the killer.'

Naomi frowned. 'It won't make Andrew any less guilty.'

Before she could continue, Binita entered.

'All the vans have been collected in,' she said. 'We don't yet know, but it's possible the killer used one or more of the garden centre vehicles to transport the missing girls.'

They discussed the various statements made by people working at the garden centre, in the light of Gloria's claim to have seen Alison being approached by one of them. There was no evidence on the CCTV footage that any member of staff had spoken to her, but the security cameras had several blind spots which staff there might have known about. There were a couple of frames where she turned and could have been talking to someone who was out of the shot.

'The cameras are trained on the shelves, not on the space at the end of the aisles,' Geraldine explained. 'They're understandably focused on the goods on sale, not on empty corners.'

'Is it likely someone could have spoken to her only when he was out of sight of a camera?'

'If not likely, certainly possible,' Geraldine replied.

'Possible,' Binita agreed.

'We just have to wait for the results of the examination of the vans,' Geraldine told Ian that evening. 'It's going to take a while.'

'How many vans are there?'

'Do you know, I'm not exactly sure. I'd have to look it up to give you an accurate figure. I think it was four but it might be five.'

60

OVER THE WEEKEND, ALL the vans from the garden centre were being tested for traces of blood or DNA. With any luck, they would find evidence that Lucy or Alison had been transported in one of them. In the meantime, there was nothing any of the team could do but wait and study the statements gathered so far. Geraldine spent all day Saturday poring over Gloria's description of her sighting of Alison, the VIIDO reports, and the statements made by the staff working at the garden centre, trying to find a coherent narrative. By the time she packed up, she was feeling frustrated and exhausted from staring at a screen all day. It was making her feel slightly queasy.

The fresh air revived her as she left the police station and walked to her car, but she was feeling drained by the time she reached home. So, she was less than enthusiastic when Ian suggested they go out for a meal, but she hid her reluctance and agreed.

'That's a lovely idea,' she lied.

She wasn't feeling hungry, but she was aware that Ian was doing his best to distract her from the case, which was taking up all her attention, and she didn't want to let him down. The first problem – which shouldn't really have counted as a problem at all – was that only one victim had been found. There was, as yet, nothing to suggest that the girls were linked in any way. All five girls, one dead and four missing, had lived within a short distance of one another. But that in itself didn't prove there was any connection between them.

'We seem to be going round in circles,' she explained to Ian as they waited for their first course. 'It's turning into one of those cases where we seem to be trying to wade through treacle to find the centre of an impossibly convoluted maze.'

Ian sighed gently.

'I'm sorry,' she said, sensing his disappointment. 'I promised not to talk about work this evening, didn't I?' She looked around the restaurant and tried to inject some enthusiasm into her voice as she added, 'It really is nice here, and the last thing I want to do is spoil it.'

Ian smiled at her. 'I suppose the idea of going out and forgetting all about work for an evening was never more than a fantasy of mine. Seriously,' he added, seeing her dismay, 'it doesn't matter. Really, it doesn't. Tracking down a serial killer is more important than – well, than anything really.'

'We don't know that's what we're dealing with,' she replied severely, glancing about to check that no one could overhear them. 'If we can only find something useful in one of the vans, then we'll be on to something. So far, we've been floundering around in the dark. But like I said earlier, I've got a feeling I might have come across a likely suspect, only, of course, there's nothing to tie him to the case yet. It's just a feeling I have.'

'So, likely to be at least as reliable as any physical evidence,' Ian grinned. 'I can hardly remember a time when your hunches haven't been spot on.'

'It does happen,' she reminded him, with a modest smile.

'You're simpering,' he said.

'I am not simpering,' she replied. 'I don't simper. I smile.'

'Well, I was looking right at you, and you simpered,' he teased her.

'You make me sound like that little girl in *Just William*. What was her name?'

Ian shook his head. Just then their food arrived. Ian began to eat, but Geraldine sat fiddling with her chopsticks.

'Come on,' Ian said. 'Eat up. This is really good. If you're not careful, I'll finish it all.' He put his chopsticks down. 'What's wrong? Would you rather use a fork?' He frowned, puzzled by her delay in getting started.

'I'm sorry,' she muttered, 'you carry on. I'm just not hungry all of a sudden.'

Without another word, she stood up and hurried to the Ladies, leaving Ian bemused and more than a little worried. He watched her as she returned and resumed her seat.

'Are you all right? We can go home if you want.'

'No, no, it's fine,' she assured him. 'It must just be something I ate earlier. The work canteen leaves a lot to be desired.' She forced a laugh and spooned some noodles into her bowl.

As he ate, she was conscious of Ian watching her and she pushed her noodles around in her bowl, eating a tiny amount now and again. The highly flavoured food was delicious but it made her feel nauseous.

'It must be something I ate,' she repeated miserably.

They both knew it couldn't be tension from the investigation, because she had worked on so many without any effect on her physically. On the contrary, she had always had a remarkably strong constitution. She hoped it wasn't anything serious and smiled confidently at Ian as she made a show of eating. But she stuck to the plain rice and noodles as far as possible, and tried to look as though she was eating more than she actually was. She wasn't sure Ian was fooled.

'This isn't like me,' she said. 'I'm sure I'll feel better in the morning.'

'Perhaps we should have arranged to go out for breakfast instead,' Ian said. He sounded slightly cross.

'It's not my fault. I just don't feel a hundred per cent,' she replied.

He shook his head. 'I'm worried about you,' he admitted.

'Well, don't be. I'll be fine in the morning,' she replied, smiling brightly. 'I'll be right as rain tomorrow, you'll see.'

She promised not to mention the case again that evening but she remained preoccupied, and they went home as soon as they had finished their main course, with Ian clutching a bag of leftovers. Her last thought before she went to sleep that night was relief that she had logged her suspicions of George Young. If she were to fall ill, someone else would pick up her report and investigate him.

'You won't slip through our fingers,' she muttered to herself.

'What's that?' Ian asked.

Geraldine shook her head. 'Nothing,' she murmured. 'Everything's going to be fine.'

Half asleep, she heard him ask her what she was talking about but she was too tired to force herself awake sufficiently to answer him. She drifted off to sleep, hoping she would see things more clearly in the morning.

61

ON MONDAY MORNING, BINITA called an urgent meeting. By the
time they convened in the incident room, everyone on the team
was agog with the news that one of the vans from the garden
centre had traces of DNA, not only from both Lucy and Alison,
but also from two other girls who had gone missing from the area
around Heslington Lane. They had found a clear link between
Lucy and the missing girls. They also had evidence that whoever
was responsible for seizing the victims had used a garden centre
van to transport them, alive or dead. If they could establish who
had been behind the wheel of that particular van on the days
when Lucy and Alison had last been seen, they would be able to
close in on the man they were urgently hunting.

Geraldine and Naomi drove straight to the garden centre to
find out which members of staff had access to the vans and, in
particular, who had been driving one particular van on each of
two recent occasions. Arthur greeted Geraldine in a low voice
and glanced around to check they weren't being observed, before
he ushered her towards his office with a furtive gesture.

'This way,' he whispered. 'Follow me.'

Geraldine grinned at Naomi before she hurried after the
manager, with her colleague in tow. The office was small, and
there was only room for two chairs, one on either side of a
small desk which was piled high with papers and files. Naomi
remained standing while Geraldine perched uncomfortably on
the one chair that was free once Arthur had sat down behind his
desk.

'Now,' he said, looking at Geraldine expectantly, 'I imagine you're here for my report? It was best to come in person. You can't trust the internet.' He shook his head sagely.

Hiding her amusement, Geraldine explained that they wanted to see the van drivers' rota.

Arthur frowned and checked his watch. 'I have my report ready to read out to you,' he said plaintively.

'Thank you very much. Can you print it out and we'll take it with us?' Geraldine suggested.

'It's fifty-seven pages,' he replied.

'Ah, well in that case, you'd better send it to us electronically,' Geraldine said. 'My sergeant will give you a secure email address,' she added, shaking her head slightly at Naomi. 'It's fully encrypted and protected by several firewalls and part of the police secure network. You'll have to delete the address as soon as you've sent your report.'

'I suppose you'll want me to sign the Official Secrets Act?'

'That won't be necessary, as long as you delete the classified email address immediately.'

Arthur nodded earnestly. 'You can rely on me.'

Out of the corner of her eye, she saw Naomi looking bemused.

'Now, before you send your report, which is going to be very helpful, I'm sure, we need to see that rota,' Geraldine said.

The exact time of Lucy's abduction wasn't known but, according to the rota, a man called Bill had been down to drive the van on the day Alison had disappeared. Frustratingly, the CCTV camera in the car park had been vandalised several months earlier, and a new camera which had allegedly been sent had so far failed to arrive. So, they had no way of confirming that Bill had driven that particular van out of the car park on the day Alison had visited the garden centre and subsequently disappeared.

'Is it possible one of your staff could have taken a van off the premises without their name being registered on the list?' Geraldine asked.

Arthur bristled. 'We have a system in place,' he replied pompously. 'No one is permitted to drive one of the vans away without clearing it with me. It would wreak havoc with our insurance if anyone did. The driver would be personally liable for any damage.'

Geraldine didn't reply, but she wasn't sure that someone intent on kidnap and murder would be particularly concerned about breaking the terms of the garden centre's insurance policy. Having drawn up a list of every member of staff who had driven the van, they began with Bill Warren, the man listed as driving the van on the day of Alison's disappearance. Keen to avoid attracting any attention to what she was doing, Geraldine decided to speak to him in Arthur's office. If another member of Arthur's staff proved to be the killer, the less he discovered about how the police investigation was progressing, the better. She sent Arthur off to fetch Bill.

'Should I email you my report first?' he bleated.

'That can wait,' Geraldine snapped. She had wasted enough time on Arthur's observations of his colleagues. 'You can send it once we've gone.'

Crestfallen, Arthur scurried off to find Bill. A few moments later, he returned with a lanky man, whose ginger hair was so bright it almost didn't look natural. When he moved under the light, Geraldine saw that his eyebrows and eyelashes, and even the downy hair on his arms, were a similar colour. He certainly wasn't the man Gloria had described, but he was on the list as having driven the van with incriminating DNA on the day Alison had disappeared. Geraldine invited him to take a seat. He glared at her, and she was glad of plainclothes constables waiting in the car park in case she needed to summon urgent back-up.

'Bill,' she said, identifying the Tuesday when Alison was last seen. 'You drove a van out of the car park that day.'

He frowned. 'Yeah. I had a delivery. You can check the books.'

'Why did you keep the van overnight?'

He shook his head. 'No way,' he replied. 'More than my job's worth. The insurance only covers us from eight to six. After that, we're on our own. It's all in the paperwork. We have to sign it before we're allowed to drive the vans. There's no way I'd want to risk a prang in one of them vans outside the hours. No way.' He shook his head as though to emphasise the point. 'Look at the time of the delivery,' he suggested. 'Then you can check when I was back in the store.' When Geraldine hesitated, he added, almost indignantly, 'Ask Len. We get the bus home together most days. He'll tell you. Len Barber.'

Naomi went to fetch Len, while Geraldine waited with Bill. A quiet word with Len confirmed that he and Bill had caught the bus home together every day for the past few weeks. Neither of them had been off work, or stayed late.

'Regular as clockwork, we are,' he told Geraldine cheerfully. 'What's this all about anyway?'

'Just a query over one of the vans,' she replied. 'Nothing much.'

'That's all right then.'

Len's name didn't appear on the rota for the vans and it turned out he didn't drive, so there was no point in detaining him, or Bill, any longer. But someone had transported Alison in that van, which had been driven out of the garden centre car park, probably on the night she had disappeared. Without any CCTV evidence, it was going to be difficult to discover exactly when it had been taken, or by whom. They couldn't even be sure the killer worked at the garden centre. The car park had no barriers, and in theory anyone could have taken one of the vans overnight. But at least they had a lead, tenuous though it was. The next step was to take a DNA sample from every member of staff at the garden centre and narrow down the number of men who had driven that one van, looking for anyone who had driven on an official journey.

62

GEORGE WAS WATERING SHRUBS outside when he became aware of a disturbance indoors. 'We have to go in,' one of his colleagues called out, waving at him.

'What's going on?' George asked.

'It's only the police again,' she replied, approaching him, her eyes bright with excitement. 'I don't know why they keep coming back here, but something's going on. Apparently, they're asking us all to give a sample of our DNA.'

'Why on earth would they want us to do that?' George blurted out. Feeling as though he had been kicked in the guts, he suddenly needed the toilet.

His colleague shrugged. 'I haven't the faintest idea.'

'But do we have to do it?'

'Looks like it. Come on, we might as well get it over with. It's not like an injection or anything,' she added sympathetically.

Realising that he must appear shocked, he forced a smile. 'You go on. I'll just finish up here or I'll forget where I got to.'

His colleague nodded and hurried inside, leaving George holding his watering can and doing his best to control his panic. It was pointless, but he wiped the handle of the watering can and pulled on his gardening gloves, before dodging behind a row of tall shrubs. Forcing himself not to run, he made his way to the back gate that was used for deliveries, and rattled it. The gate was locked. He knew where the key was kept, but he was almost certain to be spotted entering the manager's office if he went to retrieve it. He couldn't take that risk. Once he had left the garden centre, he would be able to find somewhere to hide until all the fuss died down, but first he had to walk out unobserved. Still out of sight, he stripped off his work overalls and went inside. Skirting the edge of the room, he made directly for the stand of sunglasses, slipped a pair on, and carried on walking towards the exit. Without his telltale uniform, none of the police even glanced at him. He was worried that one of his colleagues might recognise him, but they were all preoccupied with the police activity. Watching askance, he saw them lining up to be escorted into the manager's office, while Arthur ran around fussing and nagging them to be quick because customers were waiting for attention. No one penetrated his disguise.

Stepping over the threshold onto the forecourt, he drew in a deep shuddering breath. But his troubles were not over yet. It was hard not to stare at the police cars lined up outside the building, blocking the entrance. His legs wanted to sprint, but he forced himself to walk past them at a leisurely pace, as though he hadn't a care in the world. It seemed to take him hours to cross the few yards to the street, but at last he reached the pavement where he could walk more quickly, away from the town centre and towards the hospital where Linda worked. He had some vague idea of hiding there until nightfall and then finding her once she started her shift. Together, they would make their escape from York. He had no idea where they would go, and he realised it might be difficult to persuade her to abandon Robert and Noah, but he would make her understand that he had to leave. He hoped she would agree to come with him. If not, he would have to leave York alone, and she could join him later. Either way, he wouldn't wait around for the police to find him. At the back of his mind he had always known this day might come, but he had never really believed it would happen. Now he had no choice. A terrible possibility had become reality and he had to react quickly.

He walked several miles to the hospital. He was familiar with the layout, because Linda had shown him around, and there were multiple signs to guide him. Most importantly, he knew where the laundry was kept, in a walk-in cupboard off a narrow passageway. He had made a point of noting its location when he had been there with Linda, just in case he ever needed to seek refuge in the hospital. Congratulating himself on his foresight, he found the store without any difficulty, but once again he was thwarted, this time by a locked door. As he hesitated, wondering what to do next, a man in a blue uniform walked past, pushing a trolley.

'Hey,' George stopped him. 'Can I borrow your key? I left mine at home in my jacket.'

The porter was quite old, and rather dithery. 'What? I can't do that,' he replied. 'You know I can't do that. It's against regulations. You'd know that if you worked here. I couldn't do that even if I wanted to. I've no idea who you are. Who are you, anyway? Where's your ID?' He turned away and resumed pushing his trolley.

The porter was wearing a lanyard. If George could get hold of it, together with the old man's blue overalls, he would be able to move around the site unchallenged. The corridor was empty. George glanced around but he couldn't see any cameras in this side passage. Lunging forward, he shoved the porter in the back, at the same time punching him on the side of his head as hard as he could. The porter let out a yelp, staggered and lost his footing. The next moment he was lying on the floor, shuddering, while blood oozed from a wound on his temple where he had hit his head on the edge of his trolley as he fell. This was no time to hesitate. Someone could come along at any moment. George had to shove the man out of sight in the store cupboard before he was seen. Searching the man's pockets, he started to panic because he couldn't find any keys. Desperately, he looked on the trolley and found only a bin full of dirty linen. Removing a crumpled blue outfit, he heaved the unconscious porter up and into the laundry bin, pulled a white coat over him, and shut the lid. Panting from his efforts, he pulled the creased uniform over his own T-shirt and jeans just in time. A woman in a white coat strode past, without pausing to study the small pool of blood on the floor.

'Get that cleaned up, will you?' she said, with a grimace.

'Yes, I'm on it,' George replied, keeping his face averted.

As soon as the woman had turned the corner, he grabbed another pair of overalls from the bin and pulled on his gloves. Having mopped up the mess as well as he could, he repositioned the trolley over the stain, and began to walk away. Only then did he remember the porter's lanyard, which was still around the man's neck. Checking that no one was coming, he ran back, yanked up the lid of the bin and pulled the white coat aside. The porter's eyes were open, looking up at him. George gasped and started back. The old man didn't move. He just lay there, staring. Hardly daring to put his hands over the rim of the container, George reached in and grabbed hold of the strap around the man's neck. He tensed, ready to feel fingers clawing at his arm to repel him, but the porter didn't move. With the lanyard safely in his possession, he covered the man up once again, shut the lid, and walked away.

He was inside the hospital, masquerading as Peter Rampling, hospital porter, a disguise that was at least adequate. He had to stay out of sight until Linda's shift started, and he could find her. He was confident they would come up with a plan together. He just had to think of a way of convincing her to stand by him. The problem was, she was bound to ask him what crime he had committed. As he walked around the hospital, surrounded by people who spent their time striving to save lives, like his wife, he knew he could never tell her the truth. Yet he needed her help if he was to stand any chance of escape. He couldn't manage it by himself. Very soon the police would start looking for him. With time running out, he had to find a way to persuade Linda to help him.

63

GERALDINE READ DOWN THE list of employees at the garden centre. The team had been thorough in gathering DNA from them. Two employees were off work with minor ailments that day, and officers had already gone to see them at home to collect their DNA samples. Another was on holiday in Devon, but his mother had been persuaded to hand over his toothbrush, in spite of her reservations. Only one name on the list had not been ticked off.

'Why isn't George Young on here?' Geraldine demanded, staring at her screen in dismay.

'He wasn't at the garden centre and no one answered at his home,' Naomi replied, with an anxious frown.

The whole team had read Geraldine's report. The possibility that George wanted to avoid giving them a sample of his DNA lent credence to Geraldine's suspicions.

'We don't know he's been guilty of any wrongdoing, and his absence from work could be coincidental, but we have to find him,' Geraldine said. 'And we need to get a sample of his DNA tested as soon as possible.'

She and Naomi drove to the garden centre, on the off chance that he was there, and had been missed by the team collecting DNA samples.

'He could have been in the toilet,' Naomi suggested, without any conviction.

But George wasn't there. According to Arthur, George had turned up for work as usual that morning. The vans had not yet been returned by the police, so no deliveries had been booked. There was no ostensible reason why George was not at work. Arthur had no idea why George might have left early, and concluded irritably that he must be feeling unwell.

'Although why he would go off without a word is beyond me,' Arthur added. 'It's never happened before and if that is what he's done, it's completely out of order. Imagine if everyone decided to just go off home whenever they felt like it. Where would that leave us?'

One of George's colleagues had reported talking to him at the garden centre after the police had arrived. Her recollection of the timing was quite clear, she said, because she remembered having told him the police had come to take samples of DNA. That was encouraging, because it meant he had not been gone for long. It seemed quite likely that George wasn't feeling poorly at all, but was at home packing a bag, preparing to leave York.

'First Andrew, now George,' Geraldine grumbled, as she climbed into the driving seat. 'Talk about a wild goose chase. What the hell is wrong with people?'

'Could it be that they don't want to be arrested?' Naomi suggested, with a wry smile. Geraldine grunted and put her foot down until they caught up with a queue at traffic lights. Reaching the house in Main Street, they waited for a few moments and this time the door was opened almost straightaway by George's wife. She looked at Geraldine with a bewildered frown.

'You're with the police, aren't you?' she enquired tentatively. 'Have you come about the girl who died in hospital?'

'This is nothing to do with her,' Geraldine replied. 'Not directly, anyway.'

Linda appeared to relax slightly. 'What is it then?' she asked, her wary expression changing to an irate scowl. 'We don't have anything to say to you.'

'We'd like a word with your husband.'

'He's at work.'

Geraldine shook her head. 'No, he's not. We've just come from there.'

Linda looked puzzled. 'Well, if he's not at work, then I've no idea where he is. He went off this morning, as usual, and he hasn't come home. He must be out doing a delivery.'

'He isn't,' Geraldine replied shortly. 'We checked and no one is doing any deliveries today. May we come in and look around?'

'Well,' Linda hesitated. 'I don't know what you expect to find.'

'I can come back very soon with a search team who will turn the place upside down,' Geraldine said. 'Or you can let me and my sergeant in now to have a quiet look around.'

'What are you looking for?'

'May we come in?'

With a sigh, Linda stood aside to let Geraldine and Naomi enter. Geraldine kept Linda occupied, to make sure she didn't attempt to contact her husband, while Naomi went off to look around the house. Linda led Geraldine into a square kitchen and invited her to take a seat on a stool at the breakfast bar. Linda leaned against the edge of the worktop and gave terse answers to Geraldine's questions. Geraldine asked her again if she knew where her husband was, when she had last seen him, and where he was likely to be. After a few moments of desultory questions, Naomi joined them. She crossed the kitchen and went out to the garden. Through the kitchen window Geraldine watched her sergeant open the door of the shed. It wasn't long before she rejoined Geraldine and Linda in the front room.

'There's no sign of him here,' she told Geraldine.

Back in the car, Naomi held up an evidence bag containing a razor and a couple of electric toothbrush heads, and grinned. 'I wasn't sure which one was his, so I brought them both. I didn't see anything unusual, except the garden shed,' she added. 'You'd have to see it to believe it. I took some photos. I don't know if he's planning to enter a competition for the best-kept garden shed in the county, but if he did, he would win, hands down.

To describe it as pristine would be doing it a real injustice. I've never seen anything like it.'

'What's unusual about it? I mean, men and their sheds, you know. It's a thing, isn't it? I'm sure he's not the only person who keeps his garden shed tidy. '

'Yes, but this wasn't like a garden shed.'

'What was it like?'

Naomi struggled to find the right words to describe what she had seen. 'It had an atmosphere more like – oh, I don't know, more like a laboratory. The shelves were metal, for a start, and the walls were insulated in some kind of plastic. And every surface was so clean it was positively gleaming. Even the garden implements were shining as though they'd recently been polished. It wasn't like a garden shed, more like a room in a hospital.'

'Or a mortuary,' Geraldine suggested thoughtfully.

64

His MAIN WORRY WAS the security cameras, which were hard to spot. Still, as long as he kept walking, looking as though he was going somewhere, he figured no one would pay him any attention. All the same, when he strode purposefully past the same nurse for the third time, he started to feel uneasy. No one had challenged him yet, but it must only be a matter of time before someone stopped him, and when that happened there was a real danger his disguise would be penetrated. Even if he said nothing to arouse suspicion, there were bound to be people there who knew Peter Rampling. One of them might recognise his name on George's lanyard and realise something was up.

The porter he had bundled into a laundry bin was another problem. George had believed the man was dead, but he had been wrong about that before. He cursed himself for failing to make certain. The prospect of Peter Rampling recovering consciousness was terrifying. He imagined the porter yelling for help from inside the laundry bin, or clambering out to tell a member of the hospital staff about his traumatic ordeal. Before long a team of police officers would arrive to hunt for the maniac who had launched an unprovoked attack on a defenceless old man. He could only hope that the man was either dead, or else incapable of recalling their encounter.

The hospital was a large rambling conglomeration of different areas, linked by long corridors. He tramped up and down stone staircases rather than using the lifts. Not only did the confined spaces make him feel trapped, but he could occupy more time on the stairs, where he was largely unobserved. People passed him, but they were all hurrying to different destinations on different floors, and no one even glanced at him. He was careful to keep his head down, and his identity badge half-hidden from view, the name impossible to read in passing. He moved from floor to floor, wing to wing, lingering in toilet cubicles wherever he went until, at last, it was time for Linda to start her shift. Cautiously, he worked his way back to the intensive care unit. If she failed to turn up, he would be scuppered.

He saw her long before she was aware of him. He hurried to catch up with her, but before he could reach her she turned a corner and entered a room opposite a desk where a nurse was sitting, gazing around. He wondered in a panic if she was looking for him. That was unlikely, yet it was possible Peter Rampling had been discovered and hospital staff had been warned to be wary of a stranger acting suspiciously. It was even possible the police had discovered he was missing, and were working on the hypothesis that he would try to contact his wife. If that was the case, by now all staff in the hospital would have been instructed to look out for him. The police might already be there, searching for him. He had been a fool to risk coming to the hospital to find Linda, but he had nowhere else to go. In any case, it was too late to back out now. Besides, the likelihood was that the police weren't looking for him at all, and Peter Rampling was still in the laundry bin, safely dead and out of sight.

After a moment's hesitation, he decided against walking past the desk and following Linda. Instead, he would wait for his chance to approach her unobserved by anyone else. Having come this far, he was loath to take any unnecessary risks now. He could wait. A few nurses bustled past him, intent on their own work. No one stopped to enquire what he was doing, loitering in the corridor. He found an empty chair and sat down, hoping that would make him less conspicuous. But the longer he delayed, the greater the chance that the police would come looking for him. As he was cursing Linda for taking so long, the door to the ward opened and Linda emerged. Silently praying that she would walk past him, and not scurry away in the other direction, he watched her stop and talk to the nurse at the desk. A second woman had joined the first one and the three of them seemed to talk for hours. At last, Linda stepped back. He waited breathlessly to see which way she would turn.

He had to suppress a cry of relief when she started walking towards him. She drew closer but stopped before she reached him and turned back, as though she had just remembered something.

'Linda,' he whispered urgently. With her back to him, he saw her abruptly stop moving, as though she had been turned to stone. 'Linda, it's me.'

On hearing his voice again, she spun round, wide-eyed with astonishment. Taking in his blue uniform, she shook her head in disbelief.

'George,' she whispered back, taking her cue from him. 'What on earth are you doing here? And why are you dressed like that? What have you done?'

He rose to his feet and tried to smile reassuringly at her. 'What makes you think I've done anything at all?' he asked, attempting a lighthearted bravado. 'You appear to be assuming I've done something wrong. I thought my own wife would have more faith in me.'

Looking perplexed, Linda repeated her question. 'What are you doing here? And why are you wearing that uniform?' She caught sight of his lanyard and frowned. 'Peter Rampling? George, what the hell are you doing?'

'Is there somewhere we can talk?'

Still frowning, she nodded and told him to follow her. Quickly, she led him to a small side room with one empty bed.

'If anyone comes in, look busy,' she said. 'We may not have very long.'

Now the time had come to enlist her help, he realised he didn't have a clue what to say to her. While he had been waiting for her, he had thought of several ideas, none of which seemed appropriate now that she was standing in front of him, her soft brown eyes bright with concern.

'What is it?' she prompted him. 'Tell me.'

'I have to get away,' he blurted out. 'I have to hide. The police...' He faltered and fell silent, overwhelmed by the difficulty of his position.

To his inexpressible relief, she didn't challenge him to explain, but merely nodded and told him not to worry.

'You have to help me. I don't know where else to go.' He broke off, nearly in tears.

'I'm here now,' she said gently. 'It's all right. Whatever it is, whatever you've done, we'll face it together.'

He fell into her arms, shuddering with sobs, and she shushed him. Ever practical, she pulled back and spoke quickly as she wiped his face.

'You need to stay calm, and tell me what's wrong. Are you hungry?'

'No, no, nothing like that. I couldn't swallow anything right now. I'm not hungry, I'm frightened. I can't explain why, but the police are looking for me. I can't let them find me. You have to help me. There's no one else I can turn to. Please, you have to help me. I can't do this without you.'

'I'll hide you until my shift finishes and then we'll leave here together. Don't worry,' she said. 'We'll think of something. Come with me.'

Suddenly, he felt too tired to carry on. 'Can't I stay here?' he asked, with a yearning glance at the empty bed. 'Just for a while. I'll be right as rain once I've had a rest. It's just all been so overwhelming, I'm shattered.'

'Staying here is out of the question, I'm afraid. Beds don't remain unoccupied for long in here. They'll be bringing a patient in at any moment. We have to hurry, I'm due back in a few minutes. Come on, now. We need to get you kitted out in a proper uniform before anyone sees you looking like that. If I didn't know better, I'd say you looked decidedly shifty.'

65

GEORGE SEEMED TO HAVE vanished.

'For goodness sake,' Binita burst out, momentarily losing her customary composure. 'How many more people are going to disappear? This is getting ridiculous. Is there a black hole somewhere in York that we don't know about?'

An urgent alert had been sent out on all transport systems, and patrol cars were searching the streets, while surveillance was being orchestrated on every security camera on the city, but so far there had been no sight of him. His wife had been observed driving to her usual shift at the hospital, as though nothing out of the ordinary had happened. Naomi had gone to question her there, but Linda had denied knowing where her husband was. As far as she knew, she said, he was at home that evening.

'She must have known he didn't go home from the garden centre, though,' Geraldine said thoughtfully. 'That means she's lying.'

'Go and question her again,' Binita said. 'Bring her here if necessary and threaten her with obstruction if she won't tell us where he is.'

'No,' Geraldine interrupted, shaking her head. 'We can't force her to tell us anything. She works in an extremely stressful job, so she's unlikely to crack under pressure. And, in any case, we can't prove she knows where he is.'

Binita nodded. 'You've met her. What do you suggest?'

'I think it's best if we don't alert her to our suspicions. Let's just observe her. She'll lead us to him eventually, if she knows where he is. And if she doesn't, then there's nothing to be gained from interrogating her further.'

Binita nodded. 'Very well,' she agreed. 'We'll set up surveillance at every exit from the hospital. Cover the windows as well. We don't want our suspect to know what's going on. If he feels trapped inside the hospital, there's no knowing what he might do. We've already had one hostage situation to deal with. We don't want to risk another. As soon as Linda's shift ends, we need to be ready to follow her. Circulate her picture. Make this a priority. We're looking for a woman leaving the hospital at six in the morning.'

'She might not be alone,' Ariadne pointed out.

Several detective constables were sent to the hospital to find Linda. They were under instructions to observe her but not to approach her, nor let her see them. If she suspected the police were watching her, she might never lead them to George. Geraldine was disappointed that she couldn't join her colleagues inside the hospital, but she couldn't risk being recognised by Linda. Whatever happened, it was imperative that Linda remain ignorant of the police activity at the hospital. Geraldine stayed at her desk for the remainder of the night, doing desultory paperwork, as she waited to hear from the officers who were discreetly patrolling the hospital. Only two of them had gone in the end because Binita was worried that Linda might become concerned if she noticed too many strangers on the premises. It was a large site, but even so, they had to be careful and the officers changed over every few hours before they could attract attention. Only the senior staff at the hospital were aware of the situation, and even they weren't told who among their staff was under surveillance.

Geraldine finally decided to go home for the rest of the night and get a few hours' sleep. She was woken early in the morning by her phone ringing. A hospital porter had been the victim of a fatal assault. His body had been discovered bundled inside a laundry bin. Concealed in a pile of dirty overalls, he had been lying hidden for some time. The hospital doctor who examined the body confirmed that he had been dead for several hours although she was unable to give an exact estimate of the time of death because it was damp inside the laundry bin, and very warm due to the gaseous emissions from the body.

'A nice image,' Ian muttered when Geraldine read the details to him. 'I suppose you're off then.'

Geraldine nodded. The only positive aspect of the suspicious death was that the police now had no choice but to close off the entire hospital. Absolutely no one was allowed in or out without permission. By the time Geraldine arrived, there was already a commotion outside the main entrance, where visitors were being denied access.

'Visiting hours are from eight,' a large red-faced man called out. 'It's nearly half past. You've got no right to leave us out here like this.'

'It won't be for long,' a harassed looking constable was saying in a loud voice intended to carry to everyone in the small crowd that had gathered.

'Keep it up,' Geraldine smiled at him. 'I'm glad I don't have your job,' she added in an undertone and he grunted.

'Stand back there,' another constable called out. 'No one's going in this morning.'

'It's going to rain,' someone else complained. 'I can't stand out in the rain in my condition.'

'Why don't you all go home and come back later?' one of the constables asked, not unreasonably. His question was greeted by a chorus of protests.

Walking through the wide double doors, Geraldine was struck by the air of quiet activity that contrasted starkly with the clamour on the other side of the entrance. She introduced herself to a hospital administrator.

'We deal with bodies all the time,' the woman told her as she escorted Geraldine to the corridor where the laundry bin had been found with its macabre contents. 'But you don't expect anyone to be murdered here in the hospital.' She sounded faintly outraged, as though being murdered in a hospital was somehow worse than being killed anywhere else.

Geraldine agreed that murder was hardly to be expected in a hospital setting.

'It was that fugitive you're after, wasn't it?' the administrator went on. 'Although what he was doing here is anybody's guess. Who is he, anyway?' She shrugged. 'I hope you don't suspect any of the hospital staff had anything to do with it. We're in the business of saving lives, not ending them.'

Geraldine only half listened as the woman launched into a convoluted summary of the statistics for the hospital's safety record.

'No one thinks the murder had anything to do with the hospital staff,' Geraldine assured her, when the woman paused for breath.

But as she followed her escort along winding corridors, Geraldine wondered if that was entirely true.

66

THE BODY HAD BEEN discovered inside a laundry bin beside a walk-in store cupboard in a narrow corridor leading away from the intensive care unit. It didn't escape the notice of anyone on the investigation team that it had been found very close to where George's wife worked. By the time Geraldine reached the scene, the bin itself had been removed, along with all of its contents. The stretch of corridor where it had been discovered was cordoned off, and crime scene investigators were busy taking photographs and studying signs of blood spillage.

'The assault took place around here,' a scene of crime officer told Geraldine, pointing to an area of floor. 'Look, you can see where the victim bled. Someone did a pretty bad job of cleaning it up. He must have been in a rush. We found stained overalls in with the laundry, which was probably what he used to mop up the blood after hoisting his victim into the bin.' He paused, before adding, 'I say "he", because whoever lifted the body into the laundry bin must be strong.'

Geraldine nodded. 'And tall,' she said. 'If it's who we think it is, then he fits the description.'

It didn't take long for the lab to confirm there were traces of George's DNA on the lid of the laundry bin. The notion that he was responsible for the death of the man who had been discovered inside it was no longer conjecture. The body had been identified as Peter Rampling, a hospital employee who had gone missing after turning up for the night shift the previous evening. A quick check of his records had confirmed his identity as a long-time porter on the hospital staff. He had been due to retire later that year. The police team could only hope that, in killing Peter, George had contrived to trap himself inside the hospital. Unless he had departed straight after the murder, he must still be there. Security film of the past twenty-four hours had been studied and so far there had been no sign of George leaving the hospital. There was a frame which appeared to catch him arriving at the hospital an hour after he left the garden centre. It was difficult to be sure it was actually him, but it was possible. No such image, however ambiguous, had yet been spotted showing him leaving the hospital. As far as they could tell, he was still there, hiding from the police.

'Is there nothing on the security film?' Geraldine asked.

Another scene of crime officer answered. 'We had a look. The victim was tracked all the way from another floor but there's only a brief glimpse of this tall chap walking towards the unit and, whether it was by chance or deliberate, he never once looked up at a camera along here. It certainly could be the man you're looking for, but we didn't get a clear shot of his face.'

There was not much more to be gained from standing in the corridor, so Geraldine decided it was time to question Linda again. She had to be the reason for George's arrival at the hospital. Geraldine decided to take Linda to the police station for questioning. It might be easier to persuade her to talk if she wasn't on familiar territory. Flanked by two burly constables, Linda was escorted out of the hospital, with Geraldine trailing after them. As soon as they were out in the open air, a tumult of voices began to shout.

'What's going on?'

'Who's that?'

'Can we go in now?'

A constable raised his voice. 'There's no going into the hospital at the moment,' he announced. 'Visiting hours are suspended. Go home, all of you.'

The crowd had already thinned out and only a few stragglers remained, stubbornly waiting to be admitted, as Geraldine walked to her car. Linda meanwhile walked quite calmly, and seemed unperturbed at being escorted to a police car and driven to the station for questioning. As Geraldine had anticipated, she was going to be difficult to unsettle. As long as she remained in complete control of herself, Linda was unlikely to break down and betray her husband's whereabouts, if she even knew where he was. Geraldine sighed. It was going to be another long day.

Linda sat across the table, looking demure. She had declined the offer of a lawyer to assist her in answering questions, claiming that she had nothing to hide. Geraldine was sceptical about that, but saw no reason to remonstrate.

'I take it you're not arresting me?' Linda added.

As she posed the question, Geraldine was interested to see that her mask of insouciance slipped slightly. She attempted to smile, and her eyes widened in what could have been a fleeting expression of alarm. An instant later, her face resumed its serene expression.

'Should we be?' Geraldine asked.

Linda shook her head. 'I've done nothing to be ashamed of,' she replied. 'Nothing I wouldn't do again.'

'When did you last see your husband?'

If Linda was surprised by Geraldine's bluntness, she didn't show it. She didn't hesitate in answering, as though she had been expecting that question.

'He left for work yesterday morning, like he does every day,' she replied evenly. 'He hadn't come home by the time I left for work.'

'Was that unusual?'

Linda paused, thinking. 'I wouldn't say it was unusual, no. As a rule, we have supper together and then I go off after a few hours, when I'm on nights. But sometimes George comes home late and we don't see each other until I come home the next morning.'

'The garden centre closes at six,' Geraldine mused aloud, making no attempt to conceal her perplexity. 'I wonder what could keep him out all evening. You must leave for work at about half past ten. The night shift starts at eleven, doesn't it? So you saw George yesterday morning when he left the house, and he hadn't returned by half past ten, having finished work at six.' She frowned. 'Where was he between six and half past ten?'

Linda shook her head. 'He sometimes goes out for a drink, or a meal, with his colleagues,' she suggested, but they both knew she was unable, or unwilling, to account for George's movements that evening.

'Yes, we wondered about that,' Geraldine replied. 'But George left work yesterday morning, and he went off alone. In fact, no one at the garden centre has any idea where he went. The manager was quite annoyed with him for leaving like that, without a word to anyone. So, where do you think he went?'

Linda shook her head and insisted she had no idea where George had gone after he left work.

Geraldine leaned forward, and spoke slowly. 'We found traces of his DNA at the hospital, very close to the unit where you work. How would you account for the fact that he was there? Do you really think anyone will believe that was a coincidence? He came looking for you, didn't he? Why was that?'

'I've no idea,' Linda replied firmly. 'I haven't seen him since yesterday morning.'

Her voice was steady, but she was clearly rattled, her jaw taut and her eyes staring fixedly at Geraldine as though challenging her to look away first. Geraldine held her gaze.

'He didn't see me,' Linda repeated. 'But he has been to the unit,' she added, with a hint of animation in her eyes. She licked her lips and continued. 'Of course, he's been there, a few times. I work there and he sometimes came to pick me up if he had been using the car. So, of course, he would have left traces of his DNA there. But he wasn't there last night. I would have known if he was.'

Geraldine held back from revealing that George's DNA had been found on the lid of a laundry bin that had hidden a dead body, but she assured Linda that George had been in the hospital that night. What was more, the police suspected he was still there.

'Wherever he is, we will find him,' she said. 'You'll save everyone a lot of time if you tell us where he is. Obviously, you know where he's hiding. There's really no point in pretending otherwise. I understand that you want to help your husband,' she added in a softer voice, 'but he can't stay hidden from us forever. If he attempts to leave the hospital, we'll pick him up as soon as he moves, and if he is resolved to stay hidden, he won't survive long without someone helping him. And we're going to be watching you. Our only alternative is to bring in dogs who will lead us straight to him, but we don't want to do that in a hospital. We may have to, if you refuse to tell us where he is.'

Linda shook her head, wincing at the threat. 'I have nothing more to say to you. I don't know where my husband is. And now, I'd like you to leave me alone so I can get some rest.'

67

NELLIE HAD ONLY RECENTLY qualified to work in intensive care and she was finding it stressful. The hours of training and observation had been gruelling, but had not attracted the same level of responsibility she now faced. It didn't help that an experienced nurse who was supposed to be on duty with her that night had been whisked away without warning. According to one of the nurses in the unit, their colleague had been escorted off the premises by the police. Rumours were rife, and no one seemed to know exactly what was going on, nor how long her colleague would be away. So, Nellie was relieved when a replacement turned up unannounced. She didn't know the nurse who had stepped in to cover for Linda, but she supposed he knew what he was doing. Her initial impression was unfavourable, but she was too wound up to think clearly.

'We couldn't leave you to cope here all by yourself,' he said.

His kind words alleviated her concern, while his smile invited confidence.

'I only recently qualified,' Nellie admitted. 'This is my first week in intensive care.'

Almost overwhelmed with relief at no longer being alone, she couldn't prevent a few tears from blurring her vision for a second. Seeing she was a little overwrought, her colleague suggested she take a short break.

'But I'm still on duty,' Nellie protested weakly.

'Five minutes won't hurt,' her colleague replied. 'Go and take a breather. I'll be fine here while you're gone. And we won't tell anyone,' he added with a conspiratorial wink, and a glance in the direction of the desk which was currently unmanned.

'All right,' she agreed. 'If you're sure.'

'Why don't you step outside for a breath of air, or better still nip along to the canteen and get yourself something.'

'All right. I'll go to the canteen. I'll only be a minute. Can I get you anything?'

He shook his head, and thanked her, and she hurried off.

The muted hubbub in the canteen helped to calm her. Everything there was so normal. For once, there was no queue at the counter and she ordered a hot drink and waited for it impatiently. She had promised she wouldn't be gone long. It wasn't until she was walking away with her coffee that Nellie realised why her colleague had made her uneasy. Far from being well scrubbed, his hands had looked stained and quite grimy. Remembering that she had left him alone in the unit, she felt a sliver of fear shoot down her spine and dropped the coffee she had just collected.

'Oh, for goodness sake,' a woman seated nearby snapped. 'That went all over my coat. I hope you're going to pay for the cleaning.'

Ignoring the woman's outburst, Nellie ran to the nearest person she recognised, a young registrar from the intensive care unit.

'I say, are you all right?' he enquired as she collapsed onto a chair beside him. 'You look as white as a sheet.' He put his own coffee down and stared at her with a concerned expression. 'Has something happened?'

'Yes, no, I don't know,' Nellie stammered.

'I'll tell you what just happened,' the woman in the coffee-stained coat butted in, having followed Nellie with her complaint. 'She just spilled her coffee all down me.'

'No, no, it's not that,' Nellie said, recovering her composure with difficulty. 'I'm very sorry about that,' she added, turning to the woman. 'Please, let me pay for the coat to be cleaned.' She scribbled down her name and phone number on a serviette. 'But there's something else, something important. I need to talk to you,' she said, turning back to the registrar. 'Not here.'

Frowning, he suggested they walk and talk. He was due back on his rounds soon and had to get going. As they walked, Nellie explained how a man she had never seen before had turned up, unannounced, to take the place of a nurse who had apparently been taken away by the police. Nellie wasn't sure what on earth was going on, but she had heard that the police were staking out the hospital.

'Anyway,' she went on, 'this man told me he was a nurse but I don't think he can be. He seemed to know where he was and I didn't twig straightaway because, well, I was a bit flustered at being thrown in the deep end to cope on my own, but the thing is, his fingernails are filthy and his hands seem to have ingrained dirt, especially his fingers, like he works on a building site or something.'

The registrar was looking increasingly worried as he listened. Finally, he stopped her and suggested she report her suspicions to the police without delay.

'I'm not altogether sure what's going on,' he said, 'but we've been warned that the police are looking for an escaped criminal who they believe may be hiding out in the hospital. They seem to think he might be somewhere in the vicinity of the ICU, so I rather suspect you've found him. Where is he now?'

Nellie shook her head. 'I left him,' she stammered, 'looking after a patient in intensive care. Oh my God, we need to get there now.'

'You find a police officer or a security guard,' the registrar said. 'I'll join him and keep him talking. Don't worry, I won't let him know that we suspect him.'

Nellie hesitated. 'I think perhaps I should go back there,' she said, doing her best to conceal her reluctance. 'I told him I'd only be gone a few minutes and he might realise something's up if I don't return.'

'All the more reason to be quick,' the registrar replied firmly. 'Go. If he does start to cut up rough, I'll be better able to defend myself. I can always give him a shot of something.' He gave a forced grin. They were both aware he might struggle to overpower a violent adversary.

'Be careful,' Nellie said. 'I'll be back as quickly as I can, with as many police officers and security guys and porters as I can find. Don't do anything until we get there. He could be dangerous.'

Nellie and the registrar exchanged a nervous glance before she turned and hurried off, leaving him to make his way alone to the intensive care unit where they suspected a wanted man was masquerading as a nurse.

Having enlisted the support of a burly security guard, Nellie was relieved to see a uniformed police constable, but he was initially reluctant to budge from the entrance to the hospital. He wasted valuable seconds checking with his senior officer that he should abandon his post to accompany Nellie, while she fretted anxiously, worried about the young doctor who had gone to the ICU alone. As she hurried her escorts along winding corridors and waited impatiently for the lift to take them up to the right level, she was torn between fear that her supposition would prove correct, and fear of discovering she had overreacted and there was no unauthorised person in the unit at all. She might even have dragged the police officer from his post guarding the main entrance, and so enabled the killer to escape unchallenged. Alarmed, she pressed the lift button again and again.

It took the lift less than a minute to take them up to the right level, but Nellie felt as though she had been trapped in there for hours. The doctor might, even now, be lying dead on the floor, and his death would be her fault. When the doors finally slid open, she leaped out of the lift. The corridor leading to the unit was quiet. As they arrived, Nellie recognised a nurse seated at the desk with a slightly bored expression on her face, clearly oblivious to the drama playing out nearby. Nellie darted over to her.

'Have you seen anyone?' she blurted out in a frantic whisper. 'Two men?'

The seated nurse glanced at the security guard and the police constable and raised her eyebrows. Before Nellie could explain, there was a resounding crash as some heavy metallic object fell to the floor in a side ward, and they heard raised voices.

'What the hell's going on –' the nurse on duty cried out.

The policeman dashed towards the source of the disturbance, with the security guard at his heels. Nellie leaned against the desk, trembling, staring at her colleague who stared back at her for an instant before reaching to raise the alarm. A few seconds later, the policeman emerged from the side room, clutching a handcuffed man by the arm. The captive was dragging his feet and looking at the floor. The young doctor staggered after them, supported by the security guard. The doctor's nose was bleeding, and he looked dazed. Nellie rushed forward.

'I'm okay,' the doctor assured her. 'No real harm done, thanks to you. It could have been a whole lot worse if you hadn't got here so quickly.' He gave her a lopsided smile.

Without thinking, Nellie flung her arms around him, sobbing with relief.

'Are you sure you should be working in intensive care, if a broken nose sets you off like this?' he laughed.

68

EVERYONE IN THE OFFICE cheered when they heard that George had been collared in the intensive care unit at the hospital.

'Fortunately, he didn't get his hands on any patients, although I gather it was a close shave,' Binita told the team as she came into the room, beaming. 'It seems he turned up in the intensive care unit, bold as brass, claiming to be a nurse. Can you believe it? He was even wearing a nurse's uniform. I think we know who gave him that. He attacked a doctor who managed to overturn a trolley and make a din which raised the alarm.'

Geraldine was looking forward to questioning George. It was a foregone conclusion that he would be convicted of abduction and assault against Lucy, as well as the disappearance of Alison and probably three more girls. With the weight of evidence against him, she thought it likely he would make a full confession. Certainly, she intended to lean on him to tell them everything, in exchange for the police informing the court that the suspect had been quick to cooperate fully with the investigation. But first, she had to finish with his wife, who would hopefully be able to add to their information on George. She and Ariadne went to question Linda again.

'We have your husband safely behind bars,' she told Linda, who stared anxiously at her across the interview table. 'He won't be going back to work for a very long time. In fact, I doubt he'll ever leave prison alive.' She sighed and did her best to appear sympathetic.

'You seem to be convinced he's guilty of some terrible crime,' Linda replied, her face taut with suppressed anger. 'I suppose it hasn't occurred to you that you might have got this all wrong, and in your hurry to make an arrest you've accused an innocent man?'

'We have proof that your husband transported Lucy Henderson in a van from the garden centre –' Geraldine began.

'He wasn't the only person who drove those vans,' Linda interrupted her. 'It could have been any one of the staff at the garden centre driving the van when that girl was in it. What makes you think it was him?'

Geraldine stared at her coldly. This wasn't a court of law, and she didn't have to answer Linda's questions.

'We found your husband's DNA on Lucy's body,' she said. 'The proof is there.'

'All you have is proof that he met her and spoke to her,' Linda replied, not unreasonably. 'You seem to be deliberately overlooking the fact that she was alive when she was found and brought into the hospital. He never saw her in hospital, so he can't possibly have killed her.'

'She was brought into the hospital unconscious, and the injuries she sustained in the attack killed her.'

'No, they didn't. You're wrong, you're wrong! She didn't die from any attack,' Linda said, her voice rising in agitation. 'It's true she died in hospital, but her death had nothing to do with George. Nothing! It was me. I killed her.' She glared frantically from Geraldine to Ariadne, as though willing them to believe her unexpected confession.

'Why would you do that?' Geraldine asked, making no attempt to conceal her disbelief.

'Lucy was brought into the hospital.' Linda had regained her self-control, but her hands remained tightly clenched at her sides. 'When she told me what had happened, I knew she was talking about George. And I knew what you would do to him if she recovered. I couldn't take that risk. I know George never wanted to hurt her. He's a gentle soul who only thinks of others.

But the proof you found wasn't proof of anything because he never killed her. She was alive when she reached hospital and I killed her in her bed. It was easy,' she added, with sudden calm. 'If you check her meds you'll see I'm telling the truth. So, you can let George go. I'm the one you should be arresting, not him.'

'I suppose you think you're being noble, sacrificing yourself to save your husband,' Geraldine said.

She wasn't sure whether she ought to admire Linda or be appalled by her.

'George would never hurt anyone,' Linda insisted. 'Let him go. He doesn't deserve to be treated like this. You have no right to keep him locked up. He needs to be at home. He's an innocent victim in your vile scheming to find a suspect.'

'We have reason to suspect George was involved in Lucy's abduction.'

'I just told you, anyone could have been driving that van. Why don't you listen to me? You should be questioning all the other staff who drove the garden centre vans. You picked on George, and now you're digging your heels in. But you'll have to release him in the end, because he never murdered that girl. I keep telling you, it was me.'

Geraldine pressed on, ignoring Linda's outburst. 'We have a problem with letting George go, because Lucy wasn't his only victim. There's at least one other victim we suspect he transported in a van from the garden centre. What we don't know is what he did with her body. She appears to have vanished. I don't suppose you know anything about that, do you?' She sighed. 'You wouldn't tell us if you did know. But your loyalty serves no purpose. We'll find out the truth, one way or another. As for your husband, he'll never leave prison alive. You might, with a good defence lawyer. But George,' she shook her head. 'There's no possibility of his walking away from this. Your sacrifice has been for nothing. And the chances are you'll be convicted as an accessory, now you've admitted that you know what your husband did.' She frowned. 'You really should have kept your mouth shut, Linda. Your lying hasn't helped George.'

'Alison didn't die from a drug overdose,' Ariadne added. 'It was a blow to the head that killed her.'

'George is definitely going down,' Geraldine resumed. 'And now, I'm afraid, you might be joining him. If you'd had any sense at all, you would have kept quiet and tried to stay out of trouble. At least, you would have been able to visit him in prison. But I'm afraid it's too late for that now. The person I feel really sorry for is your son, having not just one but two parents in prison for murder.'

Linda dropped her head in her hands and her shoulders shook as she sobbed. In other circumstances, Geraldine would have felt sorry for her.

69

'I WANTED TO LET you know that we've caught the man who killed Lucy. We know you had nothing to do with it, but you must understand that we had to be sure.'

Jason looked up at the dark-haired inspector who gave him a formal kind of smile. He lowered his gaze without bothering to stand up. He barely listened to her when she spoke, but sat staring at her polished black shoes, trying to imagine Lucy was standing in front of him. Only Lucy had never worn sensible flat shoes, not even to work. There was no point in trying to pretend. There was no point in anything any more. Not until the second iteration did he begin to register what the detective was telling him.

'Do you understand what I'm saying?' she asked him.

He heard her, but her words confused him.

'What do you mean?' he asked dully.

'Just what I said. We won't be questioning you any more.'

Slowly the words reached him. 'Lucy,' he stammered. 'Do you know what happened to Lucy?'

What the inspector told him next was impossible to take in, it made so little sense.

'What does it mean?' he muttered. 'What are you talking about? Why would anyone want to –' he broke off, unable to repeat the terrible words.

'All I can tell you is that the evidence is irrefutable,' the inspector said. 'We have her killer in custody and he's going to be in prison for a long time. After all you've been through, I wanted you to know straightaway. Do you understand?'

He wanted to shout at her that no, he didn't understand. He didn't understand anything. Just a few weeks ago, everything in his life had been coherent and there had been a clear plan for the future. Now nothing made sense any more. He felt a sudden urge to seize the smug inspector by her shoulders and shake her and scream at her about the injustice of life and death. Why Lucy? Nothing about it made any sense.

'I understand,' he said.

His voice sounded flat, and he didn't raise his head. He should have been pleased by the news, but it made no difference to anything. He was left with an empty house and a solitary future. He had never lived alone. On leaving university he had continued to share a ramshackle house with other students until an inheritance from his grandfather had enabled him to put down a deposit on a house of his own, years before he had anticipated reaching that position. By that time, he had met Lucy and they had moved into the house together. Apart from his efforts with a paintbrush, just about everything in the house had been arranged by her: the furniture, most of it second-hand, the rugs, and the curtains she had made. He didn't really like all of her choices. The fabric she had selected for some of the curtains had struck him as fussy, but he had been duly appreciative, her pleasure at his praise reward enough for his forbearance. Now, every room in the house was filled with reminders of Lucy. He understood the inspector was trying to be kind, but her efforts were futile. How could he feel anything but empty inside when his life was over? From now on he would be no more than a shell, alive on the outside, dead inside. He nodded his head.

Closing his front door behind the detective, he felt giddy with grief and leaned back against the wall to prevent himself from keeling over. Without warning, he began to sob uncontrollably. He slid down the wall and sat on the floor, his knees bent and his head drooping forward on his hands, until his chest ached. He could sit there until he lost consciousness and died, and no one would ever know. He imagined the house Lucy had so painstakingly furnished falling into disrepair, the curtains speckled with mildew, the paintings discoloured with mould.

Eventually, he climbed to his feet and stumbled into the living room. Slumped on the sofa, he poured himself a slug of whisky. The fiery liquid hit the back of his throat, making him splutter and cough. His eyes watered. Miserably, he drank a second shot, and a third. Alcohol warmed his brain, making him sluggish. Losing the will to control himself, he yielded to his grief and wept without restraint, until he was too befuddled to cry any more. He had no idea how much he had drunk when he was startled out of his stupor by the insistent shrilling of his doorbell. As if in a dream, he clambered to his feet and staggered to the door. As he reached it, he hesitated. He wasn't expecting anyone, nor did he want to see anyone.

'Jason, Jason,' someone was calling his name.

'Hello? Hello?' he said.

For a crazy moment he thought he was going to hear Lucy's voice on the other side of the door and he flung it open, ready to ask her where she had been for the past few days. Seeing a man standing on the doorstep he swayed, and started to close the door.

'Jason, it's me, Ian. Let me come in.'

Jason shook his head, trying to clear his confusion. 'Ian?' he repeated, wondering.

Dimly he realised it must be Ian from his football team. He was a police inspector and Jason had approached him for help. It seemed like a long time ago.

'Lucy's dead,' he said and began to shake, hearing the words on his own lips. 'She was so young, so beautiful,' he said in a trembling voice. 'How could it happen? She never did anyone any harm.'

Without answering, Ian took Jason's arm and steered him back into the living room.

'Sit here,' he said. 'I'm going to make us some tea.'

'I don't want tea. Who the hell do you think you are, coming in here where you're not wanted, and telling me what to do? I never invited you in. This is my house. I don't want tea.' His voice sounded strange, the words slurring into one another. Leaning forward, he reached for the whisky. 'I want a drink.'

'I think you've already had more than enough,' Ian said, taking the half-empty bottle from him and holding it up to the light to see how much was left.

'Put that down!' Jason protested, in sudden rage. 'It's not yours.'

But he was too tired to remonstrate any more when Ian strode out of the room, taking the bottle with him. He lay back on the sofa and closed his eyes, muttering to himself.

70

THE YOUNGS' HOUSE HAD been searched but nothing had been discovered that could be connected to any of the missing girls: no items of clothing kept as trophies, no bloodstains, and no traces of DNA. An extensive team was sent in and, before long, every room in the house had been thoroughly scrutinised. Nothing suspicious was found anywhere inside the property. Having taken the house apart, the search team were turning their attention to the garden. Naomi's report on the shed had provoked some interest and Geraldine was curious to learn what the forensic team found in there. Having completed her reports, she went to the house to see the pristine garden shed for herself.

Naomi had not been exaggerating when she said that every surface had been scrubbed clean. Not just clean, the metal interior sparkled under the strong lights of the forensic examiners as though the owner wanted to use the shelving as mirrors. The garden implements looked equally polished and it was strange to see a spade without a speck of dirt on it. Even the broom appeared to have been washed. The place stank of bleach. Geraldine stood in the doorway, looking in, and watched the white-coated forensic officers at their work, painstakingly bagging up tools and sprays, and checking the floor for shreds of evidence that had been overlooked. By now, no one was in much doubt that something untoward had taken place in this strangely sanitised shed.

'He must have had a reason for keeping it so clean,' Geraldine said and a scene of crime officer nearby called out in agreement.

'Whatever it is he's been hiding here, we'll find it,' he said.

Geraldine tried to feel reassured, but she was worried. The whole scene was so bizarre.

'Do you think he could have kept the missing girls in here?' she asked the officer who had answered her.

He shrugged. 'It's quite small,' he replied uncertainly.

That was what Geraldine had been thinking. The shed was square, with metal shelving units around three walls and a small skylight to let in a little daylight. One naked light bulb hung suspended from the middle of the ceiling. It wasn't switched on as the forensic team had brought their own powerful lamps, but presumably the light bulb worked. There was enough room to store a small mower, a garden broom, and a rack of garden tools. Beyond that, there was space for one person to stand and move around comfortably, but it was difficult to see how two people could fit in there, even standing up. All the same, there was definitely something very strange about a garden shed being so clean.

Geraldine suggested the search team turn their attention to the garden itself.

'What are we looking for?' someone asked. 'Ripe fruit?'

'There's a pear tree,' someone else said. 'Might be ready for eating.'

The garden was well maintained, with several fruit trees. A lush lawn was bordered on three sides by well-stocked beds of flowers of all colours, vibrant and healthy looking. Clearly, George and Linda took great pride in keeping their garden looking lovely.

'The earth has been well maintained everywhere,' one of Geraldine's colleagues said. 'It looks like he was putting down a mixture of compost and leaf mould along the back, to help the fruit trees flourish.'

'Mulch,' another officer corrected him, 'it's called leaf mulch, not mould.'

'So, he's been putting compost and leaf mulch down to cover the earth?' Geraldine asked, as a thought struck her.

She looked around, wondering if there could be another reason why the ground had been so carefully covered over, but the idea was too preposterous to countenance. All the same, it could explain why the missing girls had simply vanished. She shuddered.

'What if they never left York at all?' she asked Binita.

'That seems likely,' the detective chief inspector replied, 'but where are they? The problem is, we can't find them, wherever they are. There's no trace of them in York and no evidence they ever left York. Where could they be hiding out?'

Hurriedly, Geraldine explained her idea.

Binita shook her head. 'Do you think that's possible?'

'It makes sense, given what we know.'

'There's only one way to find out,' Binita agreed grimly.

The dog handler sounded slightly surprised at Geraldine's request.

'So, that's a private residence?' he enquired.

Having confirmed the address, he arranged to meet Geraldine at the property that afternoon. Geraldine recalled the garden, beautifully maintained, with well-stocked flower beds surrounding a neatly trimmed lawn. Now the moment had arrived to search it, she felt a flicker of regret. It seemed a shame to dig anything up, on the prompting of a vague suspicion. But four girls had disappeared, and a fifth had been discovered caked in mud, as though she had been buried alive. This was no time to hang back. As she was hesitating, the dog handler's vehicle drew up and a burly man jumped out, with a large dog on a leash. Geraldine hurried forward and introduced herself, and the dog handler in turn introduced himself and his companion, Ringo. Geraldine reached down to pat the dog who wagged his tail ponderously, in a dignified show of appreciation for her attention. In the back garden, she gave the dog handler a garment that belonged to Alison. Having sniffed at it, the dog vacillated for a moment, as though considering what to do. Then he leapt forward.

After trotting eagerly across the lawn, sniffing at the ground as he went, he paused for a moment, nose to the ground. Dashing forward once more, he crashed through a line of shrubs and stopped in the shade of a pear tree. He raised his head, barked once, then lowered his head and began scrabbling at the earth. The dog handler pulled him back with a word of praise, and nodded at a constable who stepped forward with a spade and started gingerly scraping at the earth. Geraldine stood nearby, watching. The constable let out a sudden yell and started back as he uncovered a hand, horribly discoloured in the early stages of decomposition.

Geraldine pulled out her phone. 'Looks like we've found one of our missing girls,' she said. 'Let's see what else we can find. We'll need a full search team here to dig up the Youngs' back garden.'

71

ANDREW BROKE DOWN AND sobbed loudly on hearing that the charge against him had been altered from murder to physical abuse. It was not clear if he was crying with relief or distress.

'Abuse?' the lawyer queried, wrinkling his nose as though there was a foul smell in the room. 'That is a serious allegation to make in the absence of any witnesses.'

'We know exactly what happened,' Geraldine told Andrew. 'Apart from the evidence, we have your own statement where you admit to hitting her.'

'Slapped her,' the lawyer corrected her. 'My client never hit her. He slapped her. It may not be something you approve of, but it's not unusual to do that when women become hysterical.'

Clearly, the lawyer had been speaking to Andrew and they had come up with a story with which to build a defence. Geraldine wondered how successful that would be in court.

'Tell me how you hit her,' she urged him gently.

Andrew launched into a rambling account of what had happened, more or less repeating his earlier statement. Halfway through he tensed, and a fraught expression crossed his face.

'I never intended to harm her.' He glanced anxiously at his lawyer. 'She was – she was hysterical when I found her. I thought I'd killed her,' he muttered. 'That's why I panicked and ran. I couldn't be found with the body. I knew that everyone would think what you're thinking. But it's not true. I didn't hurt her. I slapped her face but that was all, I swear. She was still alive when I left her, making an unholy racket.'

There was little more to be learned from Andrew and they left him to confer with his lawyer. But having made a statement, and confirmed it in a second interview, he had very little wriggle room. He would escape a murder charge, but he would probably be sent down all the same.

'He just left her lying there, unconscious,' Naomi fumed. 'If he'd called an ambulance straightaway, they could have arrived in time to save her. We would have nailed George as well, with the information Lucy could have given us, and this would all have been over weeks ago. Who knows? We might even have saved another woman's life.'

The interview with George was another matter altogether. He stared at Geraldine as though he had no idea what she was talking about as she charged him with the abduction and murder of Alison and three other women who had been reported missing, and the attempted murder of Lucy Henderson.

'You abducted her and buried her, thinking you had killed her,' Geraldine said. 'But she was still alive and she escaped.'

George glanced at his lawyer, a thin, tense-looking young woman with blonde hair greying at the roots. The lawyer gave an almost imperceptible nod.

'I have nothing to say to you,' George said. 'No comment.'

'What happened when you met Lucy?' Geraldine asked.

George shook his head and refused to answer.

'Lucy escaped,' Geraldine pressed on, 'only to be murdered by your wife.'

That startled George into speech. 'This has nothing to do with Linda,' he blurted out. 'She knows nothing about it.'

'Possibly she didn't, until Lucy recovered consciousness in hospital and told her what had happened.'

'This had nothing to do with Linda,' George repeated, his face flushed with suppressed anger.

At his side his lawyer stirred.

'Lucy told her enough for Linda to realise who had bundled her into the van.'

'No,' George protested, losing his self-control. 'That can't be true. The girl died in hospital. She never woke up. Linda told me what happened. Linda's a nurse. She saves people. She had nothing to do with what I was doing. She didn't know anything about it.'

Geraldine stared at him. Clearly, he believed his wife was innocent. There was a bitter satisfaction in telling him the truth.

'It was an unfortunate chance that put your wife in charge of Lucy's recovery,' Geraldine said. 'Once Lucy had described you, Linda probably showed her a photo she carries in her wallet, a photo of you. That was when Lucy identified you as the man who had tried to kill her. She was lucid at that point, you see. She had regained consciousness and might have made a full recovery, but your wife wasn't prepared to risk that. She murdered Lucy to protect you.' Geraldine paused. 'Thanks to you, your wife is going to be locked up for a very long time. Because it turns out she's a cold-blooded murderer, just like you.'

'No, no,' George cried out. 'You're lying. None of this has anything to do with Linda. You leave her out of it. This is about me and my garden. No one else is involved. Just me.'

Geraldine frowned. 'Your garden?'

The lawyer leaned forward urgently and requested a moment alone with her client, but George waved her aside impatiently.

'I had to do it,' he explained, earnestly. 'I had no choice. The earth isn't rich enough to support plants any more, not if they're going to thrive, not properly. All the natural resources in the land have been exhausted, and plants are suffering. More and more toxic gases are being discharged into the atmosphere and there aren't enough plants left to absorb all the carbon dioxide. I had to supplement the soil, give the trees the nutrients they need. Most people neglect their plants shamefully, just leave them to cope as best they can without any help. But we have a responsibility to take care of our environment. We've ruined the earth, polluting it and overusing it without a thought for the soil that's in need of replenishing. You don't understand. No one does. I had to do something. And it worked,' he added, his eyes alight with excitement. 'You haven't seen my garden.'

'Yes, I have,' Geraldine replied. 'Only you couldn't describe it as a garden any more. Not since we dug up the bodies.'

'Dug them up? Dug?' George stammered, half rising to his feet. 'No, you can't do that. You have no right. You leave my garden alone, you hear me?'

'Are you really telling me you killed people to benefit your garden?' Geraldine asked, scarcely able to believe what George had said.

He nodded. 'I had to do it. I had to take care of my garden. Linda had nothing to do with it. You have to leave her out of it.'

The lawyer shifted in her seat. 'I think I need a moment with my client,' she said quietly.

72

'WHAT A PAIR GEORGE and Linda turned out to be,' Geraldine said to Ian later that evening, after she had told him the outcome of the investigation. 'What about us?' she went on. 'Do we make a good pair?' Ian laughed, but she gazed at him seriously. 'I'm not joking.'

He grinned, not suspecting that she might have a reason for asking him. It was her twin sister who had suggested she have a test, after Geraldine had been feeling unwell for some time. She had kept her condition to herself, but her sister had realised something was wrong as soon as they met.

'We're not identical twins for nothing,' Helena had said. 'I can see you're not your usual self.'

'What are you talking about?'

'You've lost your bounce.'

No one else had guessed the reason for the change in Geraldine. Ariadne had been worried that her friend was feeling under the weather, but the truth had never occurred to her. Even Ian had been easy to fob off with her claims that the case was worrying her. The nausea had not lasted long each day and had been easy to hide. But she definitely hadn't been feeling well, and, eventually, she had made an appointment with the doctor, who had suggested she take a test. The result had been a shock, and for a few days she had said nothing, afraid Ian would leave her. But she knew it was unfair to keep him in the dark. Her condition was going to change life for both of them.

'Fancy curry tonight?' Ian asked. 'It'll have to be a takeaway. I'm too knackered to cook.'

'Wait. There's something I need to tell you,' she said, and stopped.

'What is it?' he asked.

There was no easy way to tell him the news.

'I'm pregnant,' she blurted out. 'If you want to move out, I'll understand. I mean, this isn't something we've discussed and –'

She stopped, seeing Ian was smiling at her. He put his arms round her and pulled her close. Geraldine thought of the promises she had made to her colleagues, and the bonds she had formed with them, but there was an unspoken bond that had arisen between her and an unknown person from the future, a commitment that was already overshadowing all the others she had made.

'Whatever happens, I'm keeping this baby,' she told Ian, breaking away from his embrace almost fiercely. 'But I've spent so long working with the dead, I'm not sure how I'm going to cope with a new life.'

'We'll find out together,' Ian said, pulling her close and cradling her in his arms.

Acknowledgements

I would like to thank Dr Leonard Russell for his medical advice.

My sincere thanks go to the team at No Exit Press, when it was part of Oldcastle Books: Ellie Lavender for her invaluable help in production, Alan Forster for his brilliant covers, Lisa Gooding, Hollie McDevitt, Sarah Stewart-Smith and Paru Rai for their fantastic marketing and PR, Jayne Lewis for her meticulous copy editing, Steven Mair for his eagle-eyed proofreading, Andy Webb and Jim Crawley for their tireless work at Turnaround, and Jem Cook for his help with my website.

I am indebted to Ion Mills and Claire Watts for their continuing faith in my books. It's been quite a journey for us all, and I hope you have enjoyed watching Geraldine's career progress as much as I have.

I am equally indebted to Jamie Hodder-Williams and Laura Fletcher at No Exit Press, now that it's part of Bedford Square Publishers, for their faith in Geraldine Steel. I am sure we will all enjoy a long and flourishing relationship with her – although we might not manage another 20 books! Who knows?

I am extremely fortunate to be working with all of these gifted professionals, and really happy that Geraldine's career is not over yet!

It's hard to believe that Geraldine and I have been together for fourteen years now. My editor, Keshini Naidoo, has been with us from the very beginning. Geraldine would never have reached book 20 without you, Keshini!

My thanks go to all the wonderful bloggers and interviewers

who have supported Geraldine Steel: Anne Cater, Bookstabons, Books Cats Etc, Emma's Things To Read, Bookish Jottings, What Janey Reads, Bookographia, Mrs Jay Reads, Chapters Of Vicki, Two Ladies and a Book, Crimeworm, Stacey Hammond, Books By Bindu, Fully Booked, Green Reads Books, Scintilla, Armed With A Book, Book Prowler, She Loves To Read, Lynda's Book Reviews, Penfold Layla, Fantasy Bookcraz Mum, The World Is Out, Redhead Reviews, and to everyone who has taken the time to review my books. Your support means more to me than I can say.

Above all, I am grateful to my many readers around the world. Thank you for your interest in Geraldine's career. I hope you continue enjoying my books.

Finally, my thanks go to Michael, who is always by my side.

A LETTER FROM LEIGH

Dear Reader,

I hope you enjoyed reading this book in my Geraldine Steel series. Readers are the key to the writing process, so I'm thrilled that you've joined me on my writing journey.

You might not want to meet some of my characters on a dark night – I know I wouldn't! – but hopefully you want to read about Geraldine's other investigations. Her work is always her priority because she cares deeply about justice, but she also has her own life. Many readers care about what happens to her. I hope you join them, and become a fan of Geraldine Steel, and her colleague Ian Peterson.

If you follow me on Facebook or Twitter, you'll know that I love to hear from readers. I always respond to comments from fans, and hope you will follow me on **@LeighRussell** and **fb.me/leigh.russell.50** or drop me an email via my website **leighrussell.co.uk**.

To get exclusive news, competitions, offers, early sneak-peaks for upcoming titles and more, sign-up to my free monthly newsletter: **leighrussell.co.uk/news**. You can also find out more about me and the Geraldine Steel series on the No Exit Press website: **noexit.co.uk/leighrussellbooks**.

Finally, if you enjoyed this story, I'd be really grateful if you would post a brief review on Amazon or Goodreads. A few sentences to say you enjoyed the book would be wonderful. And of course it would be brilliant if you would consider recommending my books to anyone who is a fan of crime fiction.

I hope to meet you at a literary festival or a book signing soon!

Thank you again for choosing to read my book.

With very best wishes,

Leigh Russell